AN INSPECTOR'S SENTENCE

Thanks, as always, to my wife Joan, for her patience, understanding and innate good sense. Also for her courage to tell me where it was all going wrong.

I am indebted to Mel Starling, former colleague and long time friend, for giving me the germ of the idea for this book, supplying technical details and for allowing me to use his experiences gained from his many years as a criminal investigator.

Thanks to Maxwell Kay for the cover design.

A very big thank you to Colette Kay for all the technical and publishing work that is way above my understanding.

Chapter 1

Inspector Tony Sewell's large and unkempt frame took up most of the doorway of interview room. His creased and crumpled face displayed no emotion other than that of slight boredom. His suit jacket, with gaping pockets and bulging elbows, had long since surrendered the lines and contours originally endowed by the tailor. His dark, lank hair, carelessly pushed back, was surrendering to grey streaks. As he entered, wafts of stale tobacco odours swirled in with him. Impassively he scanned the faces of those present, then slumped into a chair and nonchalantly flicked through the file of documents he had brought with him. A man in his late twenties attired in an overstuffed checked suit sitting opposite proffered a business card and ventured to speak. His small eyes danced with friendly expectation.

 "I am Martin Watson from Dearing and Jennings Solicitors. I am here today to represent Mr Hicks who........."

This opening shot, accompanied by an uncertain smile, faded back to silence as Sewell lowered his paperwork and, leaning back in his seat, gently patted the air downwards with an open hand. As Watson stumbled to a halt, he was a met with a slight nod from his intended audience to indicate that by reverting to silence he had acted in a manner which was both desirable and acceptable. The quiet in the room ticked on. Muted voices from the main office echoed gently along the corridor sweeping up against the closed door of the small room. Dropping the file on the desk, he announced, "Right, I am Inspector Sewell. This interview will be recorded. Could I ask those present to identify themselves for the benefit of the tape?"

His voice was slow and mellow and had a distinct East London hard edge to it. He nodded to his right. A thin, pale complexioned young man strapped into tight jeans and a black leather jacket addressed the assembly. "I am Constable Stephens from Newington Green Drugs Squad."

Sewell looked around the room and, continuing his indifference, finally addressed the man sitting opposite. "Right, Mr Watson, from wherever, now's your chance."

"Oh yes, Martin Watson from Dearing and Jennings Solicitors, I am here today to represent Mr Hicks who, at this stage, does not want to........"

"Perhaps Mr Hicks could introduce himself." Sewell's interjection was quiet but positive.

Watson cleared his throat and took a breath. "The thing is, my client, Mr Hicks, has indicated to me that he does not, at this point, wish to make any comment or answer any questions or to acknowledge any matters put to him today." Watson spoke with a slow shrugging motion, his eyes almost closed. He seemed satisfied with his opening gambit. The inspector blinked slowly.

"So, he doesn't want to speak. Are you saying he has nothing to say?"

"Yes, that is correct, he wishes to exercise his right to remain silent."

Hicks, a small, haggard, wiry man with loose black curly hair reaching down to his collar, stiffened, his upper body rocked slightly so as to confirm the accuracy of his lawyer's presentation.

The inspector looked to the constable and formed a downward curve with his mouth. He spoke in a quiet matter of fact manner.

"OK, fair enough, I'll be off then. Constable Stephens, fancy a pint do you? If we are not wanted here, we might as well make use of the time."

He closed the file, tucked it under his elbow and rocked back in his chair.

"Before I go, I should point out the details of your client's arrest. He was stopped at Dover having driven an old clapped out Ford Transit off the ferry from Calais...."

"Yes, Inspector, that's a point, the reason for stopping my client on a highway has never been made clear."

"As I understand it, a traffic officer thought one of his tyres may have had tread below the legal limit."

"Was the tread pattern below the required depth? Has that ever been established?"

"I have absolutely no idea, I think you would have to ask the traffic officer at Dover"

"Inspector, I don't think that the courts take kindly to police officers engaged on fishing expeditions. As you well know, matters pertaining to the importation of prohibited drugs are laid to Customs and Excise." The lawyers eyes twinkled with self righteousness.

Sewell checked his watch. "Is that so, well, well. Actually your client, our Mr Hicks here, has been arrested on suspicion of possession with intent to supply, not importation."

Watson flushed with impatience. "Then the officers searched my client's vehicle."

Hicks, the suspect, remained mute, shook his head and pursed his lips so as to assist his lawyer's indignation. "What was the reason for the search? What legal authority did the officers have to conduct a detailed search?" The lawyer gave the desk a smart slap with his hand to emphasise his displeasure at the cavalier behaviour of the law.

"Mr Watson, it was by sheer chance that a drug sniffer dog was in the immediate vicinity and it indicated the presence of prohibited substances in the Transit. It was thought that a search would clear the matter up one way or another. And it did. So what's your point?"

Watson, his chubby fingers grasping a ball point pen as if it were a miniature sword, proffered it towards his adversary. "My point is, my client has been clearly set up. He was asked, as a favour, to collect a vehicle which had previously broken down near Calais. He went over and returned on the same day. Perhaps he may have been rash, but he is out of work and is short of funds. The sum he was paid to go to France was not a lot. He desperately needed money. He assures me that if he had any idea, any idea at all, that the vehicle was being used for the transportation of drugs, he would have run a mile. The few pounds he was paid is not in line, in my experience, with what an international drug smuggler would demand."

"So your boy is an innocent dupe, is that what you are telling me?"

"Yes, exactly."

"I see. Mr Hicks, Kenneth David Hicks, Kenny to your mates, how are you? We haven't met for a while have we Kenny? I know you don't want to talk about getting your collar felt for this one, but could you tell me what you were doing, where you were residing sort of thing, about eighteen months ago?"

Hicks's jaw sagged in response to the question, turning he earnestly sought the assistance and support of his brief. Watson took up the challenge. He smiled knowingly as he spoke.

"Really, Inspector, not only is that a pointless question, it is outside the Judges' Rules and, I would suggest, is duress. You know that such matters will be struck out of any transcript of this interview." The policeman did not break his stride. "Your client, our charming Kenny here, eighteen months ago was finishing a five year stretch for supplying large quantities of class A drugs. That does not square with him being an innocent victim."

Watson was, by now, smiling benevolently and addressed the inspector as if he were gently admonishing a wayward child. "Inspector, not admissible, not allowable, you are wasting your time, my time and my client's time."

Sewell gathered the documents from the desk and stepped towards the door followed by his constable.

"Right, let's stop pissing about shall we? Can you confirm that your client, Kenneth David Hicks, will not answer any questions put to him today?"

"That is correct." The response was earnest and precise.

"And is it correct that your client has instructed you on the basis he was merely collecting a van from the area of Calais and had no idea that it contained a large quantity of prohibited drugs?"

"That is correct."

The only animation from Sewell was a slight knitting of his eyebrows. He paused for some moments before he continued in a quiet and unhurried fashion.

"Did our Mr Kenneth David Hicks here tell you what ferry he took out from Dover in order to collect this van?"

4

Hicks sat upright registering shock on hearing the latest delivery. He ventured to join the conversation. "Oi, what's he getting at." Grabbing Watson's arm, he continued, "You want to stop him, go on, make him pack it in. He can't say them things. It's the law. Go on, tell him."

"Right, Watson, now we seem to have your client's attention. I will ask you again, what ferry did he take from Dover. I am sure that you have covered all the details of the journey." Watson was now sensing Hicks's growing discomfort.

"As I made it clear at the start of this meeting, my client, as is his legal right, does not wish to make any replies."

Sewell checked the time then addressed his junior colleague. "Do you know what, Constable Stephens, I think we are going to make that pint in plenty of time."

He regarded first an increasingly agitated Hicks, and then the lawyer who was by now flashing questioning glances at his charge. The inspector's display of boredom continued.

"Right, your boy does not want to speak, that is fine by me, yes, absolutely fine, Mr Watson, because we are going to charge your client anyway. I should inform you that we have certain matters that we will offer in evidence and as such we could, if he did decides to speak, disclose them to him before charging. I could take them into consideration. If it is still 'no reply' good, it will save me a lot of time. We have video showing your boy leaving Dover, in the van, some days before his return."

Watson swallowed his alarm on hearing this previously undisclosed piece of information and moved to present some words. Sewell raised his hand to stay the solicitor's intended offering, holding it until he was satisfied the status quo had resumed.

"We have copies of his tickets which confirm the details of travel." He allowed these details to find their mark. "From Dover, we are informed, he travelled to Belgium where he met with certain individuals. Again we have video footage and witness statements are being collected from the appropriate authorities as we speak. He then travelled back to Calais in the Transit. Are you getting the picture, Mr Watson?" There followed a period of uneasy silence. "Right, Hicks, you will now be charged as being the sole participant in this venture. Of course, as you know, Mr Watson, that once he is charged, we cannot re-interview him further, so he won't be able to change his story and any question of how far up the food chain he actually is, cannot be discussed. Constable Stephens, if you could take Hicks and his brief to the charge room, then after that, what do you fancy, the White Swan?"

Hicks shrugged off the restraining arm of his lawyer and, with his face clouded with rage, rose to his feet and roared, "Do something, for Christ's sake do something, don't let him go. I'm being fitted up. Sort it, get it sorted. Why do I always get bloody useless kids for my brief? Haven't they got any real lawyers in your office, son? Stop him, for Christ's sake stop him."

Sewell edged towards the door and smiled back into the room. "Obviously bail will be opposed, there's not a snowball's chance of him getting it. So, Hicks, you might as well get used to a long stay. Mind you the good news is that by the time you get out this time, you'll be entitled to a bus pass."

Hicks looked about searching for a suitable riposte to give vent to his billowing anger. The best he could manage was, "You bastard, you bastard, you can't do that. I'm not going down for all of this." He grabbed his lawyer's jacket and, with his anger reaching a climax, screamed at him,

"Tell him for Christ's sake tell him, get him back. You're meant to be my brief, do something, don't just sit there, get it sorted. He can't do this to me, he can't."

Watson looked stunned. Sewell, standing in the doorway watched as Hicks struggled, without success to form a rebuttal. He smiled. "Right, Mr Watson, it's been nice and all that, but I'm off now. Constable Stephens will take care of you. Come on, Constable, quick as you like, get him charged and then it's your round I believe." Sewell started at a brisk pace along the corridor. A perspiring Watson gave chase.

"Inspector, I really don't think that was…. it really wasn't…, you didn't allow my client to…." Now his previous measured received pronunciation faded to reveal a broad northern accent. Sewell looked at his watch and sighed somewhat impatiently. "What are you saying? Are you suggesting that I have acted improperly? Have I done something wrong according to the Learn Yourself Law In Three Easy

Lessons book?" He straightened his back, tilting his head upwards with closed eyes. Watson made no attempt to take advantage of the pause. Sewell looked down at his quarry. "You were given ample opportunity to represent your client. You and Hicks both made it clear that he didn't want to answer any questions. If you were unprepared or unprofessional, I'm afraid that is nothing to do with me. What do you normally do, wills, conveyancing, divorce? You are not a criminal lawyer are you?"

The lawyer thrust his hands into his jacket pocket and bowed his head. "I have only recently moved to this firm. I thought that some criminal work would broaden my experience." There was no reaction from the officer. "Look, Inspector, could I have ten or fifteen minutes with my client? What you disclosed in there, well, I assure you I had no idea."

"That's what these guys are good at, shooting some story that sounds OK until you look into it."

"Yes, I see, I am sure that considering what we are now aware of, he will be more co-operative. I'm confident I could make him see sense and ask him to recognise that he played a lesser role in all of this. Obviously he wasn't aware, neither was I, that you and your colleagues have been conducting extensive surveillance."

"That's what we do, Mr Watson, that's our job. Now I will give you fifteen minutes, no more. When I go back in, I don't want any messing about. I fully expect that your client will be able to give a complete account of his role and the identity of the others involved."

Sewell's tone was moving from being didactic to avuncular. "You never know, maybe, as we speak, we may be about to round up some others who may well be involved with Hicks. They may even be undergoing interviews now. If that is the case, I can assure you, that from experience, they would have no hesitation in dropping their mothers in it if it meant doing less time. Maybe they are dropping Hicks in it right now, saying that he is the mastermind. Who's to say? After all, he was the only one to actually have his hands on the drugs."

Watson mentally juggled the points of the conversation. "You're not taking the piss are you? I know I haven't done much criminal work, but I have been a solicitor for some time."

"Mr Watson, what you have got in there, in that interview room, is a bloke with form as long as your arm. He's not the brightest, not by a long chalk. There is as much chance of Hicks putting a job like this together as my granny flying to the moon on a kite. He is a dumbo, he's just the driver. What he needs to do, if he wants an easier ride, is to give me chapter and verse. Names, locations, any other vehicles, destinations, intended customers, the full monty. As you now know, we probably have most of this from our surveillance but there might be one or two gaps. You have to make it clear to him that he must be dead straight with us, or he is looking at pulling a very long custodial. If he tries to have me over, I'll know all about it. So there you go, full details. Remember, if his mates are singing their hearts out, they will probably drop him in it, you know, big up his role in all this, they will say he is the main man. It's up to you and him. If I'm honest, I really don't give a monkey's what happens to somebody like Hicks."

"Yes, Inspector, I see. You do have some of the others involved in this under arrest don't you?"

"What do you expect me to say? At the moment, I am waiting for information. You do realise that our cases are usually based on target work. We monitor these teams while they are putting the job together. We are able to rely on certain sources of intelligence. Obviously we cannot discuss how we do that, but I am sure that you can hazard a guess. Most of our cases start a long time before the offence is committed. By the time it happens we are likely to know the who, what, where and when."

"I am aware of the basis of your operational procedures, Inspector. It's not exactly a secret; tapping phones and the like. Look, I will speak to him, make him see sense. Ten, fifteen minutes, that OK?"

"Alright, but I need to get things moving, so no longer than that. Constable Stephens, I'm afraid we will have to put that pint on hold. Cup of tea in the canteen?"

Constable Stephens watched as the lawyer made his hurried way back to the interview room and being satisfied he was out of earshot he spoke.

"Inspector, Sir, Tony, if I may, when the bleeding hell did we do surveillance on Hicks or anybody else involved in this? Are you just pulling a stroke? So did we do surveillance?"

Sewell walked on passing the file to Stephens.

"Constable, Mark, if I may, we didn't"

"Right, so all that bullshit about times and places was a guess was it?"

"Sort of, we had a team at the top of Princess Parade at Dover just outside the docks waiting for another one of our heroes who was supposed to be bringing in a load of heroin. He never turned up. The information we had that he was using a van, but the description didn't fit Hicks's. Our blokes were about to call it a day when the local Special Branch working at the immigration control desk, gave them a bell to say that there was a driver called Hicks who's details fitted our Hicks, a well known druggy. Within minutes they saw Hicks's wreck chugging up the hill. They were booted and spurred with nothing else to do, so they gave it a tug. The drugs dog went nuts, they found the gear in a false roof space, well over two hundred kilos. They reckon when they opened the doors, they didn't need the dog, the whole thing stank of resin."

"So how come you gave it all this horsefeathers about times and dates?"

"Paperwork, where all the best evidence comes from. Dover Special Branch found his outward details, even got him on cctv. He left a fuel receipt in the cab, that showed he filled up in Ostend the day before he came back. If he's picking gear up, he's got to meet up with a team over there, arrange to stash it, then drive back here for the hand over. Him and his half daft brief have convinced themselves that we have been on his tail and have the full SP."

"So, you guessed it, you just bloody winged it. You cheeky bugger, you bloody guessed it."

"Mark, my old mate, it wasn't guessing, it was brilliant deduction. Years of experience, ages studying the criminal mind. Genius, if I may be so bold. All we have to do now is hope that Sherlock Holmes in there doesn't start thinking."

Within ten minutes, the officers were met by Watkins who was displaying an attitude of smug excitement. "Inspector, I think you will find that he will now be willing to co-operate. However, I must ask for your assurance that his role in this matter will be shown as that of a minor player. I would ask that this is made clear on the tape recording."

"Yes, sure, provided he co-operates fully."

The three men returned to the scene of the previous attempted interview. Hicks, having been advised most earnestly by his solicitor, now saw the merits of forgoing any idea that he should adhere to the doctrine of heroically sacrificing himself on the altar of thieves' honour. His indignant rage was now supplanted by a mournful acceptance that his future could now be planned out with a degree of accuracy and that he was likely to encounter some old acquaintances. He agreed that, on the advice of his brief, he would 'cough the lot' including naming all of his cohorts. In less than an hour of interviewing, the officers had garnered the information they sought. Sewell switched the tape machine off. "Just one thing, Hicks, the mobile phone you had on you didn't show any of the numbers of the others involved. Where is the one you used for this job?"

Hicks, now in a state of abject surrender and hoping that further co-operation might reduce the time he has to stare through bars, raised a pitiful gaze. "Like I said, my story was that I was just picking the van up for a mate; a bloke I met in the pub sort of thing. I knew if I did get a tug and you found the phone with all the numbers on it, I would be stuffed. Not from you lot, but the blokes I was involved with. See, it would link me to them. If your blokes got hold of it, I would be in for a bloody good hiding."

Sewell feigned mock surprise. "Really, well I never thought of that."

The whiff of sarcasm flew past Hicks without making contact. "Oh yeah, we usually use a couple of phones." He hoped that his, somewhat injudicious offering would count as further currency in his future legal dealings.

"So where is it?"

"I posted it to myself from France."

"Where to?"

"My drum, I'm on my own now, so nobody is going to touch it."

Sewell, now showing more alertness, spoke to his constable.

"Get that sorted will you Mark. Have a word with the Sorting Office. It probably hasn't been delivered yet, so you can pick it up from there."

Slowly getting to his feet, he announced, "Right, Hicks, now you will be charged for your part in this matter. You have done yourself a lot of good, believe me." The last sentence wasn't delivered with any conviction. Watson smiled quizzically, scratched the back of his head then straightened his tie. "Inspector, isn't there the matter of the surveillance material and footage? You know, the video tapes and statements of other officers, the logs that you have kept, all that. Should you not put that to my client for him to comment on it? After all if it is not produced now, it may not be adduced as evidence at the time of the trial." His weak smile was accompanied by a faint grimace. Now sensing that, very probably, all was not well, with diminishing confidence he continued. "I mean he must have the opportunity to speak to the evidence you have; to be given the chance to comment on the surveillance material."

Sewell leaned back in his chair and, with a slow flat delivery said," Surveillance, Mr Watson? There was no surveillance, no, none. Fortunately, your client has seen sense and co-operated fully."

"Inspector," Watson was now juggling with the embarrassment about to be visited upon him of being led up the police station path. "You said there had been surveillance, you made it quite clear there had."

Sewell sighed somewhat dramatically and regarded Watson with an expression of mild amusement. "Surveillance? Oh that, I lied." He casually instructed the constable, "Get him charged, Mark. We'll brief up the duty team to nick Hicks's mates. Then we can have that pint."

Chapter 2

The large black metal gate at the Roman Way entrance into Pentonville Prison was complemented by the high featureless grubby brick wall that embraced it. From inside the smaller inset door a warder poked his head outside and took in a breath of the free air on offer. It was drizzling. He turned and nodded. From behind the guard a man in his early fifties dressed in beige slacks and a leather jacket stepped into the miserable day, he drew heavily on a cigarette then threw it down. From a large Mercedes parked a few yards away, two men emerged accompanied by a thin pale faced young woman whose skimpy, tawdry attire did little more than trace the outline of her sparse frame.

 In turn the men embraced the latest addition to free society and engaged in vigorous back slapping. The elder of the two, a large heavily built man moving with a slow rolling gate, was the first to speak. "Harry, Harry mate, good to see you this side, it's been a while, quite a while."

The second, much younger man, with less deference than the first, echoed the same sentiments and continued. "You lost a few pounds, Harry, it suits you. You're looking good. The boys are all waiting for a meet, they're down at the Erskine Arms. We'll have a right good old drink up. There's a bottle of champers in the car, got a very nice meal sorted out for you, real nice bit of scoff."

The older man's slight smile suggested that the meal on offer may not actually reach the highest standards of cuisine.

The younger man nodded towards the young girl. "Oh, yeah, we thought after five years, you might need a bit of company." The remark was accompanied by a nodding leer. He turned towards the car and flagged the waif forward. Grey of pallor and hollow eyed, her efforts to seductively slink along the pavement were somewhat thwarted by her struggle to remain steady and upright. This condition was caused in equal parts by the effects of imbibing one or more substances and the fact that she hadn't come to terms with the high heeled shoes she had borrowed. As she stumbled towards Harry, a grimace, which had the shadow of a smile, pierced her blank looks. "Oh yeah, Harry, we like sorted this girl out, you know, just in case; you know what I mean, like I say it's been a long time."

Although transmitting this information by placing his mouth as close to Harry's ear as he could, this act of conspiracy was rendered somewhat redundant by the volume of his voice. He turned to the vacuous looking girl.

"Come over here, darling, come and say hello to Harry, he's still the boss in these parts. What's your name, darling?" As she mumbled he nodded.

"Right, I see, Nadia. Harry meet Nadia."

The older man, in a growling whisper put forward his defence. "Sorry, she was Mickey's idea."

"I could have guessed that." Harry clearly was less than impressed. His lack of enthusiasm was not noted by Nadia's temporary manager. "Harry, we are going to have right old session. Come on, darling, Nadia, yeah, that's nice."

Harry appraised the tottering girl without showing any emotion. He was about to speak when he caught sight of a figure standing on the opposite side of the road. He stepped back slightly and straightened. He looked across with an expression of slight impatience whilst nodding his head in acknowledgement.

He was looking at a small, dowdily dressed woman in her mid seventies. Her thin, grim face was etched with lines which spoke of a life where trust was a concept that did not offer a measurable return. Pleasures were reserved for the acquisition of tangible items but not for much else. Bold black mascara drew lines marking the boundary between eyes and the flesh beneath that had long since lost its tussle with gravity. Bright red lipstick followed and overlapped the area where her lips, now deflated, used to occupy. Wrapped in a shapeless brown coat and with thin bony hands, she held a large shopping bag. Her demeanour was that of one who was present but questioned her right to be there. However, from under her bowed head she shot fleeting glances at the scene opposite.

At first he merely mouthed the word, then gave it voice. "Mum, Mum, what you doing here?" He started to cross the road, turning to his recently arrived companions. "Get rid of the slag, do you hear me, get rid of her right now. All of you, piss off, leave the keys in the car, just piss off." Dodging the traffic he crossed over. "Mum, what you doing? You shouldn't have come all this way. I told you not to at the last visit. How did you get here? Hope you took a cab, it's nice to see you, Mum, yeah, nice." He bent and gave the small woman a lingering but loose embrace.

"I came on the bus, Harry, don't want to go wasting money on cabs and such." She nervously searched his face. "When I saw you friends and that young girl, I didn't want to spoil it for you. I haven't spoiled it have I? I could always get the bus back and I could see you later. I knew you would be having a celebration with your mates. I didn't want to spoil anything." She spoke as if addressing the pavement at her feet, only meeting his gaze whilst uttering the last sentence.

"Spoil anything, spoil anything?" his protestations were effusive; overly so. "You're my mum, you're worth a hundred of them. Mum, you should have taken a cab. You know the money's not a problem, never has been, has it? I don't understand why you didn't use a cab. Look at you, you're soaking wet, you didn't need to get all wet. Tell you what, I was going to come straight home and have a cup of tea with my mum. That's what I was going to do. See my mum straight off."

"You was always a good boy to me, Harry, a real good boy. Why don't you go with your friends, then you can pop round later, tomorrow maybe." Her voice was soft to the point of whimpering.

"In the afternoon probably 'cause you'll have a thick head in the morning, like you always used to. It's lovely to see you out again, Harry. Don't go back in there, you don't want to go back inside. You should keep away from the likes of them, they always get you into trouble."

He looked across to his erstwhile greetings committee and gesticulated that they should not delay their departure. As they tried to flag down a cab, the younger of the two men could be heard asking, "Is she paid for or what? I mean you don't want to let it go to waste."

Harry took the large bag from his mother and held her arm as they crossed the road. She squeezed his arm with both of hers and pressed her head onto his shoulder. "What you got in here anyway, Mum?"

"I got some new clothes for you, Son. New shoes, nice pair of slacks, them that you like, shirt, lovely jacket. Got it from Mr Jacobs, he knows your size, I told him you lost a bit of weight. He did it for a very good price, nice man."

"Mum, you shouldn't have bothered, I told you not to come all the way out here."

"I just wanted you to look nice. I knew your mates, if that's what you call them toe rags, would turn up and you would have a bit of a celebration. I didn't mean to get in the way. Why don't you get off and enjoy yourself. I've seen you now, so that's alright." Her voice increased in clarity and volume as the taxi carrying the two men and the girl rattled away. "Come on, jump in, you should be in the back, travel like the lady you are."

"No, I'm going in the front with my son."

The car nudged its way through the London traffic and glided to a halt outside a large, grubby yellow bricked double fronted terrace house in a side street of Barking. "There we go, Mum, home again. It's been a while."

"It has that, Son. Let's hope you stay out this time, I don't want you going back to that place, never. Could you do that for me, Harry? I don't want to die with you inside."

"Die, die, Mum? Nobody's going to die, especially not you. You'll see me off."

"That's what I'm worried about."

He slammed the car door behind him and mother and son, stood, and for a moment while he surveyed the property. "It's done you proud this old place, Mum. We've had some good times here haven't we? Do you remember the old days, some of the parties we had when dad was alive. He was a right character."

His mother sniffed the air loudly, her voice stiffened. "He was a right crook more like it, and a useless crook. No money always getting caught. All them blokes he brought back here, all villains, all the old time villains. I blame him for getting you involved with all those types that got you into trouble. Thought it was all a game, I used to worry myself sick, like I do for you."

"Let's get inside, Mum."

In the street where the house nestled, neighbours and onlookers started to take an interest in the recent arrival. Sometimes it was the flick of a curtain or a stolen glimpse from behind a front door held slightly ajar. Others, by way of paying homage, stood in the street waving lazy salutes and, with measured timbre, called his name. "Harry, Harry mate. Good to see you. Nice to see you back again." One of these, an older resident, dressed in a shabby collarless shirt and shapeless brown trousers held in place by wide red braces, purposefully shuffled towards the former inmate in his slippers. His thin wispy grey hair was complimented by patches below his jaw where islands of long stubble gave silent testimony to his diminishing skills with a razor. He placed his hand on Harry's shoulder and gently shook it. His grizzled, sagging features studied the younger man's face. Rheumy eyes that held shadows of regret of an unfulfilled life, fixed onto the younger man. Before he spoke, he seemed to swallow down the excesses of his emotions.

"Harry, son, it's good to see you, it really is. Good to see you back here where you belong." Here he hesitated. "Harry, can I ask you, did you see much of my boy when you was in there? Did you see him?"

"Yeah, I used to see him a bit, Mr Roberts, yeah, he's doing OK. He's managing his time, you know what I mean, he's getting on OK. We used to have a little chat sometimes, he's a nice bloke. Haven't you been to see him? I mean if the bus and all that is a problem, I'll get my boys to drive you over. Just let me know, it ain't a problem Mr Roberts. Just tell my mum if I'm not here."

The old man was now loosely fingering the lapels of Harry's jacket. "Thanks, son. Thing is, we had a bit of a bust up and he's told me not to come. I went once but he wouldn't leave his cell. He's got quite a stretch to go and things are......" Here he took a shuddering sigh, "....things aren't too good. See, I don't think I'll be around when he gets out. I just want to see him, Harry." As the old man spoke, he gently brushed Harry's shoulder.

"Mr Roberts, tell you what I'll do, I'll get word to him and point out that it would be a good idea if he would see you on visits. I feel sure we can persuade him. Just leave it to me, Mr Roberts, and when you go, it won't be on the bus, my boys will take you there."

The old man's hand slid slowly down the lapel. "Thanks, son, it means a lot." Then spurred by sudden inspiration, he looked up and into Harry's face with grim determination. "If I ever hear of anything, you know, going on, something you might be interested in like, I'll give you the nod. I owe you that. Just like I used to when your dad was alive, we was good mates in them days."

He stepped back to take his leave, as he did so he gave a cursory nod to Harry's mother, "Mary." She made no reply, but her mouth tightened defining the corrugated lines that creased her top lip. As the old man shuffled back towards his doorway, she spoke in a ringing tone careless as to what audience was within range.

"You want to watch that old sod, he's a nasty piece of work. I'm not surprised his son won't see him. Round here they say the son pleaded to the job even though he wasn't there. Did a deal with the old bill, we all know old Roberts did it himself, but let his son do the time. He's been saying he's on death's door for years now. The sooner the better I say. Get off you miserable old bastard." This last contribution was responded to by the merest backward flick of the old man's right hand as he shuffled towards the sanctuary of his home.

"Come on, Mum, he's not that bad, these things go on, I know what I am doing. You never know, he might be useful one day. Come on, let's have that cup tea, and then, Mum, I'm going down the pub with the boys and hang one on. I'll stay at my place tonight, it's all been sorted out."

Mother and son stood in the kitchen as the kettle steamed up the windows. For periods of time she didn't speak but, with apparent unflinching affection, held her son in her gaze. "You've kept the place nice, Mum, see you had some work done, new kitchen, very nice, smart, very smart. Who did it for you?"

"Vera Mullins's boys, nice lads."

"They didn't charge you anything did they?"

"No, I tried to give them a few bob, but they wouldn't hear of it."

"Too right they wouldn't."

As the two entered the lounge, Harry nodded towards a large flat screen television. "That's a bit flash, Mum, use it for watching the horses? Nice one." As he spoke he was aware of a stiffening in his mother's attitude and saw her look at the device as though it was about to reveal a terrible secret. "Hang on, what's up?" He confronted his parent, standing immediately in front of her. "What's up, Mum?" She looked away. "Mum, where did you get that from? You're not going to tell me he got it for you. Come on, Mum, tell me."

"Yes, your brother got it for me. He just came here one day with it and said it was for me. I didn't know he was bringing it. He just turned up with it."

Harry gave a sigh of extreme exasperation. "I'm sure he did. Has he 'just turned up' with anything else? No other goodies?"

"He got me a telly for the bedroom, not as big as that, but a nice one."

"And?"

"Oh, and a computer, a lap top. I don't know how to use it, can't even switch it on."

"Mum, you realise all that stuff will be off the back of a lorry. You know what his lot are like, always on the make. Right, I'm going to junk all this and get you legit stuff."

"Don't worry about it, Harry, he was just trying to help a bit. I think you're a bit hard on him."

"Hard on him, is that what you think. He of all people should know better. Look, what if the old bill come round here to turn this place over, which they are bound to do with me just coming out. The first thing they are going to do is ask for receipts for all this stuff. They can trace it from the serial numbers. Next thing, you're done for receiving, they use that to put the screws on me. They would just love to give me a hard time."

"Harry, he knows what's going on, he can pull strings, fix things like."

"Look, Mum, all that gear is going. I'm going to get replacements from proper shops and give you proper invoices. You think he can fix things, you don't know what goes on with his lot, all stabbing each other in the back. No, Mum, it's going, I'll get the boys to bring some new stuff round, You got to be careful you know. Would you trust any of his lot?"

The strained silence was broken when the doorbell rang. As his mother opened the door, Harry could hear muffled voices. The door to the room was pushed open by the mother and from behind her a heavily built man casually walked into the room. "Hello, Harry, I heard you were out. Thought I'd drop round."

"Well, well. I hear it's Inspector Sewell now, climbing up the ladder. Right, what do you want? You didn't take long to get round here, did you? If it's to have a look, you've seen me so now you can sling it. Just to let you know I'm getting rid of that telly and the other stuff you have dumped round here."

"I can stay as long as I like." The inspector moved further into the room as if to emphasise his authority. "Still king of your patch then, Harry? What's it now then? Half a dozen streets round here. Hardly a big time operator, not quite Al Capone are you? Got your dedicated team around you? What, old Jack, he's a bit past it by now don't you think? And that half daft kid, all muscle and no brains. The big boys up the West End better watch out, within a couple of weeks you'll be making a move on their territory."

"You're all mouth. I make more than you ever will, just a deadbeat copper."

"At least I've got time to spend it."

"I think you should push off, there's no room for cops here." From the quiet of a corner the mother's voice cleaved the air.

"That's enough, enough do you hear. Harry, of course he can stay. You used to be mates. I want you to stop all this stupid nonsense and be mates like you used to be. Can't you give it another go? It's what I would like. All said and done, you are brothers anyway."

Chapter 3

The door was marked 'Chief Superintendent Upton' Sewell walked in without ceremony.

"Eric, you wanted an update." Before he had finished speaking he had slid into the chair opposite Upton and had thrown several files, unceremoniously, onto the chief superintendent's desk. For a fleeting moment Upton considered upbraiding his inspector for his lack of respect for a senior rank and for his overfamiliarity. The idea rapidly evaporated and left his mind directly opposite its entrance point. It was always this way with Sewell.

"Yes, Tony, just thought we would have a catch up, see how things are progressing. Anyway, never mind all that, how are things with you? Any sign of a woman on the horizon? You need a woman around the place, you can't be happy all the time." Sewell had the grace to acknowledge the remark with a faint smile. "You've been divorced for years now, you've got to have somebody to look after you."

"Yeah, but who wants a beat up, washed up, pissed up old copper who never has time to go home, such as it is. There's been one or two flings, but I don't want to get stuck with something at my age. I'm too, sort of cantankerous I suppose, I like my own space."

"You need to ease up, Tony, you look like shit, you really do. You're what, about the same age as me, fifty two, fifty three? You are up for your pension very soon, you've got your thirty years in. You want to take it easy, make sure you are around to collect it."

"I suppose, Eric. I have been thinking about it."

"Tony, in your day, you've been a good copper, a very good copper. I wished I had a dozen like you, but now, you worry me. I don't want serving officers dropping dead on my patch. Do yourself a favour, take your pension." He searched Sewell's face for signs of a reaction, as usual there were none. His chair creaked as leaned back into it.

"Tony, you've got to look after yourself. You should take some time off; you're shagged out. You've got that little flat on Harbour Road haven't you, living off take aways and booze. Why don't you take a break for a few weeks. I can have a word with the doctor, he can sign you off for a few weeks, a month if you want, with some lurgy, Wapping and District swamp fever, something like that."

"Cheers, thanks for that, but what would I do? Probably just sit around the flat all day then go down the pub. No, I'm OK. I can hang on, I'm fine. I can't take any time off just now, I'm in the middle of this money laundering team, it's only a few more weeks to go until we get all that we want, then we can knock it, then I could take some leave."
Upton leaned forward and while attempting to inject some authority announced, "Well at least think about it. Anyway, good job with this drugs team. I see our friend Hicks is back in the frame, looks like he dropped all his mates in it."

"Yeah, I just stood on his toes a bit and suggested it might be a good idea to introduce us to the rest of his mob. Bunch of bozos, once one of them bottled it, the rest caved in."

"How's this money laundering job shaping up? How does that work? " Sewell did not rush to reply. "It's quite slick really. The punter who wants to launder his cash, gets his instructions by phone. He is told to go to a corner of a back street. When he arrives he is sent a text from the Middle East. The text is the last six numbers of a ten or twenty pound note. He is approached by a bloke who shows the note with the numbers on it. The punter knows it's safe to hand the dosh over."

Sewell paused to see if his boss had been following his detailed description. Upton became aware of the silence and nodded knowingly. Sewell continued. "We did a number on the bank, can't say too much about it, but we have a source. We have full cooperation but nobody, especially the bank management, knows anything about it. We put the squeeze on somebody associated. It was a case of helping us or go down for a couple of big rackets. So, we more or less have access to all the records we need."

"Tony, I'm not going to ask any questions about it, you probably wouldn't tell me anyway."

"You are absolutely right, if I told you I would have to kill you. Everybody thinks we are getting voluntary assistance from the bank. "

"I thought as much. Anyway, how much are we talking about?"

"At the moment it's running into millions, about ten or twelve, something like that."

Upton tapped his desk with a pen. "Right. How are the observations going?"

"Yeah, good, got a good obs team, a good bunch. Once a punter has handed over the cash, we tail him then we can identify who he is and where it is all coming from. Look, I'm OK, you don't need to worry about me."

Upton gave a tight lipped smile. "It's not you that I worry about, it's me. If I've got an officer who is working all the hours God sends, a lot of those hours unauthorised, and he has a work life balance problem, not to mention drinking excessively," here he raised a hand to stifle any form of protest, "and he drops dead. Then I get it in the neck. I'm the one facing disciplinary issues. No, Tony, it's all health and safety these days, not like it used to be." Sewell had seen the look of exaggerated earnestness on an increasingly repetitive basis and made for the door. "I hear your brother is out." The inspector took in the view of the general office as he paused at the door. "Look, I know he's your brother and all that, but be careful. If he kicks anything off, it can't be this nick that investigates him. Because of who you are, it'll be some faceless rubber heel squad that will do the business." Sewell paused but sensed there was more to come. "I have to ask you this. Have you seen him, or do you intend to see him?"

Without looking back he said, "He's my brother. Is that why you want me out of the job? You don't have to worry. What happened, what you did, was a long time ago, I've almost forgotten it." Inwardly Upton winced.

The inspector stalked through the open plan area and retrieved his jacket from where he had left it, draped across his desk. The time on the office clock showed it was approaching six p.m.

"Constable Stephens, get your coat, you've pulled."

"Why, Inspector, I didn't think you cared, this is so sudden."

"Yeah, where's the rest of the team?"

"The ones that aren't on shift are in the Feathers. The rest will stay till the plot goes quiet and the bad boys go home."

The quiet babble of conversation that swirled around the bar rose to a muted cheer as the inspector and his constable entered.

"Boss, what brilliant timing, the lads were just saying it's a pity that Tony's not here, 'cause if he was it would be his round."

"Cheeky buggers."

One of the assembled, a young constable, rose to his feet. "It's all right, Guv, I'll get them in."

"Sit yourself down, Sean, I'll get them. I don't want you lot wingeing behind my back, calling me a tight arsed old man." A howl of mock protest went up. "Oh, yes you would."

As the evening progressed, members of the group peeled away at various intervals. At nine thirty only the inspector and his loyal constable, Mark Stephens, remained. Sewell spent increasingly longer periods staring silently into his glass. When Stephens stood, it seem to take the older man by surprise. "What? Where you..."

"Guv, Tony, I've got to get off home. With all the hours I'm doing, my missus is beginning to think I am a figment of her imagination, she says the kids see Father Christmas more often than they see me."

"Come on, Mark, just one more quick one, just one more. Listen, I meant to tell you I got a bollocking from Upton today. Look, get another one in, here I'll pay for it, and I'll fill you in."

"Tony, I know what you are like, it's always one more. Right, one more and that is it. Then I'm up the road. I'll give the factory a bell and get uniform to drop you off home. Shall I tell them half an hour?"

With drinks refreshed, Stephens looked on with growing signs of impatience, checking his watch more than once.

"Go on then, what happened with Upton?"

"I was on the beat with him when I first started, as much as a crook as the rest of them."

"So you've said in the past. What was he up to today then?"

"He wants me out of the job that's a cert. Says I can't manage my time."

"He never did, can't manage your time, now I wonder what made him say that?"

"I think he is saying I am washed up and should pack it in. Says I have 'lifestyle issues' and a problem with drink. That's how they talk these days, load of bloody nonsense. Do you know, in the old days there were some coppers, I mean good coppers, who couldn't work a day shift until they had a few belts of Scotch inside them. They were bloody good coppers, they did a bloody good job. Now look at it, all human resources and health and safety mumbo jumbo, what a waste."

"So you reckon Upton is trying to push you out the door, I don't believe it. I've got to say, Tony, you have been caning the booze lately. Is there something up? Anything thing I can do?"

"Don't you start for Christ's sake, I had enough with that little weasel Upton."

Stephens reached across and touched his boss's arm. "Tony, we're all with you, it's a good team. But, some of them are beginning to worry about you. You spend more time on the plot, loads more, than anybody else. We know if there's any criticism about what we're doing, or how we're doing it, you will always back us up. If there is a bollocking to be handed out, you do it, then it's over and done. But........I think you should watch out for yourself."

"Do you know what, you sound just like Upton. I don't need sodding lectures. I can handle it."

Stephens sat upright not hiding his impatience. "Tony, I called uniform. There will be a car outside in about five minutes, they'll drop you off at your place."

"Yeah, yeah, OK, look I'm sorry if I sounded off at you. You're a good bunch of lads. Sorry, OK? Right, I said I'm sorry, is that enough for you?"

Stephens kept watch for the marked police car that was to take Sewell home. Almost as an aside he said. "I hear your brother is out. How does that work for you"?

"He's my brother. What do you want me to say?" By now the alcohol had introduced a thick note of belligerence. The marked police car pulled up to a halt outside Sewell's apartment block, he slid out. "Cheers, guv. See you tomorrow."

"Yeah, cheers, boys, thanks for the lift." He stood by the entrance and fumbled for his keys. As soon as the car was out of sight, he pointed his face towards the nearby Red Lion.

It was after midnight before Tony Sewell, now devoid of any coordinated movement, pushed and fell against the door to his one bedroomed flat. He did not notice the odours of stale tobacco and partly consumed and maturing take away food seeping from containers. Any post that had been delivered that day joined its predecessors as it too was scraped along the doormat and against the wall into the growing pile of bills and junk mail. In the small room that served as both lounge and dining room, he threw his jacket at the back of a chair, it missed and crumpled to the floor. His confusion at this caused a slight shrug of indifference. Beside the whisky bottle there was a photograph that he had placed facedown on the table that morning as he left. Armed with a generous measure of spirit, and a cigarette, he turned the photo over. "Hello, girl. I'm sorry. Did I tell you that? I should have." It was almost six in the morning before he woke, still sitting on the shabby settee. His glass remained untouched and the cigarette had added yet another scorch mark on the coffee table. He sat up, stretched and pulled away the cobwebs of sleep from his face. He looked at the picture again, then put the image of his former wife back in its approved place.

Chapter 4

In a small back street bar close to his East London apartment, the recently released Harry Sewell, now rapidly adjusting to life on the outside, was being lauded by those acquaintances he had seen very little of for the past five or so years. Although the drinks were piled around him, his intake was very limited. He embraced and hugged well-wishers and friends with much back slapping and constant repeating of their names. He insisted that the bar staff gave the assembled throng whatever drink they wanted, and more. His reason to be there, and his only reason, was to establish if there had been any takeover bids for his diminutive fiefdom.

"Here, Harry, tell Sid that one about the deaf judge, go on. Sid, you'll love this."

Harry thought it would be churlish not to oblige. "Yeah' well this geezer's up in front of this judge who's deaf as a post. The judge says, 'Cavendish, have you anything to say before I pass sentence?'

The client says 'Fek all yer miserable old bastard.' The judge taps the clerk on the shoulder and says, "Clerk, did he say something?"

The clerk turns to him and says, 'Fek all you miserable old bastard. 'My Lord the judge says, 'That's funny, I thought I saw his lips move' "

The hearty and prolonged laughter this evoked said more about Sewell's status than the merits of this, by now, rather hackneyed tale. However, it gave Harry a degree of comfort. The evening was progressing to night time. The landlady of the bar, a gaudily attractive woman in her early forties, threw yet another tight lipped glare towards Harry. He responded in a much less obvious manner. Her husband continued to serve and to engage in conversation and chose to ignore his wife's flashing signals.

Harry nodded to two of his guests, the men who met him at the prison gates, who then rose and followed him into an unoccupied side room next to the bar where the buzz and energy generated by his associates was greatly subdued. "Are we still on for our next outing? You boys still with me? You said you fancied something, you said that didn't you, both of you. I've got a tasty warehouse number lined up."

"We are, definitely, Harry, but don't you think you should give yourself a bit of a rest, bit of a break like? You've only just got out. The old bill will be waiting for you to pull some stroke. If it's a warehouse, it's a bit like your old style. I reckon if you pull it, and you are the boss after all said and done, they will be sniffing around you the next day."

"That's all right, Jack, I'll have a few good boys backing me up for my alibi. I've been playing cards all night with my mates, and her over there, she will cover for me from when we packed up. Look, I know there's a bunch from the north of town who have got eyes on my patch, a right load of bandits. I want to show them I'm running things here and I've still got the bottle to do business my way."

Jack, a shambling bear of a man who always seemed to wear a slight knowing smile and was dressed, as usual, in his trade mark black suit, weighed up the chances of success of another of Harry's ventures, which in terms of history, indicated increasingly lengthening odds. But the chance of a heart pumping venture that sparked up his soul with a fizz of electrical energy generated by guessing what side Lady Luck would allow the coin of chance to land, infused his being. There was also the loyalty which was ingrained in him towards his society and Harry. Although his pulse had started a quicker tick over he opted for his normal nonchalant stance. "So, what you got? Something a bit tasty?" Harry smiled then turned towards the younger man, shorter, heavily muscled and casually dressed. His raised eyebrows asked the question. "And you, Mickey?"

"Harry, what I reckon is that we need some business, I could do with a bit of a tickle, something to get me out of the house. Her, she's driving me nuts, wants a holiday, wants a new car. Her sister's having an extension to the house, so she's up for that an' all. Driving me nuts I tell yah. Yeah, I'm up for a bit of a tickle."

Harry nodded his approval. "What I've got in mind is this warehouse down near City Airport. There's a couple of them down there that only have duty free fags and booze. High value, easy to move, no trouble shifting them. The way I see it, if we go in at night, we could be in and out within twenty minutes, max. I've got it sussed, I've covered all the options."

Jack's pulse was feeling the effect of the throttle. "You've got somebody on the inside. Go on, tell me you have."

"Yeah, sort of, we don't need much inside help apart from the alarms. Nothing else, we don't need it. I've had a lot a time on my hands recently, as you know. The whole thing has been thought through, I've really gone into it, this one is as safe as houses. We don't use a big team, just a driver for a wagon and a couple inside to do the loading. That's it, we are in and out, bosh, that's it. Home and dry with a load that we can shift dead easy. Boys, I tell it's a real earner."

By now Mickey was picturing what his new extension would look like and was paying scant notice to Harry's plans. Jack brought what scant professionalism he had, into play. "You sorted out alarms, cc tv, getting the truck registration and description changed. Got punters lined up, we don't want to hang on to the gear longer than necessary."

Harry smiled knowingly. "Boys, it's all sorted, like I said, I've had a long time to think this one through. I tell you, it's sorted." There was mute approval from his two companions.

Mickey was the first to enquire. "So, what's the SP then? Are we going tooled up?"

Harry winced at the use of street language. "No, we are not going 'tooled up', we are using our brains for a change. What is it with you always wanting to be tooled up? It's not the wild west, no guns, right, I mean it, Mickey." Mickey accepted this expected admonishment with almost good grace. Harry's eyes fell away from him as he continued. "I want a small team. We'll need a driver for the wagon, a couple to go in and sort the load out, couple of look outs. And, oh yeah, a lad or somebody we can trust, who wants to make a couple of hundred quid for a couple of minutes work." Mickey was hooked. Having decided on the size and type of house extension, he was able to give his attention to the proposed method which would enable him to pay for it.

Three days after the idea of raiding a warehouse was first floated, at three in the morning, Harry and his chosen squad of helpers were in place. They had parked a recently acquired car in a large industrial estate, just yards from a fence that surrounded the warehouse of choice. Harry handed his two companions dark balaclavas. The three men approached the perimeter mesh wire fence on foot quietly and unhurriedly. With a practised casualness, Mickey isolated the alarm that threaded itself along the wire mesh fence and had opened a sizeable gash in the metal work.

Almost by way of a complaint, he commented, "These blokes deserve to be done over, that system is rubbish. Couldn't keep my old granny out. Somebody should have a word, get it sorted like."

"I wouldn't suggest it just yet, Mickey, not a least 'til we've had it on our toes from this one."

"Yeah, see what you mean, Harry. But it is rubbish."

The three men walked, at an almost nonchalant pace, towards the warehouse entrance. Mickey hadn't finished complaining about the lack of external security.

"Mickey, will you shut it"

"Sorry, Harry," Mickey paused. "So all the other security has been sorted then? Alarms, cctv, all that?"

"Told you, Mickey, sorted, done and dusted, no problem."

The men stood by a metalled shuttered door which was inset into a larger version and allowed the appropriate transport access. Mickey surveyed the surrounding area. "Nice night, but it's bloody quiet; like the grave."

"I'm sorry to disappoint you, Mickey. If I'd known you were looking for some nightlife, we could have arranged a disco or something. Go on, what you waiting for?" Mickey produced, with a somewhat theatrical flourish, the tools of his trade.

"Are you sure the alarms been done? If it ain't, it's not a problem."

"Mickey, did I tell you the alarms have been sorted out? Didn't I tell you?"

"Yeah, suppose so. Anyway, Harry, where's our wagon? It should be here by now. We can't hang about, we need to get it all shifted."

"It's on its way. I told you, it's all been planned out. Go on, do your stuff."

Mickey appraised the locking system on the door and again did not hold back in expressing his dismay at the how people who should know better were using inferior systems to protect their property. He inserted the appropriate implements into the lock. "Do you know, it's insulting, a ten year old kid wearing boxing gloves could get through this in a minute. No pride these people." Then with a flourish, he bowed to his accomplices and unfolded an inviting arm. His other hand pushed the door open. Immediately they were hit with an ear piercing screech and flashing lights which seemed to point directly to the three intruders. Nobody within a wide radius would have been unaware that there was some form of activity.

"What the bleedin' hell? What the Christ? Harry." Mickey was now shouting above the recently introduced screeching alarm. "You said all the alarms had been taken care of. You said, you just told me." To demonstrate his growing displeasure, Mickey strode off towards the gap in the fence telling himself, by way of a complaint, that Harry definitely said the alarms had been turned off. Jack stood in front of Harry, his arms splayed.

"Harry, what the..., what's going on, Harry?"

Harry stared back impassively, then started a laugh which quickly grew into a full throated guffaw.

"You should see the look on your faces. No, you really should. You know what though, I wouldn't worry about it, Jack." He made a slight gesture with his head which indicated that they should follow the clearly disgruntled Mickey. Having regained access to their chosen mode of transport, Mickey gunned the engine and crunched the gears.

"Whoa, hang on, Mickey, where you racing off to? Slow down."

"Slow down, Harry? In a couple of minutes, this place will be crawling with the old bill. I think that we should not be here when they are, if you get my drift."

"Mickey, keep driving along the road we came in on. About six hundred yards up that way, there is some off road parking. Just tuck the car in there. Come on as quick as you like."

"What, are you having me on?"

"Drive, Mickey, just drive."

Mickey slammed the steering wheel with both of his hands. Jack, in the back, gave all the appearance of one who was finding the scenario slightly amusing. The driver continued to display his disquiet.

"It's a dead end, if they come up that way, we're stuffed. It's a narrow road, they can easily block us off. Harry, I've got to tell you, I have concerns, some very serious concerns."

Jack, from the gloom of the rear seat spoke in his quiet and unhurried manner. "If Harry says he has got it sorted, then he's got it sorted. Haven't you, Harry?"

"I told you boys, I have thought about this for a long time, it's all boxed off."

Mickey was still assaulting the steering wheel. "Tell me then, how do we get out of this if they come up here and clock us?"

Jack, by now, was slumped back into his seat and smiling. Harry turned towards Jack.

"Jack mate, pass me that bag, cheers." Harry settled the bag on his lap. "Mickey, about ten yards from the car park, which we may get to some time tonight if you decide to get your foot down, there is a narrow foot bridge over the canal. The other side of that bridge there is a car. In my pocket are the keys for that car. For the old bill to get there by road, that is if they ever work out what is going on, they'll have to go around the area and over the road bridge, it's about two and a half miles. That gives us a good five to ten minute start. We are long gone." By now their vehicle was heading towards the selected parking area.

Mickey, showing his concern snapped, "OK, Harry, how do we know if they are coming our way?"

By now Jack thought he could assist. "I take it, Harry, that in that bag there is a radio which scans the police transmissions."

Harry smiled and patted the bag. Mickey's disquiet was growing in line with his lack of comprehension. He pulled into a parking slot and brought the vehicle to an abrupt halt.

"So what do we do now?"

Harry turned on the radio that was balanced on his knees. "We wait."

"What for?"

This time Jack filled in the blanks. "We wait for something to happen. Isn't that right Harry?"

"Spot on, Jack, spot on. So, have you sussed it yet?"

"No, mate, but I'm happy to tag along."

The radio gave forth. "Any mobiles in the area of Browns Lane and Waite Road to attend Fuller and Larkin warehouse. Alarm activated, the key holder has been informed."

After a period of about five seconds, there was a response. "Yes, control, this is mobile Sierra Mike Twelve. Can you show us as attending, enroute, e.t.a. five to seven minutes. Can you confirm the key holder has been notified?"

"Yes, yes, Sierra Mike Twelve, he confirms he is attending and has given an e.t.a. of about fifteen to twenty minutes from now."

"Thank you, control, Sierra Mike Twelve listening. Will advise you when we arrive."

Mickey regarded Harry with a look of deep concern. "Harry, the filth are on their way to about five hundred yards from where we are sitting. Shouldn't we be doing something? And you knew, you bloody knew that them alarms were working didn't you? Why didn't you tell us? You put the fear of Christ up me, you bloody did."

"OK, I knew they were still on, but Jesus, you should have seen your faces, it's been worth it just for that. I was just having a laugh, that's all. It was all sorted, all according to plan." Mickey gave a slight grunt to show that he was not entirely satisfied as to his boss's behaviour. Harry appraised the device on his knee. "I must say these radios today are much better than the ones we used before I went down. Very neat, clear as a bell."

Within five minutes flashing blue lights flickered impatiently across the quiet dark void of the night. Soon they had stopped outside the gate of the warehouse. "Control, Sierra Mike Twelve. We are at Fuller and Larkin Warehouse on Browns Lane. The alarm is still active. The main gate is closed. There is no indication of intruders at the moment, but we'll have a look around. We will wait for the key holder before going into the premises."

"Thanks Sierra Mike Twelve. Control listening." Ten minutes later the headlights of a car pulled up beside the police patrol. The two pairs of headlights passed the entrance and stopped in front of the metalled shuttered entrance. A minute later the alarm was silenced. The police radio confirmed the key holder had arrived and stated that they were going to have a 'look around'.

By now Mickey's concern had turned to intrigue and he had decided that a silent watching brief would be appropriate. Ten minutes later the police radio buzzed. "Control, Sierra Mike Twelve."

"Go ahead, Sierra Mike Twelve."

"Yes, Control, we are at Fuller and Larkin Warehouse, Browns Lane. Report of alarms being activated. It looks like some kids have tried to get in, or somebody who doesn't know what they are doing. Somehow they have by-passed the alarm on the fence and cut it open. They got as far as the door, which they managed to open, then, bingo, everything lit up. They didn't get inside. The key holder has confirmed that nothing has been taken or been disturbed."

"Sierra Mike Twelve, Control, do you intend leaving now?"

"Yes, Control, we are on our way now. Sierra Mike Twelve out." .

As this exchanged started, Harry sent a text from his mobile. He turned to the rear passenger.

"Jack, just wait for this. Just give it a couple of minutes." For a short space of time, each man seemed to be reflecting on some inner personal issue.

"Control, Control, to all mobiles, all mobiles." This time the voice at the other end of the radio sounded urgent. "All mobiles in the area of Poplar Road, reports of two cars on fire."

Mickey sat up. "Poplar Road, that's not far from here, it's only a couple of roads away. What's going on there then?"

Harry smiled. "What's going on is that my boy is earning his crust."

"All mobiles from Control, the incident at Poplar Road, it now seems that four cars, no hold it, five cars are on fire. The Fire Service is on its way. This may be a demonstration or political activity of some sorts. Senior officers will attend."

Harry nodded his approval. "Five cars, I must bung him an extra ton." Various radio broadcasts indicated that the fire and police authorities were proceeding with haste to the scene of the torched vehicles. Harry reached for his mobile and punched a number in. "Oh, hello, is that Fuller and Larkin, Warehouse operators? Oh, good, I take it you are the key holder and that you are currently at the premises. Good, Look, I am Inspector Morrison from the local CID." With that the scanning radio blasted out, "All mobiles, all mobiles, to proceed to Poplar Road and now Mill Lane which runs off Poplar Road, where there are reports of further car fires." Harry covered his phone and whispered, "What a boy." He resumed his conversation. "I'm sorry, sir, looks like the local lads have got a bit of a problem. I've been notified that you have had a bit of an incident. Could I have a word with my uniformed colleagues who are with you?" The voice at the other end explained that they had recently departed only seconds ago. After a further radio interruption relating to the fate of the burning vehicles, Harry continued. "Sorry about that sir, it looks like the incident is escalating. It could be a long night for our blokes. As I was saying, I am from the local CID and I was wondering if you minded us having a look at your place? From what we were told, it seems like kids some had a poke at your place. We've had a few similar attempts round here, so we really would like a quick look around, take a few pictures, that sort of thing. Is that OK? We will be with you in about two or three minutes. Stay, inside, keep the place locked. If the barrier to the area is electronic, I would keep it down just in case. When we are outside, we will call you on this number. For the record, sir, could I have your name. Richard Drake, thank you Mr Drake, be with you soon."

Mickey's mood took an immediate swing upward. "You cheeky bugger. You're just going to drive straight in and knock it. He's inviting us in, I don't believe it, what a stroke."

Harry quietly accepted the implied compliment. "Now then, Mickey, you can drive back down there now."

Mickey's growing excitement impaired his ability to receive communications. "And all them torched motors, the old bill will be well tucked up. All the cctv cameras will be sweeping the streets looking for them what done the motors." He seemed pleased with himself for being able to unravel Harry's rationale. "Mickey, if you could just drive so we can get this sorted before daylight comes. Come on, off you go quick as you like."

Whilst they were covering the five or six or hundred yards to the barrier at the warehouse, Harry made the call. "Mr Drake, it's Inspector Morrison, I'm with my two colleagues and we are just outside your premises now. Could I ask you to raise the barrier please? If I may be a bit cheeky, is there any chance of a cup of tea, there are three of us, all milk and two sugars." As he spoke the continuing actions in respect of the nearby conflagrations were helpfully being relayed over his radio scanner by increasingly concerned real police officers. He smiled as the circus added a touch of reality to his ruse. The car glided through the barrier and halted a few yards from the metal door that the three men, not more than half an hour ago, stood in front of. A beam of light from the opened door illuminated the path they should take. The warehouse keeper stood smiling as he anticipated company that would help pass the time which was already starting to drag. "Evening, gents, the kettle's on."

It didn't appear unusual that the three officers all had their heads held low as if butting against a strong wind. However, when the faces came into focus, he, for a split second, wondered why Ronald Reagan together with Jimmy Carter and Queen Elizabeth would be calling at this time of night. Reality struck him about the same time as Harry's fist connected with his jaw and sent him sprawling. As he slammed the door behind him, Harry started to work. "Right, you sort him and I'll get the truck down here, we don't use these ones, they are all fitted with trackers." Mickey started to tape the dazed man to a chair using a thick balaclava as a blindfold. He stood back to admire his work then applied the finishing touches, a pair of head phones which pumped, at considerable volume, heavy metal music into the slowly clearing brain. Harry pointed at Mickey.

"Kill the alarms, phones and cctv. Take the disk or tape, whatever they use these days, out. Get his mobile"

Mickey followed the instructions then turned to Harry. "Why?"

"Why what?"

"Why the bloody Queen? Why couldn't I be John Wayne or Elvis or something, not the bloody Queen. It's an insult, a right insult."

From behind the privacy of his mask, Harry grinned. "Sorry, mate. I thought you would look good in it. Suited you. I didn't mean to insult you or anything."

"Not me, you plank, Her Majesty. Our family shows respect to Her Majesty. My mum is a big fan of Her Majesty, she says she is an example to all women as to how to behave themselves properly. If my mum gets to hear about this, she'll rip your tackle off." The mask hid the wince.

The tractor unit, pulling a canvas sided container backed through the now fully opened access point. With two fork lift trucks on the go it was packed to Harry's satisfaction within twenty minutes. Harry's urging was constant. "Come on, gents, fags and booze, fags and booze." As others toiled, two men wrestled a tarpaulin from inside the cab and started to unroll it. By the time the vehicle was ready to leave, its white roof had been changed to black and the canvas tied to the sides displayed the logo of a fictitious Dutch logistics company. As the engine gunned into life, Harry stood back in a pose of admiration. "I never thought that getting to know a sail maker on the inside would ever be any use." He banged the cab door as a signal it was time to leave and shouted up to the driver, "Keep well away from the Poplar Road area, I got it from the radio there's road blocks all around there. You'll be on the North Circular in a couple of minutes." Then with a note of amused irony, "I think it is something to do with a load of cars that have had their petrol tanks tampered with. Kids today, what would you do with them? Right, it's been a bloody good night. If any of that crew from the north of town ask who did this, tell them it was me. I'm back in business and this is only the start, a little penny tester. They better keep to their patch. Right, off you go, I'll see you in about twenty five minutes at the unit. It's all opened up so just drive straight in."

As he spoke those others who had been assisting him, slipped away like shadows retreating from the light. He turned to the slumped figure of the bound warehouse keeper and tapped him on the shoulder and removed the headphones. The man immediately sat upright and threw his head upwards and from side to side in a vain hope that his powers of observation might pierce his blindfold. "Right, mate, we're off now. They'll find you in a couple of hours, you're gonna be good, mate, you'll be good." He started to leave but then placed a hand on the man's shoulder. "You don't want another load of heavy metal do you? We got some good stuff if you want it." The very vigorous head shaking suggested that this was not what was wanted.

Chapter 5

Tony Sewell nodded to the staff in the estate agency as he made for the rear door that would take him up to the store room which was now the observation point he and his team we're using. He was met by Mark Stephens who was armed with a large sandwich in one hand and a mug of tea in the other. Another officer was positioned at the window behind a pair of binoculars and assorted cameras. "Hi, Mark, how's it going? You all right, Raj?" Raj Patel shot a glance over his shoulder. "Yeah, fine, Tony, I will be in another five minutes when Mark takes over." Stephens finally finished his snack and with a degree of exaggerated bonhomie, announced, "Tony, good to see you." Sewell peered through the net curtains which acted as camouflage for those inside. He looked along the road to where there was a cul de sac off the main road. "Much been going on?"

Patel, without looking away from the object of his attention informed his boss that, "Our boys have been busy little crooks today, five deliveries. It looks like the three runners we identified a while ago are the main players. Since Technical Support hacked their phones, it confirmed what they are up to. The punter gets his text from the Middle East which is the number of a bank note, a ten or twenty. The launderer shows the punter the bank note, he checks that the number matches the text, and then they are in business."

The inspector stood back in mock surprise. "Hacked their phones, Constable Patel? Hacked their phones. You mean since we obtained a Home Office intercept warrant."

"Like I said, Tony, since we hacked their phones, it has all become a lot clearer."

Sewell occupied the seat next to Patel. "So, what have we got?"

"The usual, the types you would expect. Our mobile surveillance crews have covered most of the traffic and have more or less fingered them. But, about ten days ago, we clocked a punter who was a bit outside the run of these toe rags, not your average punter. A posh bloke, very smart, suit and tie. All expensive stuff."

"Really, Constable Stephens, a posh bloke? What do we know about him?"

"We've only started tailing him, we've only taken him away three times. His form, so far, is to take a cab up onto the Strand."

"Where to?"

Stephens wiped the crumbs from his fingers on his jacket. "That's the interesting bit. Each time he goes to a pub, the Coal Hole. We've had to leave it at that. We assume he leaves by foot, but we never have enough of a team to follow him from there. We're sort of saving him until we have a good team, a full set. You know the saying, drop out rather than show out."

Patel chipped in. "We have had one of the team keep observation from a burger bar across the road from the pub watching the main door. They give him about an hour, but we haven't seen him coming out. We reckon he uses either the side, or more likely, the back entrance. If he does go that way, it's very exposed; quiet streets, open gardens."

Now Stephens elaborated. "Thing is, he's a bit sussy, bit surveillance conscious. We traced the first cabby he used. The driver told us that when he was held at a red light, our bloke gave him twenty quid to stay put after they changed to green. If anybody is following him, they either have to drive past him or show out by staying with him. Fortunately we had a couple of our guys on bikes, you know, doing the courier bit. They just pulled off the road a bit further up, got tucked into some alleyway, and picked him up when he continued."

The two constables waited for their inspector's observations. "It sounds like he has done this before. So we have got a smartly dressed criminal who knows all about surveillance, or thinks he does. Right, next time he shows, I want a full team ready to go. Mobiles, footmen, cyclists, motor bikes the lot."

Patel shrugged slightly. "OK, Tony, we'll box that off for you. I'll have a bit of a scout round the rear of the Coal Hole, see if I can sort out some obs points."

Three days later, the 'posh punter' was seen approaching a known bag man. He checked his phone, a bank note was shown to him and he handed over a sports bag. Stephens reached for his phone. "Tony, our bloke, the 'posh one', has just turned up. Are you in the office?"

"Yeah."

"Like you asked for, Tony, there is a full team geared up to tail him."

"Right, on the basis of what we know, I'll make for the Coal Hole, and get there before him. Let's hope he is a creature of habit." As he spoke, he grabbed his jacket and a covert radio in the guise of a mobile phone, then made for the station car park. "I do hope he makes it, I could do with a drink on expenses. Can you confirm that this time we have sufficient for a full surveillance. Have you got a description?"

"Yes, and yes; he's posh."

Sewell pressed his radio button. "That rules you two out." Then he heard Patel's voice.

"That's not very nice, most cutting if I may say so."

"You may say so, but what's his bloody description?" As he spoke, Sewell took the pillion seat of an unmarked motor bike and clipped a crash helmet on. Through the earpiece of his radio he heard Patel. "About, five eight, five nine, short blondish hair, no glasses or facial hair, slim build, wearing a dark grey suit. He is carrying a large pale blue plastic carrier bag and has brown shoes, in fact they are two tone tan shoes. Like a posh bloke should have."

Sewell spoke into his lapel mike. "I don't think he is all that posh, or he's a foreigner."

"How's that?"

"Gentlemen in town do not wear brown."

"If you say so."

A new voice cut across the airways. "All mobiles from Sierra Victor Five, target as described by Papa Oscar Seven has made his drop and it looks like he is calling a taxi. Papa Oscar Seven, if he moves in your direction, are you able to take eyeball?"

"Yes, yes, Sierra Victor Five."

"Sierra Victor Five to Sierra Victor Eight, if he moves in the opposite direction towards you, can you take eyeball?"

"Yes, yes, Sierra Victor Five."

The tone of the radio communications sharpened and became more clipped as the business of following a suspect started. Patel and Stephens ran down from their observation point and jumped into their vehicle. "Sierra Victor Five to all mobiles, a black cab is arriving. Wait one, the target has entered the cab, registration Alpha Zulu Lima Three Three Nine. It's a lift off, lift off, lift off, direction of travel towards you Papa Oscar Seven." Although the silence that followed was no more than ten seconds, to those involved it seemed much longer. There was a collective exhalation when it was announced. "We've got him. Papa Oscar Seven has eyeball." Patel and Stephens watched from a side street as the cab trundled past them. Patel, who was driving with Stephens acting as a passenger, allowed two cars to pass him and form a barrier between him and the taxi before he pulled out and turned into the direction the cab was taking.

Stephens confirmed, "Original direction of travel, no deviation." Their surveillance vehicle, also a black cab, was identical in every way to the thousands of others plying their trade in the capital's streets. "We have two vehicles for cover. Target approaching junction. We have an off side indication. It is a right, right, right, now we have three for cover." Seconds later the radio buzzed back into life.

"We have an offside indication." And so the surveillance progressed. Clipped radio commentaries ensured directions were clearly given and understood. Rotation of the modes of transport involved in the surveillance ensured that the money launder's cab was not followed by the same vehicle for more than three quarters of a mile. Swapping of following cars, vans, taxis, cycles and motorbikes meant that, even the most alert suspect would find great difficulty in identifying an adversary. In a quieter moment, Sewell made his announcement.

"Eyeball, Papa Oscar One, permission to speak."

"Go ahead Papa Oscar One."

"Thanks, Eyeball. To confirm, I am entering the Coal Hole. I hope our target has the good manners to join me."

The ornate but uniform sized door on the Strand opened into a space which would have taken a newcomer aback. The high ceiling looked down onto a black and white tiled floor and a long bar adorned with gleaming brass hand pumps. It was a large airy premises; items which adorned the walls gave an indication of a long and distinguished history.

"Thanks for that Papa Oscar One." By the time the real, and unsuspecting, cab driver halted outside the Coal Hole, the commentary was being given from a white van.

"Eyeball to all mobiles, target has entered the pub. Papa Oscar One, eyeball to you."

"Papa Oscar One has eyeball. The target is entering the premises. I have plenty of cover, it's fairly busy. Description as before, slight build, grey suit carrying a large carrier bag." If any of the customers did happen to notice the shabbily attired inspector, all they would see was a care worn middle aged man in a sagging suit having a conversation on his mobile phone. He continued,

"He's at the bar, ordered a drink. Can mobiles plot up on this place, cover any movement by vehicle in either direction of the Strand. He's taken a seat in the main bar. Footmen cover front and rear exits. Be aware, if he leaves by the rear, it is very exposed, into Carting Lane, about a third of the way down there is a walk through that takes you onto Savoy Hill. Minimum commentary, he's a bit close but it's OK."

Minutes passed before there was an unnecessary but deliberate transmission from inside the pub,

"Large whiskey please, a couple of blocks of ice." A tall and comfortably attractive girl served Sewell. As she did so he noticed that she was staring intently at him.

"So you came back." Her voice, smoothly rounded with an Irish lilt, was direct and unapologetic.

"What?"

"So, you're back then."

"What? Oh yes, about two weeks ago, was I a bit, sort of out of order?"

"A bit, yeah." She let the words linger as she studied Sewell's face. "Ah, you weren't too bad, not like some."

"I'm sorry if I was; you know."

"It's OK, forget it." He could see the curl of a smile stretching her lips As he spoke he kept his target in vision. Far from being an unwanted diversion, the conversation with the bar's management, served to show him as a regular and therefore much less likely to be of interest to the target. He continued. "Look, can I get you a drink?"

"Nah, you're fine."

As each new customer entered the pub, the neatly attired target surreptitiously assessed them, presumably to question if they posed any threat. After a respectable pause, a transmission cleaved the airways.

"From eyeball, no change here." Quickly followed by, "Hang on, he's going to the gents. I won't go with him. If he goes in, he's got to come out the same door. It's a bit busy, but I have a decent view." A few minutes later the door to toilets opened and he saw a man move quickly the three or four steps towards the door to the downstairs rear exit. It took no more than seconds. However, Sewell's initial reaction was to ignore this departing customer as he was wearing a long coat and a flat cap. But then, he wondered. He's about the right size, I didn't see that one go in. By now the man had gone. He pushed open the door marked 'Gents'. The room was unoccupied. He rushed down the stairs and peered through the glass of the rear door. He grabbed his radio.

"Eyeball to any footman covering the rear exit."

"Eyeball, go ahead."

"There's a bloke just left by the rear door on foot, wearing a long coat and a flat cap. Can you get somebody to have a look at his shoes?"

"His shoes, Eyeball?"

"Yes, I want to know what sort of shoes he is wearing. At the moment he is on foot going down Carting Lane towards Savoy Place."

"OK, Eyeball, I'll get one of the cyclists to scoot past."

Although Sewell could follow the progress of the subject, he thought it was taking too long to comply with his order. Then he saw a delivery cycle flash past the man. "Christ, he's going too fast to see what I want." Seconds later a light female voice buzzed into his earpiece. "Papa Oscar One from Charlie Bravo Eight, he's wearing two tone tan shoes."

Aware that there were other drinkers within earshot, he resisted the temptation to raise his voice as he spoke.

"All mobiles, all mobiles from Eyeball, the target has left the premises, on foot, by the rear door. He is now wearing a long brown mac and a dark flat cap. All mobiles acknowledge."

The well practiced replies came in order of seniority from each of the teams. Within seconds all had confirmed they had received the last transmission. He continued.

"I still have eyeball. He's going down Carting Lane towards the river."

"Eyeball from Papa Oscar Five, permission."

"Go ahead Papa Oscar Five." Sewell allowed himself a slight smile as he heard Patel's tones, one of his most experienced officers.

"Yes, Eyeball, if he continues in original direction towards Savoy Place, I am in a corner room of the hotel, three floors up, and can observe him whatever way he goes."

The smile broadened. "Thanks for that, Papa Oscar Five, it looks like you now have eyeball."

Sewell, knowing that he could not take any further part in the chase as the target may have noticed him in the pub, juggled an idea in his head, then turned towards the bar.

"Papa Oscar Five has eyeball. He's at the end of Carting Lane and it's a right, right, right into Victoria Embankment Gardens. Could I have a couple of footmen onto Victoria Embankment, to hang back in case he does a reciprocal?"

"Sierra Victor Three and Five are enroute to Victoria Embankment."

"From Papa Oscar Five, could the mobiles make sure they position their vehicles so that they can take him either direction in case he hops another cab?" Patel's request was confirmed.

"There is no deviation, he's continuing through the gardens with the river on his left hand side. All mobiles, keep out of the gardens, there is no cover. Could I have two footmen up the steps at Embankment Station, one either side of the line, that will give a clear view of him continuing through the gardens."

The last static observation point was New Scotland Yard where the reception area gave a panoramic view of the outside world. A man, slightly out of breath, in civilian clothing sitting in a chair and apparently reading a paper, watched as the target sauntered past his position. Other officers, on the opposite side of the road, were mingling with the ever present crowds at the corner of Westminster Bridge. The man in the mac and flat cap turned right into Great George's Street. He then crossed the road as part of a throng of tourists towards Parliament Square. He moved on keeping the railings of Parliament to his left. Across the road a couple were, like several others, consulting a map and looking around as if to confirm their bearings. The woman spoke.

"He's approaching our colleagues at the gate, I think he's asking directions." A pause followed.

"Oh my Christ, he's gone in. He's gone in. He showed his pass and went in. He works in Parliament."

Sewell called for the usual debriefing. "I've got to say, folks, some bloody good work today. Really pleased. It's not easy following a bloke who is as cagey as that. Raj, Mark, you handled the gardens brilliantly. We could not have gone in there without showing out, so the use of hotels and bridges was excellent, well done to the rest of the team. You all worked together very well indeed. Thank you."

Stephens piped up. "Just one thing, Tony, we had to dump our taxi down Savoy Hill, when we got back, we got a ticket. Can you sort it?"

"Don't worry, Mark, I'll get that paid." A new recruit to the surveillance team, basking in the glory of the praise heaped upon him by his boss and now confident he was one of the elite, frowned.

"Pay it, Guv'nor? We're old bill, we don't pay parking tickets, we rip them up or tell them who we are and don't pay it. What's the point of paying them?"

A soft hush fell over the room. The last speaker was now showing signs of being perplexed.

"Tell him, Mark, tell Nigel here why we pay and don't rip up tickets."

"Right, thing is, if we, like you say, rip the ticket up, somewhere along the line, somebody is going to start procedures to trace the owner of the cab. We don't want that to happen, we don't want anybody to know that the cab belongs to us. If we phoned them and said, 'Look, we are old bill, we ain't paying, can you imagine being in the traffic wardens' office when that happens? 'Here, boys and girls, this cab belongs to a police surveillance team.' Guarantee, within a day, it will be all over the City. Our secret is no longer a secret. No, the cab actually checks out to an address in Harlow, as do the other vehicles. We pay the ticket and nobody knows."

Sewell looked towards the recent addition. "Nigel, "OK?" The gentle head movements confirmed he now understood. As his bravado melted, he resumed the mantle of the 'new boy'.

"Right, first up, did we get any shots of this bloke, I mean clear shots so we can identify him?"

"We got some reasonable ones from Parliament Square. I could do some nice postcard size if you want."

"OK, Bill, I'll have half a dozen of each." His pause changed the tone of the meeting.

"Right, we are not really sure, but this could be political. Obviously our bloke has access to Parliament, so we need to keep it tight, very tight. I want the cards from your cameras, anything on phones will be sent to me then deleted. I do not, under any circumstances, want any copies made. I will be the only one with access to the photos. I don't say this lightly, but as we have no idea where this is going, it could be something or nothing, or it might be some scam which might embarrass some politicians, we need to keep it tight. Nothing, I mean nothing, will leak from this team. If I find any pictures floating about, those responsible will be out, no 'ifs' no 'buts'. The log book will say we lost him in the crowds at Westminster Tube. If any of you made any notes today, I want them now. Do not make copies. Right, that's it, off you go. Mark, Raj, could you wait behind."

The chastened assembly drifted away. Sewell's warnings, judging by the brooding silence, seemed to have made an immediate impact. "Right, you two. I don't know what is going on, but I'm going to find out. If any of that lot try to tap you up on the story, I want you to suggest that, according to enquiries we made after today, these are authorised undercover payments going out to some government spook somewhere. If you hear of anybody blabbing about it, I will know about it straight off, right. Yes, Raj, you've got something to say."

"Look, Tony, if this is all tied up with politicians, and we don't know that yet, shouldn't we just kick it upstairs and let the brass deal with it? We might be in over our heads with something like this."

"Raj, what do you think will happen if I went to see our lords and masters today and gave them all this? What do you think, what do you know will happen? Even if it is iffy, it will be all secret handshakes and glasses of sherry and will die a death. I want to find out a bit more then, when I have chapter and verse, and if I need to, then I will go to the right level. If some bent bastard of an MP is bang at it, I want him crucified."

The room was silent. Stephens opened. "What are you going to do? Like Raj, I think you could be on very dodgy ground, we all could be."

"All you two have to say, like in the debrief, he was lost at Westminster Tube, that's all. You carry on with the obs on the launderers as usual. If our bloke reappears, you do not take any action, nothing. You just let me know when he turns up, that's it, nothing else. I will handle the upstairs bit, all official, when the time is right. Can I have both your agreements on that? "

Stephens responded with an immediate, "Sure you can, Tony, you don't have to ask."

Patel held back. "Well, Raj, what do you say? I can make it an order if it makes you feel happier."

"I've always played it straight, Tony, with you and with the Force. If I don't know anything, there's nothing I can say. But, I tell you now, I will not cover anything up."

"Fair enough, Raj, you're good coppers, both of you."

Raj took advantage of the opening. "Tony, just make sure you put that in our annual reports, that's if you are still here."

"Yeah right, thanks for that vote of confidence, Raj. OK, like I said, you just give me a heads up when matey shows up. Put it in the obs log, show that you informed me. Thanks, that's all lads."

Sewell knew, that despite his threats, word would leak out, probably sooner rather than later. Indeed, various whispers floated around. A sharp phone call from Sewell was the safest way of dealing with the matter rather than risking the spectacle of a public flogging. Over the next two weeks or so, Sewell was informed on five occasions that the target, now named 'the Posh Man' had arrived at the area where he handed a bag over after following the usual procedure. As were his instructions, the man was not placed under surveillance. However,

Sewell was advised of the transaction, he immediately made his way to the area adjacent to the Houses of Parliament and positioned himself at a distance so that, whilst mingling with the numerous tourists, he had a view of the entrance gate. Usually, after about an hour and a half after the money was handed over, he saw the 'Posh Man' show his pass to the police officers guarding the gates and go through.

Checks at the bank identifying the cash involved for the last six or seven weeks, showed that deposits averaged in excess of two hundred and fifty thousand pounds and that, to date, a total of over three million pounds had been handed over by him. The paperwork indicated that the recipient was an organisation in Dubai known as Abass Asset and Fund Management Bank. However, this appeared to be the first of several randomly use finance houses where the money remained for no more than a couple of hours. As such, attempts to trace the ultimate destination would be all but impossible.

By now Sewell had photos which clearly identified the man, but he needed a name. In his office he did some homework as to the locations of retired officers. It was a warm Thursday afternoon when he was standing outside Parliament's gates where he was now a regular, if anonymous, visitor. He strolled over to his colleagues manning the portals. About sixty yards away and heading to that same spot was the 'Posh Man.' As he started his conversation, the target moved closer.

"Hello, lads, Tony Sewell, DI, could you tell me if Malcolm King still works here? He was a sergeant with me years ago." The officers furrowed their brows and slowly shook their heads.

"Sorry, Sir."

Then a voice from the back said, "Malcolm King, use to be CID?" Now the target was less than forty yards away. Sewell appeared pleased.

"That's right, that's him. It just that one of our blokes is retiring and we were trying to find out if Malcolm would come along." Now Sewell could see the object of his intentions no more than thirty yards away.

"Sorry, Inspector, Malcolm retired about eighteen months ago."

"That's a shame, we tried to find him where he used to live, but he's moved. I tried to find him through our HR lot, but these days it's all data protection."

"We get that all the time, bloody data protection, health and safety, what a load of nonsense. Anyway, Sir, he moved to Portsmouth to be closer to his daughter."

"That's right, I knew he had family down in that neck of the wood. To be honest, I forgot it was his daughter. Old Malcolm was a good bloke, bit dangerous to go drinking with at times, but a good copper, shame, at least I tried."

With that, the target brushed past him and flashed his Commons pass. Sewell was about to walk away when he jerked a thumb towards the figure disappearing into the embrace of the keeper of democracy. "Isn't he that MP who was on the telly? Didn't he just do some massive gig for charity, swimming and running, stuff like that?"

"That was Haden-Grant, he doesn't look much like that bloke. No, that's some parliamentary aid or assistant. He's from one of them Baltic states, what's his name now?

A voice from over the constable's shoulder assisted, "He's Darius Karvonen he works for the Department of International Development and Aid, them that dish our money to a load of foreigners who don't need it. He's an assistant to Atwood, now he's a bit of a character."

"You know, I was sure it was Haden-Grant, maybe it's time I retired. Thanks guys." As Sewell walked away, he drummed the names Darius Karvonen and Atwood into his brain. He needed to remember them. In his office it didn't take him many hours to put together a report which covered all he knew about Darius Karvonen and his boss in Parliament, Terry Atwood, the Chairman of the International Development Committee. Every time Karvonen made a drop of cash, an equivalent amount, less fees, was transferred to the Middle Eastern finance facility. and every time he made a drop, he also made a phone call.

Prior to becoming an MP, Atwood's claim to fame was that he had inherited a reasonable fortune and substantial property from his father. At the time press reports suggested that he successfully fought off claims from other family members who demanded their rightful share of their father's estate. Atwood, with a flourish, produced a new will which had been drawn up shortly before the father's demise. A solicitor stated that he was present when the new will was drafted and that all the legal conditions were met. The solicitor was not unknown to Atwood.

In his office Sewell sifted what material he had gathered so far. It was clear that there was, at this stage, a growing body of evidence that would directly implicated Atwood in wrong doing, and it all pointed towards to the fact that large scale fraud was in play. A few minutes of research on the internet showed that the International Development Committee handed out over seventeen billion pounds a year including almost a billion on consultancies and countless millions to various countries, some of which had been described, by a previous prime minister, as the 'most corrupt countries in the world.' Several newspaper articles were attached to his report, most of which criticised the lack of clarity and accountability, levelling at the committee its inability to trace where these vast amounts of aid really ended up. What Sewell considered he had established was that he had more than enough intelligence to make it worth mounting an enquiry into how a parliamentary aid, working for one of the world's biggest hand out schemes, was able to pay millions of pounds in cash into a foreign bank which, in reality, lay beyond the clutches of any legislative powers that were available to the UK government.

As he locked the report in his desk drawer, he reached for his phone and punched in Upton's number.

"Chief Superintendent Upton."

"Blimey, Eric, that's a posh voice."

"Oh, Inspector Sewell, er Tony, what can I do for you today? You going to tell me you are actually taking retirement any last?"

"Listen, Eric, I've got hold of something which could possibly be big, very big, has the potential to be explosive. If it's what I think it is, it would make the news around the world."

"You are retiring. At last."

"No, Eric this is so big, that I need to go straight to the top, Commissioner or Deputy Commissioner, it is definitely on 'a need to know' basis."

"Are you pulling my plonker? What you on about?"

"Eric old luv, I really, really cannot tell you. It is better that you don't know. I am deadly serious, I need to see the top brass and I need to see them as soon as."

"What is it, Tony, what's it all about?"

"I am not joking. I've done this by myself, nobody, and I mean nobody, knows anything about it. I really can't tell you. When, and if, it comes out, you will understand why. Now, do you make this appointment for me, or do I have to fight my way through the red tape to do it myself? It's up to you."

Two days later, the inspector lounged outside the office of the Deputy Commissioner. After being summoned in, he unburdened himself and related the facts he had uncovered complete with a copy of his file. The deputy listened in silence and tried to mask the growing alarm he was experiencing. The intercom was buzzed.

"Sir Frank, are you free, I have an Inspector Sewell with me who seems to have uncovered something very significant. I do think you should listen to him right now."

Sewell repeated his performance in front of the Commissioner, Sir Frank Withy, who then sat back to digest the information he had just been made party to.

"Right; Inspector?"

"Sewell, Sir."

"Inspector Sewell, I will need to evaluate this, but I must say it seems to be irrefutable as to the facts you have uncovered, then I shall discuss it with a higher authority if you see what I mean. Obviously, I do not have to tell you not to discuss this with anyone at all. Irrespective of rank, nobody. In fact, you will take paid leave until this matter is resolved. Leave your address and phone numbers with my secretary and keep her informed of any plans you have for travel. I suggest that you, for the time being, remain available at all times. Who is you line manager?"

"Chief Superintendent Upton, Sir."

"Chief Superintendent Upton will be informed that you are on extended leave. He will not discuss your absence with anybody." By this time the Commissioner was bristling with self-importance, his mouth twitching slightly as if to savour forthcoming events. "Right, thank you, Inspector. I will keep you informed and if I need your assistance I will let you know." Before Sewell had closed the door on his way out, the Commissioner was holding his phone to his ear. "Home Secretary, please."

Chapter 6

"You may go through now." London's Commissioner of Police pushed the door open and tried not to bring himself to attention. Standing behind his desk was a short squat balding man in an open neck shirt and rolled up sleeves, Norman Higgins, the home secretary.

"Come in, Frank isn't it? Take a seat. Can I get you a drink?"

"A sherry if I may, Home Secretary."

"Bollocks you'll have a sherry. What sort of a bloke has a tart's drink like a bloody sherry? You can have a gin or a whisky. What's it to be?" The commissioner lowered himself with stiff arms into his seat.

"In that case, Home Secretary, a small whisky with a lot of water."

Higgins sniffed his mild disgust. "In my day, when I looked after my constituents, which I did very well indeed, you could always rely on a copper to have a decent drink with you. I suppose these days it's all political correctness. A lot of bollocks if you ask me." He thrust a brimming glass towards his visitor. "Now then, this file you've passed to me about money laundering, what do you make of it?"

As Withy placed his generous measure on the desk in front of him, some of the contents spilled onto his fingers. He hesitated, unsure as to how to proceed. He was assisted by the Home Secretary.

"Put it on the bloody desk, man, I don't reckon it will be mine for much longer anyway, if it marks it, the next lot can sort it out."

The Commissioner mumbled an appreciation, then turned to the matter of his wet fingers. With his dry hand, he fished out a handkerchief from his pocket, and with a marked reluctance, used it to absorb the offending liquid. The home secretary's eyes raised and glanced towards the view his window gave to the outside world. The commissioner, having regained most of his dignity, straightened himself in his seat so as almost to be sitting stiffly upright.

"Yes, this supposed money laundering issue, one of my officers, involved in surveillance duties, more or less stumbled across. I must say, that to his credit, when he realised that the House may be involved, he handled it himself, he was most discreet. As such he is the only officer who has any direct evidence of the person carrying the money, his position and who he works for."

Higgins wiped excess alcohol from his lips with the back of his hand.

"That's good, Frank. That's very useful."

Withy, grasping the wrong end of the politician's observations, took it as a compliment and responded with a knowing smile.

"Yes, Sir, as you can see, he has put together a comprehensive file on this matter. My officer, Inspector Sewell, is very experienced and his enquiries, which have been very thorough, have established, with a degree of almost certainty, that money from the House is being laundered and, by way of audit, how much is involved."

"Has he by Jove? And how much is involved? What sort of figures are we talking about?"

The Commissioner knew the amounts in question, but having brought his file thought it made sense to make use of it. He fingered the pages.

"Yes, here we are, it is nearly five million to date, about a million and a half over the past couple of months. "

"Bugger me, millions."

"Yes, Home Secretary, the figures are shown in the file I sent to you."

Higgins flattened the document on his desk and stared over towards the elevated constable,

"All these millions and counting I suppose."

The Commissioner, his self-importance still growing, assisted. "Yes, Sir, and still counting. When it got to the stage where we were sure that some of your colleagues may, and I do say, 'may' be involved, we recognised, that there could be certain issues which may need to be resolved between us before we proceed."

"I see, and what issues would these be?" The commissioner, now feeling more relaxed, reached for his glass and imbibed. However, the strength of the drink took him by surprise, he gave a muted cough and returned the glass to the desk.

"Sir, we are talking about potentially very serious alleged offences which, at the moment, could involve a very senior and influential politician. I am aware that there will be certain sensitivities and that we need to proceed with caution. We need to manage the enquiry in a way so as to cause the government the minimum of disruption and embarrassment. I thought, that today, we could agree a way forward, a road map to sort this out in a mutually agreeable manner."

"A 'road map', is that the way you buggers talk these day? Bloody road map. Go on then, Frank, how do you reckon we should sort this out? Where does your 'road map' takes us?"

"As you know, Home Secretary, we are pledged to pursue all crime, no matter who is involved, without fear or favour. Nobody will be immune from the legal processes. I think I recall you actually saying that."

"Did I? Oh that's right, but we were in opposition then and that other lot were screwing their expenses."

"To be fair, Home Secretary, it wasn't just the 'other lot' who were at it. You said at the time that the public would not have confidence either in democracy or the offices of law and order if these matters were swept under the carpet. I think your phrase was, 'We must shine the light of justice in such a way that there are no dark corners left.' A philosophy that I agree with totally."

"You do, do you?"

"Yes, I do. Do you think the prime minister will want to be directly involved with this?"

"The prime minister? You must be joking, he's had it, he's given up. Most of the time he doesn't know what day it is. It's like the man with the bucket of sawdust is now running the circus. You think he could manage this? Not a hope in Hell, you might as well give a mother superior an Anne Summers catalogue and tell her to make her choice. Anyway, it's probably best that he doesn't get to hear anything about this. We need to keep it tight; close to our chests, if you know what I mean."

The Commissioner leant forward in his seat his face a mask of bemusement.

"Home Secretary, I don't understand. Obviously the prime minister will hear about it, I mean he has to. When this comes out, when it becomes public, he and everybody else will become aware. I'm afraid I don't follow you."

"Listen, Frank, nobody is going to hear about this, I mean nobody. This will have to be buried."

Withy flicked an imaginary unwanted thread from his uniform jacket.

"So, Home Secretary, Terry Atwood is that big a player? As chairman of the International Development Committee, has he got the keys to the safe?"

"What makes you think it's Atwood?"

"Home Secretary, we police do not make assumptions, very dangerous habit. I know it's Atwood."

"How so?"

"Amongst other things, phone records. It's all in your file."

The Home Secretary blinked and reflected. "But nobody has applied for a warrant to tap his phone."

"Really, how do you know?" Withy was starting to feel a lot more comfortable.

"All warrant applications come across my desk, well if not my desk, an assistant. Obviously I would have been informed if his name was on it."

The Commissioner, feeling as though he had collected another snippet of information, blinked slowly and lowered his head then left it to the slightly flustered Higgins to reply. None was forthcoming.

"Not phone interceptions, Home Secretary, just phone records. We do have intercept warrants for some of the individuals who are also involved. From these we can see what numbers are involved. We traced a series of calls from Atwood's assistant, or whatever he is. We then requested, from the service provider, records of calls made and received by that phone, no warrant needed. Apparently the phone Atwood uses on these occasions is not the officially provided device. At the times when the money was handed over, every time, Atwood's boy, I think that is the right description, phoned his boss. We couldn't obtain his records, as you know they are protected. So my inspector called his number, the one Karvonen used, and he very kindly answered it. So it is Atwood."

Higgins, his lips puckered, remained silent. The commissioner, now in his stride continued.

"Our enquiries indicate, without much doubt, that he is running a scam. It doesn't take a genius to work out what is going on. His committee doles out seventeen billion pounds a year to various regimes in various countries some of which have the most corrupt heads of state. There is virtually no check on where the money ends up, and there is no effective audit trail. Billions of pounds are being given away and nobody knows to whom. It must be the easiest place in the world to run a racket from. He personally deals with heads of states. He promises an increase in funding, which in all probability has already been agreed by the committee. He knows, we all know, it will go straight into some president's pocket. In return, he gets a brown envelope, a very big brown envelope, then pays it into a some anonymous overseas account. The identity of the bank of destination is obscured by some form of convoluted transfer system. The beauty of it is, from his point of view, or so he thinks, nothing can be traced and who is going to complain? We have no idea where or to whom the money actually goes. We may know the intended country, but we do not know which person in that country benefits. Atwood's cut will never be shown to be missing and the recipients in Asia or wherever, sure as Hell are not going to rock the boat and complain that the politician he is bribing is ripping him off. It is as safe as houses, that is until my men stumbled over it." He leant forward and took a generous sip of his whisky. He sat back and cleared his throat. "Home Secretary, will you explain what you mean when you say that this will have to be 'buried?"

Higgins rubbed the palms of his hands together. "Look, Frank, what is important for us is to run the country. Stability, keep the punters happy. Give them all the cake and ginger beer they want, then we have a chance of getting back in. You do know that there will be a general election in eight or nine months' time, something like that. I am not demeaning the work you and your blokes have done, but something like this could leave a very sour taste in the mouths of our voters. As it is, things are getting very tight, you will be aware of one or two cock ups around here."

"Yes, the usual, Home Secretary. Some of your people have been hiring themselves out to the highest bidder. Doing favours to amend legislation, influencing contract bids on the supply of military equipment. Is that what you mean?"

"Yes, yes." Higgins wafted the air in front of him so as to blow the incidents away. "That was the bloody press, sticking their noses in, straight from the gutter that lot. Mind you, nothing was proved. The Standards Committee cleared them."

"Remind me, Home Secretary, just who was on that committee."

"It is a cross party committee, the findings are fair." Any showing of respect by Withy was now draining away and was being replaced by angry contempt.

"As you say, although many thousands of taxpayers pounds were used for personal gain, contrary to the rules..." Here Higgins moved to speak. Withy continued. "Contrary to the rules, only one or two of the most blatant abusers were brought to book. Is this what you want me to do now, cover up Atwood's fraud?"

"That was mainly the other side, greedy bastards. It wasn't a cover up, Frank, it was managed, handled in an appropriate manner. We must think of the wellbeing of the country, the electorate. At the moment, it looks like it's a bit close as to whether we get back in." Higgins waited to see if his words had settled in the right place.

"If I could use one of your words, Home Secretary; bollocks."

Higgins noted the response without showing any demonstrable signs. The commissioner, despite his initial hesitancy, was not going to roll over.

"Frank, let me be blunt with you, this matter will die, wither on the vine. You will not pursue it. Like I say, a general election soon, we are struggling as it is. It seems there has been a shift in favour to those public school twats. It's like we are being blamed for the economy when, as we all know, it's a worldwide recession."

58

"Home Secretary, if we could skip the party political broadcast. I want to know what your instructions are in respect of Atwood and his very big fingers in a very big pie."

Higgins realised that he was not in a position to challenge Withy's growing assertiveness by continuing the debate. "Look, Frank, it looks like Terry Atwood has had a bit of a dip; hand in the till. A bit naughty, but, well you know, it happens. How many big business men do the same? It's part of the game. I will speak to Atwood, sort him out, get him to toe the line. As I say, it happens all the time in big business."

"Yes, Home Secretary, but nobody voted for a big businessman to run the country. No big businessman made promises to improve our future and uphold democratic principles."

"Very good, Frank, you don't fancy joining our lot do you? I could see you doing a first rate job." He did not try to hide the sarcasm which came with his words. He neither expected nor received a response. He took a decent mouthful of whisky, rose from his chair and walked to a large window to face the courtyard outside. He remained there with his hands resting on the rear of his ample hips. "Right, Frank, it's actually Sir, isn't it, Frank? This is what is going to happen, no ifs or buts. We cannot, and will not, stand another scandal with one of ours. OK, he is bent, but so are half of that other lot, it goes on. If we hung out every bugger that had a bit of a dabble, the bloody place would be empty. You say this copper of yours, this inspector, has kept all this very close to his chest. I assume that only he and you know the full story, yes?"

Withy held a long silence before replying.

"Yes, he didn't even tell his senior officer. He did talk it through with my deputy, who then informed me."

"When are you due to retire, Frank?"

"What?"

"Come on, man, it's a simple question. When are you due to retire?"

"About eighteen months."

"What are you going to do then?"

"I don't know, smell the roses, get back to sailing, why?"

"Let me say this. You, and your lot, will not touch Atwood, you will make no further references to him or to this silly fandango, you will not. Do I make myself clear?"

"Home Secretary, it is not your business to instruct me not to pursue criminal activity on the basis it is a bit inconvenient for you. This is a very significant case, what would the public think if this came out? What would the voters say if they knew that the law and the government were colluding to cover up serious crimes, when the man in the street is going to prison for fiddling a fraction, a very small fraction, of what faces us in this matter today?"

Higgins was pumped with rage. "The public, the bloody public, they don't think, they follow, like bloody sheep." Realising he was shouting, he sought calm by brushing his waistcoat with his hands. Withy stood to leave.

"I think we have a disagreement. I see it as my duty to thoroughly investigate what I believe to be a serious breach of the law." He moved towards the door. Higgins's anger returned.

"Get your arse back in here, I am the Home Secretary, you are a copper. You will do what I tell you, now sit. You will obey my orders."

"Yes, Home Secretary, I will obey your lawful orders." The penultimate word had its own space and was pronounced with emphasis. A momentary raising of his eyebrows was the slightest of acknowledgements from Higgins.

Once he saw the Commissioner seated, Higgins returned to standing by the window with his back to Withy. Without turning, he spoke. "Do you fancy being a lord, Frank? You would look good in ermine trimmed robes. Fancy it, Frank? If I were you, I would give it very close consideration, very close indeed. Just think about it, a title, three hundred and fifty quid a day just for turning up. Get on committees, overseas trips, wherever you like, you know, for research. Life of bloody Riley, Frank. Think about it."

If Withy was surprised, he didn't show it.

"Because. I tell you what, Frank, this Atwood affair, is not going to see the light of day. No matter what you think you can do. You do know we have these special operations blokes, nobody ever sees them. Officially they don't exist. They are very clever, very adept at what they do. Their role is, to disrupt things, to bring about certain results. For instance, we had a situation, not too dissimilar to this one." Withy, stoney faced looked away. "A civil servant, a very senior civil servant fell over one of our more entrepreneurial ministers. This civil servant was full of the fire of righteousness. He wasn't going to let it go. I think he had God on his side. Unfortunately for him, God was having a day off. We had to do something. So, it was agreed that there was to be an unseemly sex scandal in which our civil servant played a starring role, or so it was decided. Nothing actually proved, but somehow the press got hold of it. Front page allegations, pictures of his wife, now his former wife. Of course he denied it, denied it uphill and down dale. Didn't do him any good. Poor man, he resigned. Loss of job, loss of pension. No chance of getting another position, well not a position in employment if you get my drift. Poor chap is a ruined man. Quite useful, being able to allude the odd sexual headline. You don't want to be a ruined man do you, Frank? No, you would rather be a lord. I can see it now, Lord Frank of Lower Clegheaton and Barnsley East. It suits you, it really does. Off you pop, Lord Frank, and get this sorted out. Get your inspector sorted. Tell him it's a matter of national importance that a lid is kept on this. Give him some time off, retire him; whatever. I will authorise anything you want. He does not have anything more to do with this." He glared at the police officer. "You're playing with the big boys now, it's big boys' rules. I suggest, in the strongest possible terms, that you cease this investigation into the whole money laundering business immediately. Be careful, Frank, just another eighteen months. Don't chuck away a lifetime's work and your reputation. Don't expose your family to ridicule."

"Home Secretary, this operation, the overall money laundering scheme, has been ongoing for nine or ten months now. We have been cooperating with the criminal authorities from several countries not to mention finance ministries. It's not just our money that's gone into all this. The Americans, who as you know, can become rather touchy on money laundering, especially if it is used to fund terrorism, have contributed resources, expensive resources, to this operation. If you want to pull the plug on it, several overseas government agencies will want chapter and verse as to why. They have their own 'big boys.'

They will not be best amused if all their efforts and expenses go down the drain."

"Frank, do not carry on with your little enquiry and keep our inspector bloke out of it. If the Americans say anything, we can sort it out. We've done it before, and so have they, it's a sort of mutual understanding. Now, off you pop' Lord Frank." Withy had not left the building when Higgins made a call. "Find that bugger Atwood and send him to my office immediately."

Chapter 7

On the short walk back to his office Withy, who seemed to have shrunk inside his uniform, replayed the meeting in a continuous loop running through his mind. Before he even pushed open the doors to New Scotland Yard, he had arrived at his decision. It was the only one available to him.

"Get me Inspector Sewell on the phone will you please, Jane."

"Of course, Commissioner."

"Inspector, Sewell, it's the Commissioner here. How are you?"

"Yes, Sir, I'm good, yes good."

"First of all, Inspector, I must congratulate you on the work you have been doing. Shows expertise and commitment, well done. I have to tell you, you have caused quite a stir. I have just had a meeting with the Home Secretary to discuss the results of your surveillance, quite a stir indeed."

"I see, Sir."

"Inspector, you have stumbled across a very sensitive government operation, very sensitive indeed."

Sewell noted the second use of 'indeed'.

"Is that so, Sir."

"Yes, the Home Secretary was very impressed with our ability to delve into these matters. But, as I said, it is a very serious matter, very sensitive."

"Indeed, Sir."

"What? Oh yes, because of the nature of the government's involvement, we are under strict instructions to have no further involvement with this. All actions must be halted forthwith."

Sewell noted two 'involvements.'

"So, Inspector, just to keep things in order, could I ask to you send me the case file and any associated documents? Mark it 'For the attention of the Commissioner.' I'll send a courier around to collect it. He should be with you in half an hour or so."

"I see, Sir."

"Also, Inspector, just to be on the safe side, so to speak, to comply with certain protocols, it is felt that it would be prudent, how can I put this, for you not to be on duty. Apparently, it's fairly standard procedure, so, as from now, once you have sent me the documents I have asked you for, you will be on leave, paid leave that is."

"But, Sir I.........."

"No buts, Inspector, you are on leave as from now. Six weeks, but check with personnel before you come back."

Now Sewell noted the clear imperative tone that was suddenly injected into the conversation.

"So that's understood, Inspector, all documents and six weeks leave as of now. I'm sorry if this seems a bit extreme, but under these circumstances it is the accepted procedure. Thank you, Inspector."

Sewell rocked back in his chair and exhaled a long slow jet of air. He reflected on his years of service, all the collars he had made, all the interviews he had conducted, all the evidence he had sifted through. Right now, he knew one thing; the commissioner was lying.

The next day Sewell was in the pub when his phone rang.

"Inspector Sewell, it's the commissioner for you."

"Thank you."

"Sewell, Inspector Sewell."

Sewell was not in the least bit taken aback at the notes of anger in the Commissioner's voice.

"Look, Sewell, when I say I want the documents, the file on this, I want the originals. You've sent me a load of photo copies. When I give an order, I expect it to be complied with. Now, get that stuff over to me, immediately. Tell me where you are, I'll send somebody."

"I'm on leave, Sir, don't you remember? I don't know if they will let me back into the office. I will comply with your orders, but I can only do so within the rules. They are quite rigid, there must be a clear audit trail for the movement of documents. So, Sir, if you put your orders in writing requesting all the original papers, an email is acceptable, I will comply. Those are your guidelines, Sir. And, of course, I will get a signed receipt."

"You say you are on leave, but is that really the case? There is nothing in writing, Inspector. I might say that you are not on leave at all."

"You are absolutely correct, Sir, nothing in writing yet, nothing whatsoever. But in my line of work, you know, dealing with criminals, informants and all sorts of dishonest people, I find it pays to record all my phone conversations. You know, just in case."

"Oh, shit."

The line went dead. Now he knew Withy was lying. "Bloody useless upper class, hooray Henry university prat. You've never been on the beat in the middle of freezing January night." He paid for another beer. The command from the commissioner to cover his order in writing never came. Now he was sure he was being lied to. But why? "I'm on six weeks leave, let's find out."

Sewell, knowing that management would not drop this issue, wasn't surprised when he received a command to attend his office for a meeting with Chief Superintendent Eric Upton. Upton opened the meeting.

"Tony, I don't know what the bloody Hell you've been up to, but there's a load of crap that has been dumped on my desk. I'm allowed to address you, but I'm not allowed to ask you any details, any details about anything. First thing, you are no longer on leave, you are, with immediate effect, suspended until further notice. From what I hear, and I should not say this, I understand they are going to pension you off. That's what I've heard, no other details."

Sewell showed no reaction. "Suspended on full pay?"

"Yes, on full pay."

"Why?"

"What do you expect, we've talked about it often enough, your behaviour, your attitude."

"Thank you so much, Eric, I take it that you did not hold back in supplying all the information they needed to nail me. One minute I'm a hero for flushing the sewers in parliament, now I'm a villain. Go on, Eric, what else?"

"You are to hand over all case files, note books, evidential material. This is to include all copies and originals. And of course, your warrant card."

Sewell slouched back into his chair. "Thing is, Eric, what exactly is a case file. If it has not been given a number or been logged into the system, is it a case file? I don't think so. Tell you what, go back to the Commissioner and ask him what exactly is he looking for. If he can be more specific, I'll see what I can do."

"Christ, Tony, you are pushing your luck."

"Really? What are they going to do? Suspend me again? Retire me twice? I tell you what I have got. I've got the Commissioner by the nuts. The politicians have got him by the nuts. And the politicians will be grabbing each other's' balls like there's no tomorrow. I'm the one holding all the cards, or all the nuts if you like. Tell them to go screw themselves, tell them never take a skunk on in a pissing competition. I'll send you my warrant card later."

"Tony, I can't back you in this one, you're on your own."

"Back me? When have you ever backed me? You've spent your career stabbing your mates in the back and covering your own arse. You have never backed anybody but yourself."

Upton opened his mouth to speak, but Sewell's verbal thrust beat him to it.

"Don't forget, Eric, don't forget what you did all those years ago. I can use that, even now. Maybe you could get to like prison food."

"That was for your family, I was doing you a favour, I was looking out for you."

"Looking out for my family, don't make me laugh. You took an enormous bung. Maybe I've still got the records."

Upton summarily dismissed what he regarded as an idle threat.

"If you go down that line, the only ones at risk are your own family, you would be dropping them in it."

"Really? Maybe they deserve to be dropped in it. But they won't be dropped nearly as far as you, will they Eric, my old mate."

Upton bristled at the impertinence and the threat. But more, inwardly he raged at the impotency of his situation.

"Look, here's the notice I am required to give you. It confirms your suspension. I will wait for your warrant card."

"Eric, old luv, I'm going to have to do some sorting out. I don't see why I should get stitched up because of some bent politicians. If anybody gets in my way, I will not go round them. If you get in my way, or you get some team to try and sort me, I will go straight through you."

Sewell halted at the door. "Have you ever considered retirement, Eric? Might be an idea to protect your pension. I could see you settling down in Spain. Big straw hat and little umbrellas in your drink. I would start looking at some noisy shirts if I were you."

Upton watched and followed the inspector's route through the office and then from his window as he left. He punched a number into his phone.

"Hello, Upton here, Chief Superintendent Upton. Could I speak with the commissioner please. I think he will be expecting my call." He watched Sewell until he disappeared.

"Hello, Commissioner." As he spoke, he rose to his feet. "It went more or less as I expected. He seems to be very angry and appears to blame others for his situation."

"I suppose that includes me."

Upton gave an apologetic laugh and bowed slightly from the waist.

"Indeed he appeared to imply that, Commissioner."

"Did he say, or indicate, that he proposes to take any action, do anything about it, that sort of thing?"

"No, not really, he mumbled a bit, as I say he was very angry, blamed others all the time. Commissioner, I have known him for a long time, he's a bit of a hot head, always shouting about what he is going to do, but rarely does anything, in fact he spoke about retiring to Spain. I feel pretty sure that if he was allowed to retire on full pension, that's what he would do. I don't know what all this is about, obviously something sensitive, but if we gave him a back door, I am sure he would take it. It might be better than having him running around blustering and shouting the odds. You never know, he might just touch a raw nerve or two."

"Yes, Superintendent, you give the picture of an officer who runs around using intemperate language and behaving in an ineffective manner, yet his annual reports show him to be a very talented, dogged and successful investigator. And you, Chief Superintendent, have been his reporting officer for the past six years. So, do you still say he is merely full of bluster?"

Upton jerked upwards, his eyes searched for a riposte

"Well, yes, Commissioner, and indeed in the past he did perform to an acceptable standard. But his divorce and the breakup of his family have affected him, he has become too fond of the drink. Perhaps I was giving him the benefit of the doubt."

"When was his divorce, Chief Superintendent?"

"Let me see, I think it was a few years back, yes, something like that."

"It was nearly fourteen years ago. Why do you describe him, in his reports, as a first rate investigator?"

"Maybe I was a bit generous in my estimation of him and a bit too lenient with his reports."

"Chief Superintendent, is this man a washed up no hoper or is he a tenacious and gifted officer? He has certain information which, if mishandled, could be very embarrassing for this force and members of the government. Which is it? I have to brief the Home Secretary on this. I want, I need, I demand the correct information."

Upton took a deep breath and exhaled sharply. "I would have to say he is probably one of the best officers I have worked with. He has not been promoted because he comes from a family of local and active villains and it was deemed prudent not to give him too much authority in case he misused it."

"For Christ's sake, man, half the bloody Met is bent. As one of my predecessors said, his job was to catch more crooks than he employs. There's something going on here and I want to sort it out. Make an appointment to see Human Resources.

Chapter 8

It was almost a week since Harry's team had pulled off the warehouse robbery. Any interest the media had shown had, by now, drifted away as more recent ephemera had flared and died. The public wanted news. The police investigating the robbery started with an intense flurry and had even questioned Harry as to his whereabouts at the time the venture took place. The plain clothes officers who hammered on the door of his expensive apartment, weren't local. He had expected this because his brother was a local cop and there was to be no allegations of family collusion. "Open the door, Sewell, open it or we will break it down."

Harry threw the door back and stood in slacks and a short sleeve shirt, smiling at the assembled officers. "Hello, boys, you lost or something? Anything I can help you with?"

"We would like to come in and discuss some matters with you."

"Oh, you mean that warehouse job. You took your time, I was expecting you days ago, and no."

"No what?"

"No, you can't come in, unless you've got a warrant. But you haven't got a warrant, because if you did have, you wouldn't be standing there like vicars at a choir meeting. No, you would have been through this door quicker than greased weasel shit. So, you haven't got any evidence against me, have you? You're here on a fishing expedition, sorry, boys that ain't going to work, so bye for now."

Harry knew what was coming next, he could write the script. "Look, Sewell, maybe you would rather we did this at the police station."

"Oh, officer, please, you're not still trying that. You've been watching too many cops and robber films. If you want me to go down to the nick, then you will have to arrest me. If you are not too sure on the procedure, I can help you, I've been through it once or twice. Now then, tell me you have got evidence, or piss off."

"All right, OK. Look could you tell me where you were last Saturday night?" If it checks out, then you are in the clear and we won't need to bother you again."

Harry brushed his chin with his hand and gave a display of mock concentration. "Let me see, last Saturday night. Yes, I was playing poker with some mates down the pub, a good game, I won a few quid, a profitable evening. It didn't break up until after three. Yes, I would have to say it was a very profitable evening."

"And where did you go after that?"

"Nowhere, I stayed there."

"Who with?"

"The landlady, she's what you might call a friend of mine."

"Are you saying, you stayed with this friend of yours? Just how friendly are you with her? Did you sleep with her?"

"Not a wink, mate, not a wink. Now, if you gents would excuse me, I've got my ironing and dusting to finish off."

"Right, Sewell, we will need the names of the people who you say you played poker with, just to corroborate your story. We will need to take witness statements from them."

Leaning against the jamb of his door, Harry folded his arms and looked skywards. "Do you know what, boys, I don't feel like telling you. Is that a crime? Can you arrest me for that? No, I don't think so. When you find them, as I have no doubt you will, I am sure they will all give you statements, that is, as long as it is done with my solicitor present."

Behind the man who was doing all the talking, two other officers where in whispered conversation. With heads slightly bowed, they conferred with the officer at the door. "Just one thing, Sewell, you mother doesn't live far from here, hasn't she got a bit of form?"

Harry's face tightened with rage. "You leave my mum out of this. No, no she hasn't got form for anything, not for a long time now. She's a pensioner now, she's in her seventies. Don't think you can turn her over just because I've just come out of nick."

The three police officers turned to face Sewell full on. The leader sensed an opening. "Tell you what, you come down to the station and answer our questions and your mum has a quiet life."

Harry's rage deepened. "That's blackmail, you can't do that, just leave my mum out of it."

"Your call, Harry, either you talk to us, or we talk to your mum, it's up to you. You never know, we might have to nick her. Do you want me to take her down to the station?"

The anger on Harry's face melted into a wide smile. "Thank you lads, you've been a real help."

The assured stance the policemen had held, rapidly faded. Harry continued. "You see, what I should have told you is that this door bell, actually it is a door bell, but it is also a camera and a microphone, it's one of these new gadgets. Keeps you protected from villains, you never know who is out and about the days. So there it is, you dumbos are now the main players in a blackmail film. It's what your lot call 'duress'. You've blown it, guys. You might think I am shooting the breeze and that there is no camera or microphone; your call. But what I say is this, if any of you dickheads pokes your nose around these parts again, ever again, or any of your mates, I go straight to the press and my brief with all this. Now get your scooters of my lawn and sod off."

Within twenty minutes Harry was at his mother's house. Even he noticed the smell of stale cigarette smoke that had settled into the furniture and had soaked into the walls like old conversations. "You alright, Mum, nobody been bothering you have they, nobody's been round?"

"What you talking about, Harry? Who's been round, who's supposed to have been round? No, nobody's been here. But, I'll tell you this, my boy, I know why you are worried, I know what it's all about. It was you, wasn't it? it was you at that..."

"Whoa, Mum, careful, just be careful what you are saying, know what I mean? Who is listening, if you get my drift?" His eyes bulged so as to add emphasis.

"Harry," her voice was louder, much louder than it had been, there was a pause. Now quieter and softer, "Harry, son, you're not going on about that again. Ain't any bugs or microphones or anything like that here, or your place. Harry, you have this place checked over and over again. There's nothing here, it's all in your head. You've got it on you that there's these bug things all over the place, you have got to let it go, son, it will make you ill again."

A slight jerking of his head with synchronised waving of his outstretched thumb indicated he wanted to continue the conversation in the garden. Harry pointed back to the house. "You've got to be careful, Mum, they can hear you. I think we're OK out here. Look, I've had the old bill around, trying to give me a hard time. They haven't been here have they, I mean they shouldn't, I've warned them off.

His mother drew deep on a cigarette and exhaled a narrow jet of smoke. "It's that warehouse job, isn't it? That was yours, you did that, didn't you"?

"Mum, what you don't know, you can't talk about. I can tell you this, when that job was pulled, I was down the pub all night playing poker with the boys."

"And you was playing with that cow of a landlady, don't know what you see in her, slag."

Harry demonstrated the usual degree of exasperation he felt on these occasions. "Don't be like that, Mum. I've just come out and she waited for me."

"She's married, she's a married woman for Christ's sake. She works next to her husband. How does that all work? She's stringing you along, taking the piss. You'd be better off with Violet Reid's daughter, that Judith, nice girl. Violet has been a good friend to me, a good friend for years. There's nothing wrong with Judith, never been a bit of trouble. Violet always showed me a lot of respect, always."

"She showed you 'respect' as you call it, because she is still paying off a loan from you. How long has a that been going on then? You must have had your money back ten times by now. And her daughter, she's daft, she's in cloud cuckoo land."

"She's a nice quiet girl, you need to settle down now, especially at your age. You want to pack this lark in. Nobody does blaggings these days, it's all computer fraud, nicking identities. Pays very nicely, that's what you should be doing, that's if you had the brains."

Harry's features seemed to squeeze to the centre of his face as his complexion reddened.

"Don't go on, Mum, don't. You always do this to me. Just leave it will you."

The old lady judged that, from past experiences, she could now start to probe Harry.

"That warehouse, Harry, it was you wasn't it? You don't have to tell me, I know you done it, it's your style."

"Mum, it's best you don't know, alright."

"Why do you do it, Harry? I don't want you going back inside. Why do you do it?" He wheeled to face his mother, his angry face thrust into hers. "Why do I do it? What else do I know? What else have I done? What else have I been taught? I get respect, around here, people respect me."

"They don't respect you, they are terrified of you. They know what you can do, what you have done. I saved you once, even if it was a long time ago. If you ever get banged up for that, you wouldn't be out for a long time." She casually drew on her cigarette, her left arm holding her right elbow, flicking the ash off with her thumb nail. She studied him to see if her barbs provoked the reaction she expected.

"That was in the past, Mum, that's all done, finished. You want to know why I do this, why I am the main man around here? It's because that's what you trained me for, that's all I've known all my life. When I worked with Dad, and I came home with a stash, you were happy enough to take it, you never said, 'Stop it, don't do it any more'. Never, you never, your eyes used to light up, you would grab the stuff and stick it in all your hiding places, in neighbours houses and sheds. You knew they would never grass you up."

"They wouldn't because of you. The last thing they wanted was a mad bloke like you going round to sort them out." She calmly flicked another layer of ash from her cigarette.

"Mum, I keep telling you, I am not mad, I am not mad. Alright, I've got a bit of a temper, all those bloody shrinks don't know what they are talking about."

"I'm sorry, Son, I didn't mean it like that, I didn't. All that stuff in the old days, it was your dad, he was a villain, it was all a game to him, it was him what done it to you. All airs and graces, poncing around like he owned the place. "

"Dad was bloody useless; small time. Not a boss like me, he didn't run his own manor, just a low life little creep. You ran him, you sorted him out. It was you who pushed him out to do some poxy little post office. If there was any trouble with any of his mates, or so called mates, you would send me round to sort it. You didn't give a toss if he got pulled and was sent down. You go on about me and my bird being married, it never bothered you, did it? When dad got potted, I don't recall you hanging about."

Her cigarette was slowly and methodically crushed beneath her foot, casually she removed a loose strand of tobacco from her tongue, examined it briefly before she flicked it away.

"It was different in them days, you wouldn't understand. And don't forget that fight you was in. Who sorted that out for you? Where would you have been if that hadn't been buried good and proper? Don't you ever forget what was done for you then. That cost, cost a lot. I saved you then."

Harry was spent, there was nothing he could throw at his mother that would wrong foot her. He realised it was time to quit.

"That's it, Mum, I've had enough. I'd be better off back inside. When you get like this, it's worse than being locked up. Why do you do it?"

His mother shrugged nonchalantly as she lit another cigarette and after examining the glowing end, exhaled a plume of smoke.

"Mum, I need a drink." He moved towards the kitchen. Her body tensed then she moved to overtake her son.

"It's alright, Harry, let me get it for you. I'll get it, what do you want, a whiskey? I'll get it. You sit in the lounge, I'll bring it in."

This sudden change from studied arrogance to obeisance jarred with Harry. The rushing in front of him, her change from a matter of fact thrower of verbal darts to accommodating mother, found an alarm in Harry's battered mind. A realisation washed through his being. He pushed her to one side and pulled open the sideboard door. He looked back at her. She thought this would not be a good time to challenge her son or proffer a form of defence. Harry moved to the cupboard under the stairs. She sighed heavily and affected a look of bored resignation.

"What's all this, how did you get hold of all this, all these bottles, whiskey, gin, cartons of fags. There's bloody loads of it. You don't even like gin. Where did.........?" Slowly his head drooped, his eyes closed, he spoke slowly. "It's the warehouse, job isn't it? It's the bloody warehouse job. I recognise the brands. Look, look at them, they're all duty free." He grabbed her by the shoulders and shook her. Her previous insouciance stiffened into fear. She had seen the rage that her son was now demonstrating, but it was a long time since it was aimed at her.

"Where did you get it from, tell me you bitch or so help me.... where did it come from?"

"It was a bloke in the pub, he said he had a few bottles of the stuff and he......" She reeled from the blow he delivered with the back of his hand, her legs buckled. He thrust his face into hers. He roared at her, "Bitch?" The word was spat out. "Who gave it to you? It was bloody Mickey, wasn't it. That little bastard, right he's had it now."

"Harry, listen, no listen to me. I gave Mickey a bell, I reckoned it was your job and I like just asked him if there was a chance, you know, of a couple of bottles and some fags. I told him not to tell you 'cause I would fix it with you. I said you wouldn't mind. Just a few bottles and some fags."

"A few bottles, you've got enough for a bloody off licence, cases of it. The old bill were going to come round here. I would have been bollocksed. I'd be back inside. All this stuff. I mean...." For a moment he was still and silent, then another thump of realisation hit him. "You're selling it, you're flogging it off. For Christ's sake, I haven't even touched it yet and you're running a sodding shopping outlet."

The rage her son was now showing was not new to her. She was now trembling, she wiped the side of her mouth with her sleeve.

"I just thought I could get some for the neighbours, they've been good to me, like when you was inside. They helped me a lot, son, it's hard for me when you're banged up, I'm on my own like, I've got to look after myself. I just thought it would be a sort of 'thank you' for looking out for me, that's all."

"You lying cow, you've never given anybody anything in your life apart from a lot of grief. Go on then, how much, how much were you charging? How much a bottle, how much for a carton of fags?"

He recognised the signs of her procrastination whilst she tried to form a defence, a ruse which she hoped would mitigate her actions. She flinched from her son's raised hand and, in a rare act, the truth tumbled from her lips.

"A few quid for a bottle and a carton of smokes that's all, about half the usual price. " She took advantage of the silence that followed. "I didn't mean nothing, Harry, just thought I'd make a few bob, towards my pension like."

He punched a number into his phone.

"Shut it, shut it you slag." The roaring volume of his voice shocked her into a judicious silence.

"Jack, I need you 'round here, my mum's place, with a van, now." Jack recognised the signs.

His voice was flat calm. "Alright, I'll box that off. How's your mum, she's OK isn't she? I mean she's alright?"

"Her, she's blown us out, she's only flogging stuff from the warehouse all down the street. She's blown us out, mate."

"But she's alright, Harry, she is alright? Harry, don't do anything until I get there. I'm coming round now. I'll get Mickey to fetch the van. I'm on my way, Harry, just hang on."

"Get Mickey, is that what you are saying to me? Get Mickey? Where is that little scrote, that cheating toe rag?"

"Harry, what's gone on? If Mickey needs sorting, I'll do it. What's he done now, that daft little bastard?"

"What has Mickey done? What he has done, is to fix her, my wonderful, caring mother, with half the stuff from the warehouse. Then she's been flogging it, to the bloody neighbours for Christ's sake."

Eventually, Jack butted in. "Harry, listen to me, I'll sort it with her neighbours. If any of the old bill have had a whisper, I'll sort it. Just leave it to me, Harry, I'll find Mickey, give him a bit of a talking to, get it sorted."

"No, this is down to me. I'm gonna sort Mickey out. He could have put me back inside. I'll put him back inside."

"Harry, listen to me, listen. Mickey would never stitch you up, never. He's not the brightest on the block, but he would never do you down. You're his hero. If he did drop some stuff off to your mum, he probably thought it was doing her a favour."

Harry glanced across at his slouched and dejected mother. "Why would anybody do this old cow a favour?"

"Harry, do you know what I think happened? Your mum has put two and two together and guessed who did the job. She knows Mickey's a bit, you know, bit flaky. You know what your mum can be like. She must have pushed Mickey into it. There is no way he would drop you in it. Are you sure she didn't, you know, twist his arm a bit? I know she's your mum and all that, but she has got form for putting her point of view across with no messing."

"Where's Mickey, Jack? I want you to tell me where he is. I want you to tell me now."

Twenty minutes later, Harry pushed open the door of the Dancing Fox pub. Mickey's immediate reaction on seeing his leader was to smile broadly. But the words he was about to use stayed trapped in his throat as he saw, and interpreted, his leader's demeanour. Mickey saw the distance between the two men shorten as Harry strode across the bar with his fixed eyes blazing. The regular drinkers, most of whom were not strangers to Harry's proclivities, immediately read the signs, abandoned their glasses and left the premises. The less informed accepted that there must be a reason why so many were now spilling out onto the pavement and decided that, perhaps, there was a merit in following them. Mickey half rose from his seat, his hands already shielding his face. The landlord, behind the bar, offered a plaintive lament, "Please" but realised it was falling on stony ground. Mickey was now stumbling backwards. "Harry, it was your mum. She said that if I didn't cough up, she would tell my missus. My girl don't know anything about the job, she's having a baby, Harry. If she knew, she would leave me. I told her I've packed all that in. She's having a baby."

The blow sent ripples through Mickey's body before he succumbed to the inevitable, and although being hindered by a couple of chairs and a table, he eventually slumped heavily onto the floor. Harry grabbed the inert figure by the collar, and dragged it through the door marked

'Gents." About two minutes later a dishevelled and blood spattered Harry stepped back into the bar as he brushed his hair back into place. The door would have slammed shut behind him had it not been hindered by an arm lying on the threshold. "Large vodka." Harry nodded in the direction of his recent outing. "He'll pay." As he waited for his drink, he brushed the skinned knuckles of his right hand. The vodka went down in one gulp and he made for the exit. At the end of the bar, he gently slapped the counter and turned back towards the landlord and smiled. "He'll be alright, in a couple of days he'll be up and about again, he's a strong lad. Thanks, George, I'll drop in later on." Only now did George, the landlord, think it was safe enough to enter the Gents to see what assistance could be offered to the broken, groaning body stretched out across the floor.

Chapter 9

Inspector Tony Sewell was into his third day of his suspension. The letter he had just read explained that the action was due to "disciplinary issues." It listed what he now should and should not do. This included an instruction to return his warrant card "immediately". He screwed up the letter and threw it across the room. "They can sod off." He examined his card, then placed it in a drawer. During his, now enforced, leisure time he had recounted and replayed the immediate events that had led to this situation. One thing was sure of, the commissioner had lied to him about the political money laundering escapade. Maybe the commissioner himself had been lied to. He was satisfied that he had fallen over a scheme which was in place solely to line the pockets of politicians and not to enhance the standing of the country. His suspicions were enforced when the inspector found it difficult, if not impossible, to contact any of his team. Even the faithful Raj Patel was unobtainable. As he was a much smaller fish than those he was accusing of theft from the public purse, he realised, or accepted as a probability, it was likely that the full weight of the establishment would be brought down upon him. He would have to be neutered or discredited, so that anything he may put forward in suggesting wrongdoing by politicians, would not pass the first post. The senior players of the press empires would be contacted and either favours called in, or new threats made. The investigations into the money laundering, would be pulled. The other interested parties, such as the Americans, would be told that the enquiry had been flawed because of a corrupt officer and that there was no chance, at this stage, of a successful conclusion. The Americans may not believe this, but they would know better than to challenge it.

"Right, I can either sit here and wait for those running the numbers to come for me, or I can get off my arse and do something. But what? There's a lot of them with more pens and pencils than me. What would they do? Stitch me up to look like a crook? Do me in and make it look like I topped myself? They could give me shedloads of money and tell me to go away, but then, if I spend it all, I could come back. No, they need to sort me once and for all, good and proper."

His phone rang, he didn't recognise the number. "Yeah"

"Is that Inspector Sewell, Tony Sewell?"

"Yeah."

"Look, you won't remember me, I was a young constable when you were running training classes. I think you had just been made up to sergeant."

"Yeah. And you are?"

"I would rather not say. It's a bit, I suppose delicate. But I think I have information that might be of use to you."

"I don't talk to people when I don't know who they are, information or no information."

"Alright, I quite understand. I am Murdoch, Giles Murdoch. I was in your group when you were running the course on the powers of arrest."

"Really, can't say I remember you. Where are you stationed now?"

"I'm not, not stationed anywhere. I left the force about ten or eleven years ago not long after your course actually."

"So how did you get my number?" Sewell was now on his feet.

"You gave us, all your students, your mobile number, said we could call you if we had any questions. It's been in my phone's memory ever since. To be honest I had no idea if you still used the same one. Look, you were very good to me on a personal level. I had certain issues that I was dealing with, you probably guessed what they were and you were very kind to me."

Sewell brushed his hair with the flat of his hand. "Murdoch you say? I think that rings a bell. So what do you want to tell me? What's this information that you want to give me?" There was a pause.

"Right, OK. My partner is a senior officer in the force. I can't give you his name for obvious reasons. That's why I left. He was progressing up the management ladder and I wasn't. We thought that if it came out that we were a couple, it would affect his career. You know what it's like. So to avoid any risks, I left so he could continue. Actually he's been quite successful."

Sewell's initial impatience was flagging and curiosity was taking its place. "Very interesting and all that, but why are you calling me?"

"Sorry, I do go on. The thing is, my partner, well I think he might have somebody else in his life and he has been very hurtful. The other night he left a file lying around the flat, something he has been working on. Your name was on the front."

Sewell slumped into a seat. "Right, I see. What was the file about?"

"It all seemed very secret. But, David, my partner; I shouldn't have said that should I? But it seems they want to get at you. Hang on, look, can't talk now, he's at the door. I will call you back."

The next day Sewell parked his car about a hundred yards from a house he knew in narrow back street and near to the footpath he guessed would be used. Tucked into a line of vehicles, he wasn't noticeable. He was prepared for a long wait, especially if a visit to the pub took place. At about six thirty he saw the thin jaunty figure with his usual rucksack swinging from his shoulder. As the jeans and leather jacket approached, he lowered the passenger window.

"So, no pub tonight then?"

Mark Stephens backed up the few paces he had gone beyond Sewell's Ford. He stood upright by the door, scanning the area, without bending he greeted his boss, his voice was an urgent whisper.

"Tony, what the bleedin' hell are you doing?"

"Get in, Mark. It's OK, there aren't any of our cars here. Come on, get in."

Checking for official looking vehicles, Mark Stephens lowered himself stiffly into the passenger seat.

"Tony, what you doing? We've been given the nod that they have suspended you, we all reckon something's up. We've been told that we must not get in touch with you and that we have to report it if you try to contact any of us. They made a right song and dance about it. They haven't actually said it, but they are suggesting that you've been up to something dead iffy. It's the money laundering politician isn't it?"

"What have they said? Who's said it?"

"It was Upton. He came round and spoke to the team. To be fair to him, I don't think he knew what was going on. He just said you have been put on leave, long term leave, but the word had already got round that it was suspension and that there may be 'issues' that have to be looked into and these were being handled by specialist senior officers. That's when he said we were not to have any connection or communication with you, he really hammered that. He said that if you tried to get in touch with any of us, we have to report it immediately."

As he spoke, Sewell checked his rear view mirror. "Did they give any indication of what I was meant to be up to?"

"No, but he made it sound serious. What is it, Tony? What's going on? I mean, I stand to get a right bollocking if they know I'm even talking to you. What have you been up to? It is this political thing isn't it. You don't want to go messing with that lot."

"What have I been up to? Doing my job, that's all, I've just been doing my job. Yes, you're right, Mark, it is the money laundering job when we followed that bloke to Parliament. That's when I deffed you lot out. I did a bit of sniffing around and it seems like somebody, some politician, is having a go with bent money. I ended up seeing the commissioner, he looked like all his Christmases had come, you know, job of the century had fallen into his lap. I assume he saw some politician, Home Secretary I think. After that it all came down on me. I reckon some nob is on a major fiddle and they either want to handle it themselves and keep it in the family, or it is a cover up. If it is, it must come from the top because our commissioner has had a meeting with the brass, so somebody somewhere knows about it.

"Look, Tony, don't get me wrong, this is all very interesting and all that, but I shouldn't be speaking with you, I could end up in the soft and pungent. For what it's worth, I know you might pull a few strokes, bend the rules a bit, but I don't think you would ever go bandit. You're too straight for that, but we have been told to stay away."

Sewell gave Stephens a look of benign amusement. "Since when did not following orders cause you any grief? Think about it, they're already covering up, so how messy is it going to get if they put you on the rack? Then they're covering up a cover up. They will be scared shitless if the Federation gets involved, powerful lobby the Federation, they won't want to see their members hung out to dry when all they have done is what they are paid for. Look, I don't blame you if you want to play it a bit pear shaped, just do one thing for me."

"What's that?"

From his pocket, Sewell produced a small cheap mobile phone. "There you go. That, Mark, is a pay as you go, paid for by cash, mobile, a burner. The user cannot be traced. It has got one number in its memory, this one." Sewell produced an identical phone. "Same as that one; cannot be traced. What I would like you to do, what I am asking you to do, is, if you are on obs and you see that bloke again, you know the Coal Hole visitor, just text me the time you see him, nothing else, just the time. He probably won't go back if he thinks he has been blown. Can I ask you to do that? Mark, they are after me, I know too much. I don't know what strokes they might pull. I just want my defence sorted out before they come for me."

Stephens took in the view from the car window. Then he held his hand out and received the phone. Without speaking he left.

Chapter 10

"Lisa, Lisa, open the door, Lisa open the bloody door." From inside the neat semi-detached on the small estate an impatient voice, annoyed at the hammering, shouted,

"What? What is it? Is that you, Jack? What do you want? Oh my God, is it Mickey, is he alright?"

Jack looked about to see if any of the neighbours were attracted by the commotion. "Come on, Lisa, hurry up."

She threw the door open and saw that it was indeed Jack. He was supporting her bloodied and bruised husband who, at that time, was demonstrating the composure of a bag of damp laundry.

"My God, Mickey, Mickey, what's happened?" In those few seconds her voice had risen to a scream.

"Mickey, Mickey, love, what's happened."

Jack, dragging the slumped and mumbling Mickey, pushed past her. "Lisa, keep it down, let's get him inside. Keep it down, Lisa. You'll have the whole bloody neighbourhood out if you keep that up."

"Is he alright? He looks a mess. Has he been in an accident? Mickey, Mickey." Her volume had not decreased. Jack dropped the groaning casualty onto an armchair. He turned and grabbed her by the arms.

"Lisa, you have got to keep it down. We don't want all the bloody street to know."

She knelt by her distressed husband brushing his hair with her hand.

"Mickey, Mickey love, what's happened, what's happened to you?" Suddenly she stood and stepped back. "He's been beaten up, somebody's worked him over. He's a mess an absolute bleeding mess. Jack, you tell me, you tell me right now, what happened, who did this?"

"He's got a few bumps and bruises, he'll be fine in a couple of days."

"A few bruises, he looks like he's half dead. I'm calling an ambulance."
Jack reached over and took the phone from her hand.

"No, don't do that, Lisa. It stays with us, in house like. If he needs
anything, I'll make sure he gets it. No ambulances, Lisa. No doctors,
nothing like that. I'll sort it."

Her initial lack comprehension was now beginning to melt. "What you
saying, Jack? What's gone on? Why can't I get him some help?" She
looked down at her husband who was by now trying to make sense of
his surroundings. As she started to speak to him, a realisation washed
through her features. At first her voice was a hoarse whisper.

"Sewell, bloody Harry Sewell, he did this, that mad bastard, that mad
evil bastard." Now she was roaring again.

Through swollen and damaged lips Mickey pleaded, "Leave it, Lisa,
leave it, it's alright, bit of a misunderstanding, that's all."

"He's a psycho, a bloody psycho. He always has been, they all know
him round here. He needs locking up, throw the bloody key away. Get
out of my way, I'm getting an ambulance."

Mickey, clutching his ribs, tried to sit up. "Lisa, love, leave it, alright,
just leave it." Her rage was being replaced with astonishment.

"No, I won't bloody leave it, I'm not having some nutter who should
be in the loony bin, beating my husband up and then I'm just expected
to stand here and do nothing like it's just another day at the office.
What happened, why did he do it? Why are you so scared of him? If
you went to the law now and complained, he would stop it. He
wouldn't dare do it again." Jack had made a call on his mobile. He was
speaking and holding his hand up in an effort to bring about some
calm. He slipped his device into his pocket. Staring directly at Lisa, he
spoke with a slow and deliberate voice that was verging on menace.

"Lisa, listen to me, are you listening? There's a doctor on his way
round here now. He'll be here in about half an hour, he's a private
doctor, one of the very best. It's all paid for, everything. We do not go
to the hospital, we do not go to the police, we do not, under any
circumstances, talk to anybody about this. Do you understand what I
am saying, Lisa? Do you understand?"

Mickey, now attempting to sit upright was nodding his head. "That's right, love, nobody knows about this, nobody. It's just one of them things."

"Mickey, I don't care what you say. I know you can be a right prat, but you are my husband and I love you, though I often wonder why. Mickey, we're having a baby, I don't want it to grow up with you hanging around all these bloody villains especially that nutter Sewell. Yeah and him here, Jack, you're just a crappy little crook too. I don't want its dad to be a jailbird. I don't care if you get a job emptying dustbins. I want you to come home at night and that I don't have to worry if you are going to have your collar felt. I just want to be a family, a normal family."

About an hour after the doctor had finished tending to Mickey, Lisa watched him as he drifted off into a deep sleep. Then she stepped into a taxi and within ten minutes she was standing outside the door to Harry Sewell's apartment. Her heart was pounding and her mouth was dry and tight lipped. Fear was draining the strength from her legs. She tried to fix those strands of her bleached blond hair that had freed themselves from their allotted positions, then she smoothed her faux fur white coat with the irregular black spots. Through all this she knew what she had to do. At first it was a tenuous short ring, then with her resolve returning she leant on the door bell so that it rang continuously. When Sewell threw the door open, the suddenness of it took her by surprise and she involuntarily stepped back. Sewell smiled down at her seemingly pleased to see her.

"Hello, Lisa, love. How are you? What you doing round these parts? You keeping all right?"

"Don't give me all that old crap, you mad bastard, you beat my Mickey to a pulp and I'm not allowed to talk about it. I want to talk about it, I want to know why."

She stepped back from the doorway. She took a breath.

"You, Mad Harry Sewell, a long time vicious crook and jailbird beat my husband to a pulp."

She was, while shouting at the top of her tiny voice, addressing the surrounding public area. One man walking a dog slowed his pace for a second but showed no interest in the announcement. Harry Sewell whilst smiling nonchalantly, pivoted his head left and right scanning the area.

"I don't think anyone heard you, love. Why don't you have another go?"

Lisa appeared nonplussed. "What?"

"I said, why don't you have another go. Maybe this time somebody might actually hear you."

"What?"

"Look, Lisa, why don't you come in? I think you could do with taking the weight off your feet. Come on, I don't bite."

"Oh yeah, but you do everything else."

"Come on, come in." He put an arm around her and gently pressured her forward. Her small reluctant tottering steps and glances towards the closing door showed her concern.

"Sit yourself down, Lisa. Can I get you anything? Tea, coffee?"

"No, I don't want anything from you. I just want to know why you beat up my Mickey."

As she spoke, she was taking in the opulence of Harry's apartment. Soft white carpets, sumptuous leather suite, through a doorway she could see a modern, very expensive kitchen fitted out with upmarket brands. Not one, but two huge flat screen televisions. Harmonised decorations and ornaments which she guessed were high value.

"Look, Lisa, the business we are in, like me and your Mickey, it gets a bit tense at times, it can be very stressful. Things get misunderstood and, well, things happen. There ain't any bad feelings between me and Mickey, not now."

Her hand grasped the front of her coat.

"What do you mean, what are you saying about you and Mickey being in business. You're a crook, a villain, you've been inside. My Mickey's not like that. Not now he's not, he's put all that behind him."

"Really, put it behind him?"

"You keep away from him, do you hear me? I'll make him keep away from the likes of you. I've got a mind to go to the police about what you done."

"I wouldn't bother, love. I think you'll find that Mickey will say he was mugged down an alley and didn't see who done it. I know the old bill round here. My brother is a copper, an inspector no less. I wouldn't start any more trouble for Mickey if I was you."

Here he paused as if a thought had struck him. "Hang on a minute." Sewell disappeared into a room. Minutes later he returned proffering a large envelope. "I hear you want a new conservatory, this might help." She eyed the package with a degree of suspicion and alarm.

"What's that?" Harry dropped the package onto her lap.

"That, Lisa, is thirty grand. It's Mickey's."

She peered into the envelope and fingered the notes.

"Thirty grand?" Her incredulity was growing. "What do mean it's Mickey's?"

"We had, what you would call, a little business venture. That's his cut, his cut so far that is." He paused waiting for the anticipated next question.

"His cut so far?"

"Yeah, we moved some of the merchandise, but there is a lot more to go. Mickey's in line for another big payout. He is due for some more." He finished his sentence with a faint smile and a gentle nod of his head. Lisa slowly licked her dry lips then swallowed.

"How much more?"

Chapter 11

Higgins was standing in his office, in shirt sleeves with his hands thrust deep into his pockets. His thick elaborately patterned braces faithfully followed the contours of his ample frame. His phone rang.

"Home Secretary, Mr Atwood is here to see you."

"Is he, is he really? You'd better show the bugger in."

Without knocking, Atwood breezed into the office and, unbidden, took a seat. He was a small, slim man in his early fifties, neatly framed and immaculately attired. Everything about him was orderly and reeked of tasteful expense, from his trimmed and crafted hair to his exquisite dark blue suit. His head was tilted slightly to one side. His eyes blinked slowly.

"So, Norman, you wanted to see me. Business, or are you desperate for company?"

His voice was low and measured. Raising his chin slightly he made a minor and unnecessary adjustment to his tie.

"I don't think I'll ever be that desperate for company, matey, and it's not about business, well not official business. So, matey, what have you been up to? What's your latest scam?"

Higgins's small eyes were firmly fixed on his subject and never wavered. His mouth squeezed shut to the point where his lips were hardly visible. He stood erect in a show of dominance and assertiveness. Atwood suppressed an ironic chuckle which was rising in his throat.

"Norman, you do get a bit precious at times. You look like an angry school teacher who has caught the naughtiest pupil pinching biscuits from the tuck shop."

"I, unlike you, didn't have a tuck shop, it was the chippie across the road. Now, I want to know why I had the Commissioner of Police in here telling me that one of his men has uncovered a money laundering racket that seems to have your finger prints all over it."

Atwood casually withdrew a cigarette from a silver case. "Did he really? I hope you had the decency to tell him, and his men, to mind their own business. They shouldn't be bothering members of parliament, they should be chasing muggers and handing out parking tickets."

Higgins wafted away the smoke.

"Look, they've clocked that lad who is working as an assistant for you."

"Ah, young Darius, yes he does assist me in so many ways, charming boy."

"Your bloody charming boy, has been observed, by the police investigators, paying large amounts, very large amounts, of cash to money launderers. They've got photos and audit trails, the bloody lot. And it all leads back to you. So, come on, what's going on? It's all to do with this Overseas Aid Committee that you're on. Are you creaming a bit off the top, is that what it is?"

Atwood straightened one of his cufflinks. "A bit off the top? Certainly not, how could you suggest such a thing? No, not at all, actually, it is a rather large bit off the top. Very large, and it's coming along nicely. That is, it was until you and your police friends seemed to have screwed it up. You did tell them to pick up their ball and go home, didn't you?"

Higgins slumped into the back of his chair, opened mouthed as he showed shock and alarm.

"Oh my Christ, what have you done? There's a bloody election coming up, it's tight enough as it is. All we need are headlines telling our voters that their parliamentary representative is nicking the family silver."

Atwood smiled nonchalantly. "Look, Norman, nobody is going to find out, as long as you chase off your police friends. Even if they do sniff around, they are not likely going to find anything, they will be able to prove. We are extremely well protected. You tell your commissioner that if any unfounded allegations are made, we'll have his job. Boot him out."

"I've already told him I would get him a seat in the Lords if he called the dogs off. So far it seems exactly what he is doing."

"There you go, Norman, I knew I could rely on you, good man."

Atwood's smile hadn't faded. Now Higgins was showing signs of exasperation and intrigue.

"Come on, Terry, let's have it. What's going on. What's this deal that is so untouchable? What would you do if I shopped you?"

"Bless you, Norman, you are not going to 'shop' me as you put it. You are not going to bring shame on the party. You are not going to give the other lot a leg up in this election and you are certainly not going to be the minister who, by a misguided act of conscience, sends the party into the wilderness for the next two to three terms."

Higgins, in a pointless exercise, shuffled some papers on his desk. "I don't know. I don't know if I can cover up a crime being committed by a senior party member. Suppose somebody leaks it. Imagine what would happen if the police decided to go ahead and investigate it fully? How do we look then? No, I think I shall have to go to the prime minister and put it to him."

Atwood greeted this nascent threat with the slightest of shrugs. "Really, Norman, the prime minister, you expect him to do something? You might as well try to teach a cat to tap dance. Now then, where do you keep the booze, old boy? The sun's over the yardarm, I could do with a heart starter, drop of whisky would be most welcome." He then sauntered over to the cupboard behind Higgins and poured himself a generous measure. "Won't you join me, Norman. I thought you might have had the decency to keep a decent malt." Higgins scowled silently. "So, Norman, you are off to see the prime minister. The best of luck with that. He will not understand a word of what you are saying, and even if he did, unless somebody kicks him up the arse, he's not going to do anything. Anyway, aren't you forgetting the golden rule, if things go tits up, he must be able to say, in all honesty, that he had no idea of what was happening, you know, plausible deniability. You wouldn't get past his guard dogs. More than likely, you would be the one put out to grass. But look, if you want to have a chat with him, go ahead, Norman, be realistic, if you tried a stunt like that, you wouldn't get off the starting blocks. His henchmen would have you bound and gagged and smuggled out in a roll of carpet. It's a non-starter, old love. You are stuffed."

Higgins searched for appropriate words, but as they started to form on his lips, so they died without seeing the light of day. Eventually he found coherence. "Come on then, so what exactly are you doing and why, specifically, do you think that nobody can hold you to account for it?"

"Norman, it's a lovely little, actually not so little, enterprise. As you know, I hold the purse strings to the Overseas Aid budget, seventeen billion quid, that's billions, Norman, billions, seventeen billion, but you know that already. The beauty of it is, that once it's gone, it's gone. Hardly any of the dosh we shell out is traceable, and it goes to some of the most what are accepted to be, loosely governed countries on the planet, with leaders who wouldn't know honesty and decency if it stood up and bit them on the bum. The only thing we are able to say about where our donations go with any certainty and honesty, is that a lot of it lands in the pockets of dangerously dishonest leaders, crooked government departments, major industries working within these countries and any other minor despot who has the sense and gumption to get on board the gravy train. I must apologise, this scotch in not bad at all. You sure won't join me?"

Higgins's feeble shaking of his head was both a form of growing surrender and acceptance of the offer to partake in the contents of his own drinks cabinet. Atwood did not stint on the measure.

"There you go, have a slug of that."

Higgins did just that, imbibing a generous volume. The two men sat in silence. Atwood waiting for the inevitable questions, Higgins's whirling mind trying to formulate them. He took another sip, then started. "How do you do it? I mean the police seem to suggest that your aid, Darius or whatever his name is, is ferrying large amounts of cash to a money laundering team. How on earth do you get hold of all that money? Where does it come from?"

"I do deals Norman, that's what I do. It's easy, because they are all greedy and dishonest bastards."

Higgins raised an eyebrow to the unintended irony.   Atwood continued.

"I agree an extra amount to be sent to their country and I receive a fee for my consideration. It's been going on for years."

Higgins took a deep breath. "What do you mean it has been going on for years? How long have you been at it?"

"I have been chairman for three years, but there have been others before me."

"Three years, you've been working this for three years? "

"Yes, with others before me, that's another thing, if you try to blow the whistle on this now, there are those, who are, or were, the great and the good, who would want to keep it under wraps. Some of them are very powerful, very powerful indeed. I don't think it would be a good idea to upset them."

"It's a bloody franchise, Atwood, handing it down from one to the other, give me strength. So who else has been lining their pockets? Anybody I know?"

"Yes, at the moment I can't say who but you will know some of them later on. Perhaps I could introduce you to some of them. Maybe two or three are closer to you than you may think. Even I don't have all of the names just most of them. Better not to bandy names around. Keep it under wraps as much as possible. I should say, Norman, there are only a few, from both sides. However, for reasons I cannot explain, others choose to play a straight bat and are squeaky clean. But as to those who have made use of the possibilities, I am not at liberty to say. Obviously it is an unwritten agreement. I think you would be surprised if I gave you a couple of names."

"It's the bloody Da Vinci Code."

"A code of honour amongst gentlemen if you like."

"Will you listen to yourself, Atwood, you are talking about 'honour' and 'gentlemen' you are a bunch of cheating, lying, amoral gutter dwellers. Do you know what, I'm of a mind to get back to the police and ask them to flush all the maggots out of this."

Atwood leaned back in his seat and slowly took a sip of his drink. His eyes drilled into Higgins's.

"As a friend, I would advise you, in the strongest possible terms, not to do so. If you feel that is necessary, then go ahead. You will not be able to prove a thing and you will have annoyed some very powerful people. But, if you feel moved, give it a go."

He took another slow sip. Inwardly Higgins appeared to recoil at this nascent threat delivered in such a casual but menacing way. He rose from his seat and stood looking out of the office window. For minutes no words were spoken. Still looking outwards, his voice calm, he addressed his colleague.

"So that's it, you get your bung and your lad trots off to get rid of it. How much? What is your take in all of this? What is, as the money boys say, your bottom line?"

"In my time I have taken a few million, no probably quite a bit more than that, actually a lot more than that. But there are fees, yes a lot of fees I have to shell out about forty per cent to middle men and the like."

Higgins, shaking his head in disbelief addressed his question to the ceiling of his office. "Christ man, his many times do you do this?"

"I've got maybe a dozen clients, that's how I like to refer to them. The funds, or more properly, the fees, I receive from them are processed through a bank in the Middle East, obviously I cannot say which bank it is. I have an understanding with them, they are very discreet, and so they should be after the cut they take, but so far they have been very business-like."

"Of course they have."

Atwood smiled. "Now you are getting the picture. Another drop of Scotch perhaps?"

Higgins exhaled long and slow. "Darius, your Darius, isn't he the weak point? If you two had, what you would call, a falling out, isn't he in a position to blow the whistle. He could claim he was acting under orders from you. I mean he's a foreigner here, he doesn't know how the system works, he wasn't sure what was going on, but when he thought it was all a bit hooky, he called the authorities in. He could open the whole nest of wriggly things."

"Ah, dear, dear Darius, he may one day turn his back on me. Perhaps I should put that another way, but you know what I mean. No, Darius is as safe as houses. He is on ten per cent and, as we speak, he is building up a substantial property portfolio back home. He is in the process of buying a very nice hotel. He has a good business brain and what he is doing now, will set him up for life."

"But he is a risk, he could cause you problems."

"Not really, you see Darius is an illegal immigrant."

"How do you mean? I thought that anybody who worked here had to be squeaky clean, an intern from the States or an EU citizen. Where's he from, Finland?"

"His passport say Estonia, that what his passport says."

"I take it he's not Estonian?"

"No, actually he's from Georgia, no extradition treaty with Georgia. His father is a big time business man, obviously with links to the government. His mother is Swedish, I think she was a former fashion model. A perk of my job is replacing 'lost' passports. So if the wheel does come off in any way, he will be deported, put on the next plane home. He is here on a false passport, I made sure of that as a precaution. Darius is in this for the money, it's purely business."

Higgins seemed to be juggling the story in his mind. Atwood's arrogance was undoing his armour of official indignation. "So, what you are saying, is that no bugger is going to blow the whistle, if they do, they will end up with a face full of omelette and nobody can prove anything. Nobody is going to complain and we deserve this because we are throwing money at a bunch of gangsters with no system of accounting for it. But I still say it would be a hell of a job to cover it all up if it hit the fan."

"Norman, everybody covers something up, it goes on all the time. If anybody started anything we, the politicians, would be in charge of Committees of enquiry that would drag on for at least ten years, I mean just look at our record. A bunch of our own misfits would say that no wrongdoing could either be found or proved. Then, if we are really unlucky, some public group would start shouting the odds. Then we put in another tame judge, after another ten years, would arrive at the same conclusion, and so on. Then it all gets lost in the midst of time. Norman, everybody covers up. The tv companies with their mucky perverts, the pharmaceuticals who in the pursuit of profits have no regards for their customers who suffer unspeakable harm from untested treatments, the banks, as we all know, the police, the civil service and of course parliamentarians who have made a practice of lying through their teeth for many, many years. Look, as you well know, currently we are supposedly spending all our time, all our efforts, in chasing the so called illegally acquired assets of some of our Chinese and Russian visitors, or so they say. If they are actually chasing them they are not trying very hard to catch them. There just isn't the time or resources to bother with small fry like me." He paused to allow the full effect of his message to sink in. There was no reply from his colleague. Atwood hammered his point home. "You are worried that if it did come to light and the public did get a whiff, it is possible we as a party could be badly wounded. But that is not going to happen, like I say, there are political heavyweights who would ensure it was buried, they know what strings to pull."

The   profundity of Atwood's compelling and comprehensive explanation, seemed to caused ripples of shock through Higgins's being. He searched for a suitable rebuttal, but even his vocabulary retreated. "Jesus H Christ, so everybody is happy are they? What about those poor beggars with nothing, those who are supposed to be getting the benefit? What about them?"

"They get their bowl of rice, they do OK. Although I deal with the more entrepreneurial side of things, quite a lot of it does seem to go to the right places." Higgins shook his head slowly.

"So you see, Norman, it is as safe as houses, nobody will go near this. The wheel may come off, but not any time soon. In a couple of years, I will realise my investments and retire to the sun somewhere. Now, a question."

"What's that?"

"Do you want in?"

Chapter 12

"Keep this tight, no names, nothing like that, I need a favour. Before you say anything, it's not a freebie, there's an earner in it for you." Tony Sewell had to wait for the reply. The voice at the other end of the phone eventually responded with sarcastic incredulity. "What, you want me to do you a favour? I never had you down as a comedian."
It was just the reply he expected, his opening gambit. The voice continued.

"How do you think you could find enough cash to bung me? From what I'm hearing you're being kicked out, had to hang up your handcuffs and truncheon. You can't even hold a plod's job down and you want me to do you a favour and score me for it. You're having a laugh."
Tony noted that the phone wasn't immediately slammed down on him, and the sound of interest was notable in the other voice.

"Not having a laugh, this is straight up. Can we meet, you never know who is listening in these days. Are you up for a meet?"
Making use of the following silence, he drained his tumbler. Eventually there was a reply. "Where?"

"Do you remember that wedding reception, it was years ago now, you pulled the bride's sister."

"Yeah."

"And you had it off with her in the bridal suite before the couple even said 'I do' ".

"Yeah, that's right. She was a good girl. I remember it now. That's going back a few years."
Tony allowed himself a smile.

"Yes it was, but you do know the place I'm talking about? "You do remember it, don't you?"

"Yeah, it's where we…"

"Not now, not on the blower."

"As if, just testing."

"Look, I'm going to be there about half eight tonight. I know I don't have to say this, but make sure you're not followed. Don't use you own car, it will be picked up by cameras all over the place. Use some of your blokes to keep a lookout just to make sure. I'll be on my own, like you say, as far as my old firm is concerned, I'm dead and buried."

"Yeah, my heart bleeds for you, look at me, I'm crying."

After a brief silence, the voice at the end of the phone resumed in a more measured tone.

"This will be worth my time? I don't want you jerking me around for fifty quid and a packet of crisps. It's got to make me smile."

Tony was now feeling more relaxed now that the conversation had bloomed.

"Make you smile? You'll be laughing your bloody head off."

The wedding venue of all those years ago, a no star seedy pub come hotel, now was a wine bar that, in the intervening years, had not striven to raise previous standards. The sort that it cast its tawdry net at was the supposed young high flyers from the business world, but in truth landed punters from the less lucrative end of the market who found employment in the surrounding grimy streets where businesses were often transitory. Tony made sure he was not accompanied by unwanted representatives of the law. He entered the near empty premises which was generously illuminated with undulating blue and pink neon. As he sat at a table in a gloomy corner, a young girl, who eschewed any thoughts of developing a welcoming approach to customers, dealt a distressed plastic cased menu of considerable vintage. She rattled off 'today's specials" in a robotic tone whilst, at the same time scratching her armpit.

"Large Scotch, water on the side, no ice."

"You not eating then?"

Tony handed the menu back. "I'll let you know." He had almost finished his drink, which in itself was not to be taken as a measure of time drifting past, when he saw who he had been waiting for. The figure, dressed in jeans and an open jacket, ambled towards him. The two men appraised each other without speaking. The young waitress closed in for her sales pitch, before she started, Tony, whilst eyeing his companion, gave his instruction.

"Large vodka tonic, ice, no lemon. He looked across and for the first time addressed his now seated companion. "Still the same is it?"
Whilst softly scraping the table with a beer mat, the man replied,

"I'm impressed that you remembered." He paused. "Right, what's this all about?"

Tony waved down the impatience. "In time, in time. First off, how's mum?"

"Mum, she's just mum, she doesn't change, tells everybody she walks with the angels, at the same time she kicks shit out of the Devil."
Tony nodded slightly showing his approval of his brother's appraisal.

"She had her favourite, Harry, and it wasn't me. I didn't follow the family business, worse than that, I became the enemy. It's like I brought shame on the family. I should have been part of 'Sewell and Sons, Villains and Blaggers Limited.' It wasn't my thing really."

"You had a go, Tony, a bit of a dabble."

"That was only occasionally in the old days. I was young, thought I'd help dad out, more of a hobby really."
The two men sat in reflective silence. Harry took the lead. "It's good to see you and all that, and I mean it, now that we are sitting here together. You know, I wouldn't mind meeting up from time to time, bit like the old days. I can't remember why we had a bust up, it was probably because you were the filth. What would your firm think about me and you meeting up, being mates sort of thing?"

"I think me and my firm are coming to the parting of our ways. I've made the mistake of falling over a bent politician and they are going to either kick me out, or more likely, stitch me up so that anything I say will be down do a disgraced bent copper with an axe to grind."
He turned to catch the waitress's attention and motioned that the drinks should be replenished. He continued. "That, Harry, is why I am here with you, I can't pretend that I am not scared. If I've upset the government, Christ alone knows what they will do to keep me quiet. I

have a good idea what is going on and who is doing it, but getting further than suspecting is the hard part. That's why we are talking. To be blunt, I'm looking for your help. I want to find out as much as I can about who's doing what. If I can get the full story and tuck it away, then if they do come after me, I can use it to threaten them that I would go public. You know, punt it out on social media, whatever that is."

He searched his brother's face for a reaction. Harry grimaced. "What's the score then? What are these political blokes up to?"

"As far as I can tell, they are ripping off a fund that is meant to be sent as aid to places in Africa and Asia. Nobody knows exactly how much is being punted out. I have found a politician who is taking a cut. I presume he is doing some deal with these foreign blokes and getting his rake-off."   Their drinks were plonked unceremoniously on the table. Harry's features showed that he approved of the scheme.

"Nice one. How do they get rid of these back handers? If they want, I know a couple of mates who could work it for them."

"Harry, please."

"Only trying to help. So how much are they stuffing in their trousers then?"

Tony did not rush to reply The delay increased Harry's interest.

"The total budget is seventeen billion."

Harry's head dropped forward, his mouth gaped.

"Sorry, did you say 'billion', seventeen billion? You don't mean million. It's got to be seventeen million."

"No, seventeen billion, each year."

Harry groped for words. "Bastards, here's me getting banged up for forty or fifty grand, and these bastards are doing loads more and will get away with it. I mean, who's going to bang up some nob politician."

"Couple of points, if I may, Harry, it wasn't just the fact you were having it away with somebody's life savings, it might have had something to do with the state you left them in."

"Yeah, I suppose. But only because they got in the way."

"Secondly, you are right, it's not very likely that a politician is going to have his collar felt, but there is always a chance. Either that or I take him down myself, with your help of course. If they are going to fit me up, I might as well get mine in first. What I've got are the facts, they are hard things to deny. When I say facts I've got the start of them, I know where I can fill my inside straight. That is, like I say, with your help."

"Right, let's get down to it, my bung. What is it, where is it and how do I get hold of it?"

"It will be the easiest, safest job you have ever done, I mean ever. It's all cash, and a lot of it. A group of bozos takes in cash then, for a price, launder it. The money is handed over in the street, then it's transferred to a kebab shop, where it's counted, bagged and paid into a bank. This is cash, Harry, all cash. Probably each handover is at least a hundred grand. I can give you the nod when one is about to happen, then you and your boys can just help themselves.

"What, these blokes are walking along the street with all this cash, and that's it? No minders, no armoured cars, nothing like a proper bank? No suspicion, nothing like that?"

"That's the way it's done, Harry, it's an easy touch for you a your boys."

"What happens then, does it actually go to a legitimate bank?"

Tony nodded. "Yeah, that's right, with our bloke the politician, it eventually does. At the start we were struggling, then we got hold of one of its junior managers. He was on the fiddle, gambling big time, using the bank's money of course. Believe it or not he kept losing. So to try to cover his losses he tried his hand at supplying coke to his mates and then their mates. Unfortunately down the line one of his customers was one of our under cover guys. It was double bubble for him. He was fiddling the bank's money for the gambling losses and his little drug racket. The bank still doesn't know he was helping himself to its cash. We told him we could do him for fraud and supplying coke. Or, if he wanted a free ride, he could let us have a look at various records when we wanted to. It wasn't us that really frightened him, it was the bank. If he got sent back home under a cloud he wouldn't have a very bright, or long, future. Nobody, and I mean nobody knows about him except a couple of my team. If it was public knowledge somebody is bound to blab or try to have him nicked."

"Bloody hell, Tony, I thought I was the devious one. Nice stroke, nice. So, how much are they taking in?"

"My bloke, never less than two hundred grand a go, sometimes two hundred and fifty, that's been done a few times, when we checked with our snout in the bank. We reckon these guys, with their assorted clients, can easily take over a million a day.

"Jesus, a million."

"That's right, and it's all hooky. That is your fee if you like, if somebody nicks it from them, they can't lodge a complaint, they can't phone the police and say that somebody has had it away with
their illegal dosh."

Harry held his hands in front as though holding a large invisible brick. "So, Tony, heavies? Who looks after all this in this curry house or whatever?"

"They have two or three heavies. We reckon they are tooled up, not first rank though, lazy buggers from what we saw. They probably have a safe room in the shop, a false wall, something like that."

"Right, so where is this money shop?"

"All in good time. Have you got a safe phone, a burner?"

"Yeah."

"Right, get me on the one I am using at the moment, only bell when you have to. Do you know, Harry, if I'm honest with you, I wasn't really looking forward to this tonight. When I think of all what's gone on between us, all that bad blood, gets blown up when we don't speak to each other. Never mind all this, I'm glad to see you again, you never know, I might come over to your side of the business."

"That's alright, Tony, as long as you remember, I'm the boss."

"Harry, you're the boss. You haven't asked me what I want you to do for me, what's involved."

"You wouldn't have asked me if you thought it was out of my league. What exactly is the score?"

"I'll tell you, Harry."

"I gathered that."

"I fell over all this during an observation job. What I have got by the tail is one of their runners. I want to use him to get me into the his boss. I know where he works, where he lives and, most importantly, who his boss is."

"How you going to do that?"

"I'm going to stand on his toes and when I'm finished he will be begging to tell me what his naughty boss is up to. I must be mad, I know I should drop all this, I could have retired. But I just can't leave it there. I suppose I've been a copper too long. I don't like villains, whoever they are, getting one over on me."

"And that's where I come in."

"Harry, that's where you come in."

Their drinks came. Details of the venture were discussed and then regurgitated. When it came time for the brothers to leave, they shook hands. "Harry, like I say, it's been good to, you know, get together. We should do it again, if only to do mum's head in."

Harry dialled a number and a car that had been parked over two miles away started to move. Within minutes it turned into a one way street where he had arrived earlier on foot. As they drove off, he looked, but there was nothing behind them. Tony flashed his warrant card at a member of staff and then made his exit through the rear of the premises and into dark narrow streets. He loitered in the shadows of a corner. With nothing to concern him, he made his way to the bright lights of a main road and hailed the third available taxi he saw. His precautions against being followed would have been very effective, if he was being tailed. His efforts were redundant. He was not being followed. However, that would not be the case for much longer.

Chapter 13

In a windowless room in an anonymous building, a briefing was in progress. "Right, we have acquired a new target who we are told is very influential. It seems that our hero is trying to blackmail a senior public figure who has considerable influence. I don't know who this public person is and I don't care, it's just another job. Our masters have made it known that the person being blackmailed is a very powerful and authoritative figure. Apparently if the blackmailer does go public, it could have major, very major, ramifications in political circles. The interesting part of all this, is that our target is a copper, a detective in-spector no less. As such, he may be known to one or two of you from your former lives. If you do know him, tell me and we will put you onto another job. Our records show that none of you, who are ex police, have served with him but, you may have been on courses, or the like, with him. The name of our bloke is Tony Sewell, Inspector Tony Sewell. Ring any bells with anybody, no, good? I have also been in-formed that this guy is known to associate closely with established criminal gangs. The suggestions are that he passes on information as to whether or not a particular gangster is currently under investigation, then arranges for evidence to go missing and even put the squeeze on prosecuting lawyers. You've heard it all before."

He paused to gauge the reaction. His head made a slow sweeping survey of his audience. The slight buzz of conversation and the tight lipped nodding indicated that his sales pitch was being accepted. "He does this for financial gain. He makes money out of being corrupt. Let me be clear about this, in the course of this surveillance, you will not attempt to find out the identity of the so called blackmail victim. If you, by chance, discover the identity, you will inform me immediately and you will be reassigned." The man paused to allow the message to sink in. "The interesting part in all this is, for a large part of his career, our target, the corrupt inspector, has been involved in surveillance and he is meant to be very good at it. At the moment, so as to keep him away from access to official systems, he has been suspended on the grounds of persistent heavy drinking and insubordination. He has not been made aware of the fact that he is now being investigated for suspected blackmailing activities. He is bound to consider that may be a reason for getting him out of the way. As I have mentioned he is, ladies and gentlemen, a drunk. Not only should this make things a bit easier for us, but if at the end of all this, nothing is found against him, we may ask him to join us. I think he would fit in well with you lot."

An appreciative, if slight, chorus of laughter showed that, at least, he was being listened to.

"So, as much as possible, we will use static devices to keep an eye on him. As we speak, lamp posts, telegraph poles and other fixed points in the street where he lives, are being fitted with discreet cameras which will have live feeds back to our HQ. Any frequent haunts will, in time, be covered. If we need to go mobile, we will use the usual, vehicles; cars, taxis, vans, bikes, motorbikes. Our hope is that he will be covered by the cctv system. Where we do have to use vehicles to tail him, they will be used once and once only. Because of the nature of this operation, it is hoped that we may be given some advanced equipment which will allow us to track him at a distance. When, or should I say, if we get these gizmos, they are to be treated as top secret. Do not let them leave your sight. This stuff has been developed by a foreign power and we, ladies and gentlemen, have been given the honour to try them out. I am expected to write a report on how good, or bad, they are so, keep me up to date." Here he paused and surveyed the room. Satisfied he was receiving due attention, he continued.

"Also, when and if we identify regular pubs or the like that he frequents, we will introduce members of this team in such a way that they will be thought of as regular punters. If it can be anticipated, I would like team members to get into his pub, or whatever, before he arrives, that way he won't be looking to see if he has been followed in.

Considering his present circumstances and background, he is more than likely to be looking out for somebody like us doing what we do."
He sipped from a glass of water.

"Why the bloody hell they suspended him and then asked us to come in is beyond me. It would have been a lot easier if they he'd just left him to carry on as normal. But who am I to question our lords and masters. So, let's be professional. Our masters, whoever they are, want pictures of him if he is seen to be associating with shady characters. So make use of all those expensive spy type gadgets you all use these days. But don't take any pictures of him on his own. We know what he looks like and I don't want anybody showing out by taking unnecessary risks."

Over the next period of days, Sewell was seen to make use of his suspension by spending considerable time in either The Ferryman pub, a five minute walk from his flat, or The Red Lion, a more upmarket establishment about a mile in the opposite direction of his most visited local. Most Fridays, and sometimes on a Thursday, after one of his drinking episodes, he made his way to Brick Lane where a curry seemed to be a suitable meal to soak up the alcohol. These were times when he questioned whether or not he was actually being followed, then the idea for him to take anti surveillance techniques seemed pointless. But on other occasions, Sewell realised it might pay dividends to not make it easy for those who may have been putting him under their microscopes.

This could give him opportunities to identify any company he might have picked up. He never did. Either he wasn't being followed, or if he was, they were very good or more likely using fixed discreet cameras installed in and around the area of his flat. He was starting to feel the beginnings of paranoia in that every time he left his flat, he looked over his shoulder trying to fix in his mind descriptions of men and women who may have shown the slightest interest in his activities. He also wrote down the registration of vehicles falling into the same category. His assumption was that, because of his fleeting encounter with a probably corrupt politician and the evidence he had to support his views together with the extreme reaction from his superiors, he was not going to have a free ride. The dark officials wanted something on him to either keep him quiet or to discredit his plausibility in the event of him making allegations.

Once or twice a week he ventured further afield, on these occasions he employed all the anti-surveillance techniques that he had acquired over the years when he was fully employed. By jumping in and out of taxis, he set his own pace and avoided many of the thousands of cctv cameras that had spread across the capital like a fevered rash. When entering one of his local hostelries he looked but never saw anyone who he didn't know, follow him in. One evening, a stranger did appear. For the area he was fairly nondescript. About five foot ten, short dark hair, three quarter length leather coat and jeans. He sat with his drink at the bar some ten feet from Sewell and spent his time on his mobile phone. The stranger swallowed the remains of his drink and made to leave. He scanned his newspaper, but deciding there was nothing in it that held his interests, he left it on the bar. On his next visit to order another pint, Sewell noticed the discarded red top and flicked through the pages of the publication, then discarded it. Across the room a couple were in deep conversation. There was no reason why Sewell should have noticed the tiny lens in the face of a wristwatch worn by the woman.

Chapter 14

"Right, Tony, I don't think you have met my guys, well hopefully not in your professional capacity, but this is Jack, and this runt here is Mickey. Mickey and me had a little coming together, but it's alright now." He turned and planted his smiling face in front of Mickey's. "It's alright now, ain't it, Mickey? All forgotten; little lesson?"

"That's right, Harry, a little lesson."

Harry Sewell either ignored or dismissed the rumblings of resentment and anger in Mickey's voice that, to Tony, were as noticeable as the fading bruises which carelessly adorned his features. He had joined his brother in a back room of the gloomy cheerless East End bar where Harry, on previous occasions, held court. In his journey, Tony had taken the usual precautions to avoid being followed. His relationship with his brother was thawing. Harry seemed pleased to be reacquainted with his sibling. Tony, inwardly, held the relationship in reserve, it was a necessity rather than a warm instinct. Harry smiling, addressed his audience. "Right you two, this is my brother, Tony, who is, or was, old bill, an inspector no less. Him and his bosses have had a falling out, and Tony is now out of a job. Now he is looking for my help and that means you two can help me."

Jack sat in half shadow at the edge of the dim yellow glow given off by a feeble lamp. Mickey hunched himself over the round pub table. They mumbled cautious salutations.

"Now Tony wants some information, which means screwing some bloke's flat."

He turned to face Tony. "That's what you want; that's right ain't it?" Tony nodded his agreement. Harry continued. "The place is an apartment in Saundersness Road up the Isle of Dogs, or Canary Wharf as they call it nowadays. Mickey, this is up your street."

Mickey did not rush to join in.

"Oh, right. How old is the place, what sort of security has it got?"

Tony clasped his hands together and leaned forward. This was a considerable step for him. He was now moving from enforcing the law, to actively breaking it. He took a deep breath then plunged in. "OK, the apartments are over twenty years old, they were the first of the new developments on the Island. They have electronic gates for access to the car park on ground level. Pedestrians use a gate to the side. There is always a security bloke, an old guy, who keeps an eye on the gates. He does the opening and closing. If he knows the person who is coming he'll open up for them. But to the rear, there is a footpath between the river and the wall to the car park. It is only a hop over the wall, which is about five foot and you are in. Kids do it all the time. There are large parts of the car park that the caretaker can't see."

Mickey's interest was stirring. "Cameras, what sort of cameras?"

"From what I can gather, they are pretty basic. You can see what way they are pointing. From the car park you walk straight into the lift area. No codes are needed to access them."

Harry leaned forward, he knew he didn't have to wait for a hiatus in the conversation.

"Don't worry about the caretaker or the cameras, they can be both fixed. It's not a problem. If he's a local, he can be spoken to. "

Once Mickey was sure that Harry had said his piece, he felt safe to continue. "What about the door locks?"

"I'm sorry Mickey, I don't know. But as the place is so old, I reckon they would be fairly standard."

Mickey's face showed contempt and disappointment that, so far, there was to be no challenge to his technical skills. He put his disappointment away. "Alright, what's the gig?"

Tony winced and sat upright. "What's the what? Doesn't anybody speak English these days. Look, if you are asking what I want, I'll tell you. The bloke that lives there is of interest to me, a lot of interest. Not to put too fine a point on it, I want to stitch him up, I want to be able to squeeze his nuts so hard that he will do anything I tell him to."

Mickey, now starting to enjoy the attention foisted on him, ran a hand through his already untidy hair. "So, where do I come in? What do you want me to do."

"I want access to his computer. I want his password. If we are lucky, there may also be bank records."

"Is that all?"

"That's all, Mickey, just his password, once we have that I might want a bit more."

Mickey was now assuming the mantle of the lead player. "So, who is this bloke, what's the interest in him?"

Tony did not react and stared at the floor. Harry broke the silence. "It's a fair question, Tony. We need to know who it is. If it is one of your copper mates we would have to play it a bit pear shaped. We will have a go but we have to know the risks. I think you should tell the boys so they know who they are screwing."

Tony sat up. "Yeah, fair enough, I've gone this far, in for a penny I suppose. The story is that when we were doing surveillance on a money laundering ring, we fell over this bloke, the one I want you to do. It seems like he is working for, illegally, for some big player in Parliament. We followed him and found that he works for a bloke called Atwood. He is creaming cash off from a massive fund. At the last count, when I was in the ranks of the employed, we reckon he has had it away with four to five million at least. That is only for the last few months or so."

Mickey piped up. "The cheating bastard, that's corrupt, definitely corrupt. They should have the law on him. Can't trust anybody these days."

"Yes, as I was saying, when I had enough evidence, more than enough, to my mind, to start a serious investigation, I went to my boss, I mean right to the very top. He was full of it, he could see a massive fraud, but since then, he seems to have backed off."

Jack spoke. "And these blokes, when they are doing all this, I mean taking a bung, it's all cash, like bags full of readies."

"Like you say, Jack, it's all bags full off readies."

Tony watched the nodding heads of the three and could see how the interest was growing. Jack sought clarity. "So they walk around just carrying the dosh in a bag?"

"That's right, Jack, up and down the road with a hundred thousand or two. I think they should be very careful, don't you?"

The pebbles Tony casts were creating larger and larger ripples. "So I am sure, what these moody officials are doing is following me to try and stitch me up. What I want to do is get my retaliation in first. I want to stitch them up before they do it to me."

Jack, still listening from the gloomier part of the room stirred. He could see the possibilities, but wanted to know the risks.

"So, who is this punter we are going after and why?"

Mickey nodded vigorously in support of the enquiry.

"That's fair enough," Tony gathered his thoughts. "As I said, this bloke is an aid, an assistant, to the politician. Over the past weeks I've been watching this assistant, he's called Karvonen, Darius Karvonen. I've been watching him leave parliament and tracking him to where he lives. I've done it a bit at a time but basically he takes the Clipper, the river bus, from Westminster down to Masthouse Terrace then walks round to his flat. He's not the bloke that I want. But I need to use him to get to his boss and, like I said, put the arm on him, I mean put the squeeze on him big time and get him to grass up this Atwood."

Harry piped up. "But if you have blown his cover, so to speak, won't they jack it in? I mean, if they carry on carting all this cash around, they're asking for trouble."

"It did go quiet for a week or so after I reported it, There is no reason that any of the others involved would know anything about it. Then he started back at it. I get the nod when it happens."

Jack broke the brief silence that had overtaken the room.

"If this bloke Atwood is, like you say, a senior politician, shouldn't you think this through? It looks like you could piss off the government, I mean really piss them off. These guys have a lot of power, massive amounts. They control everything and everybody. If they see a giant cock up coming their way, they just might blow you away, never mind giving you bad references."

Mickey was being drawn ever closer into the proposed venture. "If he's a politician, like some big nob, aren't they meant to be honest? Do you think this geezer would really do something like this?"

Jack smiled at the young man's naivety. "Mickey, my old dad used to say that you could see more dead donkeys on the streets of London than honest politicians. If you are a politician, you can't be honest, you would never last."

"So, what I would like is to get into Karvonen's flat, sort his computer out, load it up with some stuff I've, recently acquired, a spot of tidying up then leave, it will be as safe as houses. He leaves at about seven thirty in the morning and doesn't get back until about seven thirty in the evening. I usually watch him from across the river, it's pretty much an uninterrupted view. Once I see him going into parliament, I will give you a bell. It takes him an hour more to get home, so there won't be any panic. Is that all OK? Does anybody see any problems with that?"

"No, no mate, don't see any problem at all." Tony Sewell detected a note of swelling arrogance in Mickey's reply and watched as he made sure the others appreciated his artfulness.

"No problem, So this bloke gets back to his drum about half seven then?"

"Yeah, that's right, Mickey, so you've got all day, but on the just in case basis, I'll keep an eye out for him if he gets on the ferry at Westminster early."

Mickey scanned the room, his head nodding slightly. His associates responded in similar fashion.

"Right, so using my computer skills, I access his device, load it up with your stuff, a spot of hoovering, then we're off?"

Tony tried not to rise to the cocky attitude, "Yeah, that's about it."

Mickey thought it was time to sum up. "That seems to be alright." He sought and received silent confirmation that this approach was desired. "Where's the stuff you want putting into his system?"

From his jacket, Tony produced a memory stick. Mickey took it and regarded it with a studied indifference. Putting the device into his pocket he leant onto the table so that he had to look slightly upwards to address Tony. "Sorted, mate, sorted. I can do this on my own, five minute job. Piece of cake."

"Yeah, alright, Mickey, but me and Jack will come along on as back up."

"If you want, Harry."

Tony Sewell was on the point where he felt he was being taken over. The serious concerns he had about a new career as a law breaker weighed more heavily the closer he moved towards it.

"Once you have sorted his computer, I will go back to the flat the next day. It will be a police raid."

Chapter 15

It was late evening when Jack walked the mile or so from the meeting to his home with his usual rolling gate and the steady pace of a big man. The meeting he had just attended left him feeling uneasy. For the first time he had met Tony Sewell, his boss's brother. After, when the police officer had left, Harry had proposed another escapade, another robbery. This time Jack thought the risks were high, higher than any previous outing. He tried to suggest to Harry that perhaps another less risky venture would be more acceptable, or to let some time elapse from the recent warehouse job. But no, Harry was bent on confirming his reputation as master of his little kingdom.

Jack trod the narrow silent streets at a slowing pace, his head full of thoughts, not many of them positive. The closer he got to his house, the slower the progress he made. He stood by his front door for several minutes warming the keys in his hands, his head slumped. His worried, fearful demeanour then lifted to one of casual cheerfulness like an actor entering his stage. He pushed open the door of his terraced house and slipped the key back into his waistcoat pocket. He looked along the gloomy and deserted street, a slight mist had given fuzzy halos to the yellow street lights. He quietly trod the path to his kitchen.

"Is that you, Jack, luv?" The voice trailed down from the upper floor.

"No, it's the postman, I left my bag when I was around here this morning."

"What a sauce, anyway, it wasn't the postman, it was the butcher, I thought he was coming back for his chops."

"Chops, I'll give you chops."

"Come on then, you got the kettle on? I could murder a cup of tea."

Jack smiled to himself, he knew before he arrived that a cup of tea would be called for. It always was. "Coming right up, Luv. Do you want a biscuit or anything?"

"Just tea, what time is it? I've been nodding off?"

"Just gone eleven."

Balancing a cup and saucer in either hand, he moved the bedroom door open with his foot. He sat beside the bed. "Here we are, a cuppa for a demanding wife." She plucked at a pillow as a meek demonstration of her unjustified scolding.

"I'm not demanding, is that what you think?"

Jack put the cups down, stroked her cheek and bent a kissed her forehead. He took her hand between both of his and framed a quizzical look as if searching for an answer. "Let me see, demanding? Well, I'll think about it."

He gazed into his wife's gentle blue eyes and kissed the back of her hand.

"You alright, Jack? You been alright? Been up to much? Had a good day?"

"It was good, but it just got a lot better. What have you been doing, my wife? Been up to London to see the Queen?"

"Oh, yeah, I had dinner with her, it was alright, but I don't like them corgis. Don't think I'll go again. Better off down the bingo, nicer class of people."

The two stayed quiet, looking into each other's souls. When Jack spoke his voice was soft and serious.

"How have you really been, Luv?"

"Oh, you know, not bad, not bad at all."

"Taken all your tablets?"

She replied with a hint of gentle exasperation. "Yes, I've done all my pills and all my potions."

"That's good, get you on the mend, back on your feet."

"Can we go dancing when I'm better, I used to love dancing. You weren't bad you know, a good mover for a bloke your size, no you were. Mind you, I was a bit of a looker then."

"What do you mean then? You are now my lovely, lovely wife, you are beautiful, not was."

He rocked back from the light on the pretext of sipping some tea. The gloom and the height of his hand hid the tears filling his lower lids. He lowered his head and yawned and ran his fingers across his eyes as if rubbing away the threat of tiredness.

"Been a long day, Jack? Been out with the boys. What you been up to? No, don't tell me, that's your life." There was an awkward pause. "Why don't you go down and watch the telly for a bit. I know you like to stretch out and have a drink. I'll be asleep in a minute, all these tablets knock me out."

"Alright, I'll stay here while you nod off, come on make yourself comfortable, that's it."

Jack sat immobile watching his wife as she lay silent, remaining as a sentinel until he was sure that sleep had overreached her. He tucked the duvet around her and, with his fingers, combed her hair away from her face Downstairs he stretched out on a settee and sobbed silently.

The sunlight from outside had penetrated the neat little bedroom. Jack was occupying the bedside seat as he did the previous night. His wife stirred, sleep was pressed into her features. "Jack, you been up all night? Didn't you come to bed?"

"Yes I did and I've been up for over an hour and a half, it's after nine, and look at you, still in bed. I don't know, you young girls, lying around all day."

"I know, terrible, isn't it?"

"What do you fancy for breakfast? I could do you some nice scrambled egg."

"Honestly, Jack, I'm not that bothered. Cup of tea would be nice."

"Dear me, girl, you and your cups of tea. Come on have something to eat, keep your strength up."

"Maybe later, just tea, I promise I'll eat later."

The disappointment on Jack's face was less than the sadness he tried to cover up. His wife saw clearly the emotions he was trying to hide. She tugged at the duvet and turned to the light coming from the window. The silence in the room was heavy. Jack's heart was pounding in his chest.

"Jack, we've got to talk."

"You get some rest first, then we can talk."

"No, Jack, we've got to talk, we need to. The doctor was round here yesterday, the results have come back. It's got worse."
One of them was fearful of speaking, the other of listening. Jack moved as if to thwart the message. She shook her head at him in a gesture of hopelessness. "Sit down, Jack, come on sit by me, hold my hand."
He lowered himself onto the bed and took her hand.

"Jack, we've got to stop pretending. What the doctor said, what he told me, was that I've probably got another one or two months, two months at the very most."
Jack let out a mournful sob.

"Look, it's no use pretending, we've both had an idea, we both knew, but.....but we wouldn't face up to it." Her voice was becoming more assertive. "So, there it is."

"Are they sure? They get it wrong sometimes."

"Jack, my lovely, darling Jack, it's not wrong and we both know that, it's what we've been expecting." She allowed the message to settle. "Right, what I want, is to make as much as we can in the time left." Now her voice was brighter. "I don't want to go anywhere, I don't want anything. I just want to stay here for as long as I can and be with you. Now, I know you're a bloke and you like to get out, that's alright. My sister comes round during the day for a couple of hours, then Angela, her daughter comes of an evening. So, I want you to go out, otherwise you'll go mad. But I do want you here, and I want to laugh and smile as much as we can. But, like I say, I want you here. You know what I am saying, don't you?"
With his chin on his chest he mumbled a faint, "Yes."

"Look, Jack, I have always loved you, always. But I know what you are. I've never complained, I've never tried to change you, although, at times, I wished to God I could have. When you've been inside, I waited for you, I never looked at another man, never even tempted. I know you've been up to something recently, ever since Harry got out." Jack looked away from his wife, his face filled with grief and despair.

"No, I don't want to hear what it's about, I never did. But listen, Jack, if you go inside for this one, if you get nicked for it, whatever it is, we will never see each other again. I will never ever be able to see you or hold you again. There is no miracle cure, I can't get up and walk, I'm stuck here. I have never asked you for anything before, but now I'm asking, I'm begging. Don't get banged up, do everything you can to stay out. Tell your mates about me, tell them I am dying."

The shock to both of them on hearing the last word, momentarily caused a pall of silence.

"Think about yourself for a change, What favours have these blokes ever done for you? That one time when you got sent down, they didn't lift a finger. Do it for me, Jack, please, please stay with me. Stay with me for these last few weeks. I've never asked for anything before, never. It's not too much is it?"

Jack nodded silently and held her in a gentle embrace.

Chapter 16

Mickey slid over the wall from the river pathway landing in the parking area of Karvonen's apartments and made his way to the lift area. He noted that the few security cameras in place, were conveniently positioned so as not to track his progress. Looking across to the security office he saw the incumbent. A man bent with age, attracted by the movement, glanced back at him, but then quickly averted his gaze. Less than twenty minutes before, the guard had been "spoken to" by Harry, he agreed that, "us Eastenders," stick together and don't ask any questions when it comes to legitimate business." He realised that this accommodation ensured the continuance of employment that allowed him many more days of doing not much more that sitting in a heated security office. Entry to Karvonen's apartment proved not to be a challenge for Mickey. His phone rang.

"Are you in yet, Mickey?"

"Yeah, I tell you what, Harry, there is a very nice view from here, straight across the river. I can see all of Greenwich, the Cutty Sark, everything. I wouldn't mind a place like this."

"Yeah, very good, Mickey, never mind the sightseeing, just get on with it. And keep your fingers to themselves, no nicking."

"I was just saying it's a very nice place, that's all."

Karvonen's computer was on a desk which was fitted into an alcove. The lead connecting it to the router on a window ledge dropped down behind the desk.

"Oh, that's nice, very nice, sweet as a nut." From a bag, Mickey selected a screw driver and opened up the plug. From his selection of gadgets, he picked out a small flat coin shaped item which had fittings for wire attachments. He connected this to the inside of the plug then reassembled it. He opened his own lap top.

"Come on, come on."

Within seconds his screen was populated with the message he sought. Standing back he ensured that everything was left as it was found. "Job done." However, with Mickey, old habits remained old habits. He sauntered around the apartment but nothing took his interest. He walked back across the car park area, nodded to the security guard and hopped over the wall.

Before he had even taken his seat in the car, Harry pounced.

"Go alright? You didn't leave nothing behind this time, no pliers left lying around? It's all sorted, yeah?"

"Blimey, Harry, let me get in the bloody car, will you. Yes, it did go alright, no I didn't leave any kit behind and yes, it's all sorted."

"Did you get Tony's gizmo fixed."

Mickey demonstrated a slightly theatrical air of impatience. "Not today, I fitted a bit of kit to his laptop so that when he turns it on, it shows his password."

"What, we've got to come back tomorrow? I was going to go up the West End tomorrow."

"Harry, that is not a problem, I can do it myself, everything he does, including entering his password, I can pick up on a lap top if I park outside."

"So, this piece of kit, he's not going to find it."

"I bloody hope not, cost a fortune. It's what the Israeli intelligence use. Anyway, where's Jack today? it's not like him to miss out on a bit of a tickle"

"He said he's not feeling so good, bit of a bug. I'll give him a day, then I'll get him out; a bit of fresh air, get him doing a little bit of a job."

Mickey was checking his lap top and was not absorbing the news about Jack. "Oh yes, it's only all connected, all working, you little star. Harry we are in business, next time he logs on, we get all his details. Shame about Jack, how's his missus? Isn't she meant to have something wrong with her?"

"I don't know. If you ask him about it, he just says she's not too bad, never talks about it. I don't want her keeping him indoors, he's part of the team, should be out backing us up. Right, Mickey, what's the score?"

"Next time he switches on, we get his password. If we leave the laptop in the boot of the car outside the flats, it will pick it all up. I'll come back in tomorrow, get in there and load up Tony's memory stick. I take my little box of tricks back, then, I suppose, it's down to Tony. I'll give him a bell, let him know it's all cushy."

Twenty four hours later, Mickey retreated from Karvonen's apartment, taking Tony's memory stick, the contents of which were now downloaded into the computer.

"Hi, Tony, all done, it's over to you now."

"No glitches?"

"None, all done and dusted."

"Thanks. Tell you what, Mickey, I need a constable, plain clothes. What do think about working for the law?"

"I think it would be an interesting career move."

It was nearly eight in the evening. Karvonen had been in his apartment for less than twenty minutes when he answered the door.

"Hello, can I help you?"

"Mr Karvonen, Mr Darius Karvonen?"

"Yes."

"I'm Inspector Sewell, Westminster Vice squad, this is Constable King." Sewell thrust his warrant card into Karvonen's face. Mickey, from behind, proffered an ID card momentarily.

"I think we had better come in."

"But what is all this about. I work in parliament you know."

"Yes, yes, we know all about that."

Karvonen reluctantly allowed access.

"Look, what is all this, is something wrong? Is there a problem with parliament? I work with very senior and powerful politicians you know."

Tony Sewell showed that he was less than impressed, Mickey, followed suit.

"Mr Karvonen, we have it, on the highest authority, that you are engaged in matters of a serious criminal nature. Could you log onto your computer please."

"Why?"

"Just log on."

Karvonen tapped the appropriate keys.

"Constable King, if you could do the honours. Mr Karvonen, Constable King is one of our computer experts."

"I don't know what you want, what is all this? I think I will have to call my boss. He is a very powerful politician."

"Not just yet, Mr Karvonen."

"Can I see your identity card again?"

"There you go."

"What about his?"

"Mr Karvonen, if you doubt the validity of our cards, you are free to call 999."

Mickey thought it was time to further his career in law enforcement.

"Inspector, I think you should take a look at this. It was hidden behind an email server. Clever, but not very secure."

Tony bent down and peered into the screen. He stood and turned. "Darius Karvonen, I am arresting you on suspicion of possessing and distributing pedophile images. You do not have to say anything, but it may harm your defence if you do not mention when questioned something which you later rely on in court. Anything you do say may be given in evidence. Do you understand the caution?" Sewell looked back at the screen.

"It's pretty disgusting."

"What are you talking about?" The screen was turned towards him. Shock and fear, in equal measure, rocked him. "I have never seen that, any of that before, never do you understand? I want to phone my boss. I have never, ever seen that before."

"So, you want to phone your boss. Do you remember, when we arrived, I said we were from the Westminster Vice Squad? I also said that we have it on the highest possible authority that you enjoy this sort of stuff."

Karvonen slumped ashen faced into a chair. "Who would say such a thing? Who knows me?"

Sewell took a seat and indicated that Mickey should do the same.

"Who knows enough about you to point the finger? I should also tell you that we have had our specialists going over your finances. It seems as though you have a great deal of money going through your fingers. We have traced an overseas account. Now we have an idea where it comes from." Sewell casually inspected the back of his hand. "We are getting some high level, and I mean high level, assistance on this. It seems that pornography is a substantial source of income." By now Karvonen was recovering from his initial shock and was starting his defence.

"I tell you, I swear to it, I know nothing, absolutely nothing about that filth on my computer, I find that disgusting."

Sewell looked across to Mickey. "Constable, when did they say the van would be here to take us to the station?"

Mickey had lost track of the conversation and was admiring the view across the river from the large window. "Oh, er, about half an hour." His reply was in the form of a question.

"Really, Constable, that quick? I thought there were some delays."

"Oh, yes, yes Sir, some delays. It might be more than half an hour."

"That could be a problem. We cannot start a formal interview until we get him down to the station. You have recorded the time of entry, arrest and the issuing of the caution?"

Karvonen gripped the arms of his chair. "I am going to the police station, but why?"

"Why, Mr Karvonen, because you are facing some very serious charges. If you are found guilty, you may face a very substantial prison sentence. It will wreck your life, you will never work again, either here or in any European country. Then there is all this money; could well be more charges to follow. When we go to the police station will you make sure you have your passport, we will have to keep that. Where are you from? Eastern Europe?"

Karvonen did not attempt to answer. The growing enormity of the situation was swamping him. Sewell allowed him time to rationalise the events of the evening.

"Inspector, you say you are from a Westminster police station and that you are being assisted by someone of importance. Does the name Atwood, Terence Atwood mean anything to you?"

Sewell feigned mild shock. "I never gave you that name, that name has never been mentioned tonight. Constable, can you confirm that the name Atwood has not, at any time, been mentioned since we arrived here."

Mickey was now rather more alert. "Atwood Sir? No, not been spoken of tonight, I can say that with all certainty."

Sewell indicated to Mickey that he should stick to being a rather unprepossessing police office and tone down the theatricals. A silence followed. Sewell did not want to let the moment pass. "Why do you say that, that name Atwood?"

"Officer, I am being set up here. I don't know if it is you or Atwood."

"I see, and how do you think that we could set you up, as you put it? How could we have walked in here and set up your computer with all that material. We were only here a couple of minutes before we found it. May I remind you that we had to ask for your password. We came here after being given specific information."

"From Atwood?"

"I can't say."

"Inspector, let me think for a minute, just let me think."

Sewell shrugged nonchalantly.

"Right, Inspector, I want to do a deal. If I do, I want your assurance that nothing will happen to me. If you do not detain me, I will be out of the country in a matter of hours. Even if you do detain me, I will be out of the country within a day, so, for you, for me, a deal."

"Why would I do that?"

"Because I have information about a massive scandal taking place in Parliament. I mean a really massive fraud. As I say, I don't know if you are setting me up or it is Atwood. At the moment I don't care. It's probably Atwood who has fixed all this and sent you here. All I can imagine is that something has gone wrong and he wants to make me the guilty one. I just want out, but I can give you the biggest case you will ever have."

Sewell gave the impression of weighing up the offer. "Look, Mr Karvonen I am a simple policeman, but I have been around for a long time, I've worn out a lot of shoe leather. I couldn't tell you how many times I have heard those in your situation tell me they can lead me to Mr Big, or they can tell me about a massive robbery that is about to take place. You get the picture? Do you know how many times they have told the truth? None, not once, as far as I am concerned, you are just another criminal trying to get off the hook. It won't work Mr Karvonen, no it won't. Your offence, your alleged offence, is a particularly nasty one, I can tell you what will happen. Once you have been found guilty, you will be imprisoned here in England, and I can see you getting a very substantial sentence, then you will be deported back to your own country where the authorities will have been informed about your case."

Mickey felt as though he had to restrain himself from applauding in appreciation of Sewell's showboating, he had to make do with the merest nod of his head and the shadow of a smile. Karvonen was showing signs of terror. He made direct eye contact with Sewell, and as he started to shake he shouted out.

"No, no, it is true, I can prove it, I can prove it right now, here in this room, right now."

He moved across to a large wall cupboard and knelt down. Sewell blocked his progress

"What are you up to? Constable search that cupboard, might be firearms."

Mickey moved with an exaggerated sense of purpose towards the area. Karvonen, showing signs of exasperation explained. "No, not a gun, a safe, it is the safe. Let me show you. I can prove it, I will let you see that it is a massive fraud being conducted by the MP Terry Atwood, he is using his position to make a lot of money. Now, and I do not know why, he wants to put me in to trouble. He must think something has gone wrong."

Karvonen pushed back a rack of clothes and started to open the safe fixed to the wall. He started to manipulate the combination, then he stopped.

"Officer, be assured this is the biggest case you will ever see. If it is true, I just ask that you let me go. I will be out of the country within hours. Obviously that is what Atwood wanted. If you arrest me, he would say that, for the sake of politics and the party I must be thrown out of the country. That's why he set me up like this, he is aware that I know too much and something has happened that makes him want to get rid of me. You must let me go, you are being wrapped up in a huge scandal. It is better if I go."

Sewell crossed to the safe. "If you are right in what you say, I will consider it, but I want to see this proof you have. And stand away from the safe before you open it, just in case."

Sewell pulled the safe door open. "What the hell, what is going on? You are going down my son, this is completely empty. What sort of a game is this?"

Karvonen allowed himself a brief smile. "Let me show you." He reached down to the thick door of the safe, a click was heard. Then a panel swung open revealing a space within the door. Mickey was on home ground.

"I've seen them before, very neat. We did one on a job." He stumbled to a halt. "That was a good arrest, yeah, we got three of them, all arrested."

From inside the door cavity Karvonen withdrew a file of papers. "You see, this is the proof. Terrence doesn't trust computers, so he asks me to print off the online statements. Look, let me show you on the computer. I keep my own records, I have a file for all the amounts he has paid in."

Sewell's cursory glance showed that the bank statements indicated regular and substantial payments into a Middle Eastern financial investment company. However, it was not the same bank in London where he was controlling the fraudulent drug dealing young manager. "How does this show the account holder as being Atwood? How does the money end up in this account?"

"All the funds go through a random selection of banks. It makes it much harder to trace."

Sewell was pushing for more clarification. "So, how is this Atwood's account? Where's his name"?

"Look at there, TAMP, that is Terrance Atwood MP. All the details are emailed to a private account that he keeps separate from all his official stuff. The print offs you are holding are all from his account. What you are holding is what he sends to me. Once I confirm I have it, he deletes it at his end. He is always worried that if there is a problem with the computers going down, he can always use the print outs I can print them for you now. There you are, officer. Can I go now?"

Sewell fanned the documents out in front of him. "He has more or less used his own name, that's a bit stupid."

"He has what you say in this country 'a big head' he thinks nobody can touch him. He pays a large premium for them to keep their mouths shut. Officer I would really like to go now. I promise I will be abroad by tomorrow morning."

"How much do you get out of this?"

"Ten per cent, I do all the arranging, carrying the cash, meeting with the guys who take the money. I do all the bank liaison. Stuff like that. He makes me do it."

"When is the next delivery?"

"It should have been today, but the guys never turned up, it happens. They are very careful, they can be very suspicious."

"So if it didn't happen where's the money?"

Mickey's reaction was a reflex.

"Yeah, and how much is it? Is it in notes?" Sewell tried to hide his exasperation.

Karvonen pointed to the sports bag he had arrived with. "I think it is about two hundred thousand in sterling."

Mickey pounced on the bag with the speed and deftness of a weasel on a rabbit.

"Bloody hell, Tony, it's stuffed." Without removing his gaze from the bag, he addressed Karvonen in a voice that was growing with excitement. "How much did you say?"

Karvonen flashed a look towards Sewell. "You are not policemen are you?"

"I am, he's not."

Karvonen shrugged accepting his fate. "OK, I have had a good run, I have made a lot of money. Now I go home."

"And where is home?"

From a drawer Karvonen pulled out five passports, each a different nationality and identity.

"Where do you want me to be from?"

"You are not coming back?"

"No, I am not coming back, ever."

"That's fair enough then, you will leave that money here."

Mickey whooped with joy. "Oh yes, leave it here."

Now Karvonen was finding the absurdity of the situation amusing.

"I don't suppose, you know, my ten per cent? Perhaps a chance that I could....?"

Mickey was emphatic, "No way, sunshine, not a hope."

"Mr Karvonen, my 'constable' has spoken, sorry no ten per cent."

"So, can I go now?"

"You can, if you to tell me everything you know about all this. Names, contacts, who he speaks to at the bank, everything, the whole story, especially where and who the final bank is." Sewell sat at a table making notes and after an hour said, "So that's it then, that's the lot?"

"It is as much as I know, now there is no reason now for me to hide anything. Can I go?"

Sewell stuffed the statements into his coat pocket.

"You can do what the bleedin' hell you like. You can even go to the Coal Hole on the Strand and put a disguise on in the gents."

"What?" Karvonen couldn't hide his shock on hearing this.

"You heard. You leave this place now. Pack a bag and your passports and go. You will leave the keys, computer, parliamentary pass and your mobile with me. I want the passwords for your phone and laptop. If I hear of any attempt to contact anybody, we now have evidence of your involvement in child porn and money laundering, wherever you are, we will bring you back here. If you are extradited, you will go down for a very long time. Now go."

Within twenty minutes Karvonen was preparing to leave with Sewell now in possession of the parliamentary aide's electronic equipment. Whilst Karvonen was stuffing his basics into a flight bag, Sewell had instructed Mickey to copy all contacts from the recently acquired phone and laptop details onto his phone. Later Mickey threw all

Karvenon's equipment into the fast flowing river, the tide was racing out to sea. "He won't be needing these." Once Tony Sewell had identified the modes of address used between the two parliamentary employees, he felt it was worth a chance in making contact by email.

"Terry, I have been raided by the police, they were at my apartment when I got home a couple of hours ago. They didn't find my phone or laptop, I hid them by the lift when I saw my door was open, I thought I was being robbed They said it was about money laundering. I didn't say anything. I don't think they were sure because they did not arrest me, but they questioned me a lot. Terry, if it is a problem I will need you to help me, you must help me. I don't know what to do now. I will stay away. When I get a different phone I will contact you. Please tell me it will be safe for me. I will not leave the country, they might be looking for me at the airports. You always said if there were problems I should not worry."

Sewell sat back and admired his artfulness. "There you go, our Mr Atwood MP will be having an attack of the vapours once he picks this up. He'll be flailing around in the dark. He'll be looking for more information; he needs more information. Of course, what he wants to find out is, was it me? He has put the blocks on any investigation, so he may assume I want to get my revenge in first. And he will want to know what has happened to his money and more than that, any evidence against him that has come from Karvonen. Come on Mr Atwood, a reply would be nice." After an hour or so, there was no reply. Sewell, still reclining in Karvonen's apartment, snapped the lap top shut.

"It looks like our MP hasn't bought it, no reply. He and his boy must use some security code or something. Well, at least Atwood now knows he's been rumbled. Let's see what happens."

Chapter 17

Upton's phoned buzzed. "Sir, there is an ACC Morris here to see you; he's with Superintendent Mayne. They don't have an appointment, but say it is very urgent."

Upton paused, he was still smarting from the verbal reprimand he received from the commissioner over his tortuous explanation about the inconsistencies in Tony Sewell's competencies. Was this, he wondered, the follow up visit he had been dreading, a more robust sanction perhaps?

"Assistant Chief Constable Morris, you say. The only one I know is from up north somewhere. Never heard of a super called Mayne. Did they show you their IDs?"

"Yes, Sir, it all seemed to be in order."

"Did you notice what force they are from?"

"I think they said OST 34, Sir."

"OST what? Never heard of it. Ask them what it is about."

Upton squeezed his ear to the phone, but could not decipher the conversation.

"I am told it's an operational support team, Sir, that has only recently been set up."

"Operational Support? What the hell, oh, send them up."

The first to enter Upton's office was a tall man of heavy build attired in a somewhat distressed rain coat. His style was very confident and relaxed, he had an almost distracted air. Following him was an officer in the livery of an assistant chief constable. Without speaking, the man in the mac, who gave the appearance of ignoring his more senior travelling companion, approached the Chief Superintendent's desk and took a seat.

"Yes, do take a seat, Superintendent."

Upton rankled at his visitor's lack of deference he thought his rank commanded. However, the air of indifference being exuded by the now comfortably seated man, saw his sentence drift to an inconclusive ending. The assistant chief constable showed signs of being ill at ease and hovered at the doorway before finding a chair. Whoever the plain clothed man was, he wasn't a police officer.

"Chief Superintendent Upton, I have already taken a seat. Do you always waste time on redundant matters? Not a good management tool."

Upton could not hide his reaction to the lack of courtesy from a junior officer. But his displeasure gave way to concern. "Just who the hell are you? What are you doing here? I've a good mind to……"

"To do what, Upton? Stop my pocket money? Give me a jolly good thrashing."

The visitor took Upton's phone from the cradle and punched in a number. "Hello, it's Mayne. Could you put me through to the commissioner immediately? Hello, Commissioner, and how are you today? Good, look, I'm with Upton, I'm afraid he is not being very cooperative. You couldn't give him a nudge could you? Thanks ever so much."

As Upton reached for the proffered handset, he noted that Mayne seemed to have an almost chummy relationship with the commissioner. His doubts about him were reinforced.

"Commissioner?"

"Upton, you are to assist Superintendent Mayne in every way possible, do you understand?"

"Yes, Sir, but I was….." The line went dead.

"You say your name is Mayne and that you are a superintendent. I take it that is neither your name nor your rank. Are you actually a police officer?"

"Upton, I wouldn't want us to become bogged down in minor details."

"You are MI5, the funny farm people, something like that, aren't you?" Mayne swatted away the intrusion. "I am here today to talk to you about one of your inspectors, Anthony Sewell, who is currently under suspension. Now you will tell me everything you know about him, cases he was working on, current and past relationships. If you lie, or mislead me, or disclose any part of this or subsequent meetings to anybody at all, it will probably mean the end of your career and your pension. So, do I have your attention?"

Upton, as best he could, remained impassive throughout this verbal assault doing his upmost not to show any reaction and set himself the task of remaining indifferent. He nearly succeeded.

"So, you want to sack me, Sonny. You think you can come in here with all this bullshit and expect me to jump through hoops and kiss your arse. I don't think so. I suggest that you take your public school snottiness and get out of my office."

Mayne, who appeared pleased with himself and quietly amused, leaned back in his seat, regarded Upton then broke into a smile.

"Jolly good, nice try, sorry, no cigar. Absolutely, I do expect you to jump through hoops and kiss my arse. I think you have homed in on the situation very quickly, well done. And yes, I can destroy your career, or what you consider your career to be and will have no hesitation in doing so.."

The ACC quietly cleared his throat. Upton energetically, and unnecessarily, adjusted various items on his desk.

Upton, trying to bite back on his anger, decided on a line of attack. "You think so? Is that what you think? We will see about that. I will call the Federation right now and tell them I am being threatened by somebody who obviously is not even a police officer."

He grabbed his phone.

"Yes, put me through to the Federation office."

His disquiet grew in parallel to the prolonged impassiveness of the smiling Mayne.

"Chief Superintendent, if I may save you the price of a phone call, you see, I do not take orders from your commissioner, it's the other way around. Nor will I countenance any intrusion from a union rep. Now, I think we should start again."

He reached over and gently removed the instrument from Upton's wavering grip.

"You couldn't order a pot of tea could you? Just fancy a nice cup. Tea, Mr Morris?"

The ACC who was slightly surprised at being included in the proceedings, indicated that refreshments would be acceptable.

Mayne spoke in an almost bored fashion. "Right, now then, the object of my attention today is, as I said, the now suspended, Inspector Sewell. You have known him since you more or less joined as bobbies at the same station. Was a good officer, now, still a competent, if a somewhat wayward inspector who is honing and developing drink problem. Right, so far?"

Upton nodded. "Prior to his suspension, he was running a surveillance team investigating a money laundering scam. That is right isn't it?"

Upton's "Yes" was more of a hiss.

"When we went through his team's files most of his targets were identified and their backgrounds established. However, there was one target who seemed, initially, to generate a lot of interest. But then it all stopped very abruptly. From what he told the commissioner, this person has access to Parliament."

Upton accepted that the pause was an indication for him to speak. "All I know, is that he told me he that had got hold of something big, very big, need to know stuff. He said it was better that even I didn't know about it. He asked me to arrange for him to see the commissioner, so I did. That's all I know, nothing more. He did not tell me what it was about, I still don't know what is involved and I did not ask. Next thing is, I am told to suspend him, that came from the top. It was clear something was going on and it was a cause for major concern, but I did not know, nor do know, what it was all about. I spoke to some of his surveillance team, but they were not giving anything away. I thought it was best to leave it alone, so I did."

The arrival of the tea service saved Upton from further explanation. He realised he was starting to talk without first thinking the question through.

Morris took it upon himself to dispense the tea. Having done so he sat back as a silent observer. "Right, where were we? So, Upton," at this point Morris winced at the abandonment of Upton's rank and interceded.

"I think that Chief Superintendent Upton deserves the courtesy of being addressed by his rank."

Mayne momentarily weighed up the message. "Do you really, Mr Morris? Thank you for that. Now then, Upton, as I said you and Inspector Sewell go back a long way and that you were on the beat together at the start of both you careers. His father was a small time crook and he has a brother who appears to be a long established and hardened criminal, did this concern you?"

Upton's wheezing laugh mocked the question. "You what? Was I worried about his brother Harry, being a villain? Half the coppers in the force have got relatives with form. Some of them make Harry Sewell look like a saint. There has never been any suggestion, ever, that Tony Sewell was bent. He was never involved in or interfered with any enquiries involving his brother. Basically Tony was a first rate copper, if I'm honest, he should have been promoted years ago. But the powers that be, wouldn't give him a leg up because of his family connections."

"Yes, I noticed that. It must be about thirty years ago since you arrested Harry Sewell for public disorder. What was that all about?

Upton's stiffening was almost imperceptible. "Like you say, it was a long time ago. No idea what it was all about, can't remember. Harry was always a bit of a handful even as a teenager. You have been doing your homework, Mr Mayne."

"OK, Chief Superintendent Upton, here's what it's all about. Sewell appears to have fallen over, what he believes to be, a money laundering enterprise involving a senior politician. We have questioned his team. At first they all lied saying they lost the target, that is the politician's assistant, at Westminster tube. When our questioning became a bit more persuasive, they told us the guy went through the MP's entrance, after that Sewell seems to have gone solo. Whether or not this is the case is of no consequences to you. You will not make any noises about this whatsoever, not to anyone. We, that is a section from my organisation." Here a raised hand from Mayne stopped the obvious question from Upton. "We have had your Tony Sewell under surveillance. He has given us a hard time, which is interesting because it shows he expected this sort of attention. He doesn't appear to be aware of recent technical developments. Over time we have managed to mark most of his outer clothes, coats and jackets, with a spray. It is colourless but with certain visual aids, the marker can be seen from quite a distance. The spray contains micro pellets which can be tracked, the range isn't all that brilliant, but it enabled us to build up a picture of his movements. He is now seeing his brother on a more or less weekly basis. He has also visited the apartment of this politician's assistant. This assistant has not been seen since and we are unable to track him either by his phone signals or by the use of his computer, or for that matter, any other lines of enquiry. We do not know if Sewell and the assistant are working together or if he has put the frighteners on him. It could be, as Sewell seems to have so much information, that they are working as a team."

Upton erupted. "I don't believe that, not for a minute, that's not his style. He's a clever copper. He's probably got that bloke by the nuts."

"If he has, he's disappeared. Look, Upton, this is what it is all about. You, more than anybody else, know Sewell, you have virtually grown up together; spent most of your years in the same nicks. I want you to go and talk to him, tell him that what he is doing, what he is chasing, is a non-starter. He risks causing a major political crisis. Tell him that what he thinks is some bent MP working a racket, is actually part of an overseas investigation involving the authorities from several countries. If he causes it to go belly up, it will severely embarrass this government and ruin its international reputation. Tell him that if he drops the whole thing and agrees never to go near it again, he can have his job back or retire on full pension. But he must pack it in. If not, he will, and I mean will, face the most serious of consequences. Also, he must agree to meet with me and disclose any information he has collected."

Upton sensed that matters were moving back towards him.

"So, what would these most serious consequences be? Is he likely to have an accident of some sort? If he is just cocking things up, why don't you just arrest him?"

Mayne's shrug was non-committal. "We need to manage these issues according to certain rules. Even an inaccurate and unfounded leak can create major problems."

"Shall I tell him about your lot bugging his clothes?"

"That would not be a good idea, that would be a very bad idea. These systems we are using are on loan from a foreign government, they must not, on any account, be disclosed. It would be a career limiting move, if you get my drift. You can tell him, if you must, that surveillance was attempted, but his experience in that field meant we were unsuccessful."

Upton leant back in his chair and let his shoulders sag. "So, basically, I warn him off and tell him if he doesn't behave, he will get run over by a bus. And if I cock it up, the same bus will come after me."

"Exactly, you have it one.

Chapter 18

"Hello, Mrs Sewell, Mary?"

"Yes, who wants to know?"

"I'm Mickey's wife, Lisa, Mickey Benson. Mickey's my husband."

"I gathered that. What can I do for you? What do you want?"

"Well, my Mickey got hurt and it was your son Harry what done it, he was hurt quite bad."

"That's nothing to do with me, love. If you think my Harry has done something, you should have a word with him. You know that blokes will be blokes, they have their ways. I always find it best to keep out of it, let them get on with it. Can't say that I know too much about it. Anyway, from what I hear it was a few days or so ago, he should be up and about by now, they usually are after a few days. I'm sorry, love, there's nothing I can do, like I say, best leave it to the men. I'm sure your Mickey wouldn't thank you for going behind his back and involving me in it."

Lisa Benson took a very deep breath then slowly exhaled.

" Can I come in? I think it best if I do. As I understand it, it was down to you, you made Mickey get you a load of stuff that was nicked....."

The interjection was sharp.

"Not here, love, not on the doorstep. You don't know what nosey sods are listening. You should know the rules. Come on, you better come in."

Lisa pulled her coat tighter as she moved along a dingy hallway. She was surprised that, one who had for so long wore a heavy cloak of notoriety, should live surrounded by such dowdy effects. Heavy dark curtains pulled together, despite the evidence of sun outside, deepened the solid browns of the furniture and the heavily patterned carpet. The very large flat screen television made an incongruous statement. Mary Sewell slumped into a chair. Lisa ignored the casual hand signal to do likewise and stood with one hand gripping the opposite shoulder of her coat.

"Yeah, right, like I say, there was all this nicked stuff, and you made Mickey get you a load of it. All drink and smokes, you had a load of it."

"Look, young lady, what's your point, what do you want? I'm a bit busy right now, just say your piece then sling your hook."

Lisa's words came out in a torrent.

"I know it all, I know what happened, what went on. It was a warehouse, your Harry done it. I've got proof, I can go to the law, he's only just got out, this time it will be a very long stretch, very long."

"What did you say your name was, Lisa? Look, Lisa, you're filling your knickers with wind. If you think you can fit Harry up for this job, it means you haven't got the first idea about what goes on around here. If he did do it, and I'm not saying he did, it's a long, very long way, before it gets to court. The coppers round here look after us. We look after them, they look after us. My other son is an inspector, he's not going to let his brother go down, no way."

"How come then he pulled a stretch last time? Where was your inspector son then? Where were all these coppers you say you've got in your back pocket? "

"Aren't you forgetting that your Mickey was involved, he was part of it. He'll get potted as well. He's got form, he could pull a good few years."

Lisa stepped backwards. "He wasn't really a part of it, he just sorted a car out for them, he won't go down for nicking a car.

Mary Sewell spat out her contempt. "You what? He only nicked a motor? Tell you what, my girl, go back and ask your old man to tell you the truth. Look, I never ask what they are up to, never. But word gets back to me. Listen, you never talk about it, never even if you are with family or best friends, you never ever let on. You will get to know, but you keep it very quiet. You back your husband up, you do not go around blabbing, if you drop one in it, the others will follow. Go back home, leave it to the men. They can sort themselves out. Don't get involved, don't ask questions. Now, unless there is anything else, you best be off."

Instead of leaving, Lisa slid into an armchair. Mary Sewell felt that something of note was about to happen.

"What is it now, I thought we'd had our say?"

"Look, to tell you the truth, I didn't really come round here because Mickey got a bit of a hiding. It's happened before but not as bad as this one. And it was you, because you got him to bring a load of stuff around here. Then Harry, even though he knew it was you that put the arm on Mickey, blamed him for it."

"Harry has got a bit of a temper, I'll give you that. He's caused me a lot of grief in the past, but I think he's settling down now."

Lisa closed her eyes and made fists with both of her hands. "Mrs Sewell, you've been around this type of thing for a long time now."

"Not so much of the long time."

"Oh, right. What I want to find out is when these blokes go off and do these....." Here she searched for a word..... "these jobs."

Mary Sewell took advantage of the pause. "Yes." the word, in anticipating a question, was stretched out.

"What I mean is, when they do a job, a big one, like this warehouse, how much would Mickey get? What would his share be?"

Mary Sewell's rasping laugh revealed her stained and crooked teeth. "Well, my dear, you are more one of us than I ever would have thought. Now, I imagine that you would like to get your hands on some, or more likely, a lot of Mickey's share, I take it that's why you are here."

"Of course. Mickey is my husband, he's a lovely bloke, but, he's sort of not very bright. I thought if I could manage the money for him, it would make sense."

"Why don't you ask him for it?"

"He doesn't tell me what he's up to, I didn't think he was doing all this stuff with your Harry, honestly."

"Honestly?"

Mary Sewell's response was searching. Lisa Benson, caught unawares, looked away, her flushing unease halting the flow of her conversation. Mary Sewell waited.

"He never actually said what he was doing. I suppose I didn't ask him."

Mary took her time in lighting another cigarette. "He doesn't have regular work, but you are both quite well off. Where did you think the money was coming from?"

"I didn't ask. I suppose, sort of deep down I thought he might have been up to something."

"I am sure you did, girl, I'm sure you did. So, you want to know how to get your hands on his money?"

"I suppose, yeah."

"So, Lisa, my dear, how did all this start?"

"I went to see your Harry, about him, you know, what he did to Mickey. It was horrible, so I went round to have it out with him."

"Did you really? Blimey, you're only a dot of a girl, you must be very brave or very stupid. Although Harry is my son, I'll tell you this, watch him, be very careful. He can be as good as gold one minute, but he can flip, be very careful. So what happened?"

"He gave me Mickey's share, thirty grand, I counted it."

"I'm sure you did. How do you mean he just gave it to you?"

"When we were talking, he just dropped it on to where I was sitting. He told me what it was. He said there was more to come, he didn't say how much though. I thought, well, I am Mickey's wife so we should be a team, we shouldn't have secrets. I think I am entitled to my share of what Mickey gets."

Mary Sewell digested the information. "I think you've got your share. Where is it now?"

"Here, in my bag, I haven't told Mickey yet. What do you think I should do?"

"There's no point in faffing around, you've got to tell him that my Harry gave you a bung and that you are keeping it. If he starts anything, tell him you're going to your mother's. Say you can't live like this with him being a thief and all that. Let him know that you are likely to tell your mother everything. That'll put the wind up him, that's how I started. He's got to keep you on his side. If any of the others hear that you have bunked off to your mum's place, I tell you he'll be done for. What you mustn't do is go out and splash a load of it around. The police are always watching, they'll want to know where you got it from. What you could do is go to the dog track regular; you can always say you picked a good runner and you've made a few quid. And don't put it in the bank. If they see a load of cash going across the counter, they have got to tell the law."

These continuing restrictions were starting to weigh on Lisa. "I was thinking of a car, a little sports car. Could I have one of those?"

"That's pushing it a bit, look, I know a couple of bookies up the dog track. What you do is give them a few grand before it all starts, then after each race they will say you had the winning ticket, had three hundred on it, then they give you back your money, all nice and neat. I can tell you which ones to use. Remember don't be greedy."

In a theatrical show of mock, but serious, surprise, Lisa leant back clutching her chest. "I would never do that, I'm not greedy, no not at all."

Mary Sewell appeared to consider the statement before she nodded her head. "No, my dear, I'm sure you're not. One last thing, never, and I mean never, keep any amount of cash at home. If you get turned over by the coppers, and it will happen, then they find a stash, you are in dead trouble."

Lisa's look of surprise now melted into one of troubled concern. "Where do you keep it then."

"Oh, all sorts of different places. Safety deposit boxes, bury it in a friend's garden. Actually what I could do for you, as a favour sort of thing, I could keep it for you, I've got some very good contacts."

Instinctively Lisa grasped the bag of money closer to her. "No thanks, Mrs Sewell. Thank you for offering, but I'm sure I can manage. I'll be off now. Thank you for what you told me."

"That's alright, my dear, by the way, how is your husband, your Mickey?"

Lisa initially seemed perplexed by the question. "What? Oh yeah, he's alright, just a few bruises."

Chapter 19

The chief superintendent stepped out of the marked police car, stretched slightly and tugged the hem of his uniform jacket. He gave a cursory glance to the driver who, in turn, offered a "Goodnight, Sir." He stood outside his house which was on the London side of the Kent border. The house, a large four bedroomed detached was, if anybody cared to ask, way beyond his pay scale. He was able to afford this pile because some years earlier he said his wife had benefitted from a substantial inheritance bestowed on her by a wealthy uncle. She had spent he formative years in Islington, the daughter of an insurance clerk. Her mother gaining employment as a junior civil servant. Her uncle, who bestowed such largess on her, was also from Islington. Upton bent to unlatch the gate which led onto the neatly manicured garden.

"Hello, Eric, nice place you have here." He straightened and looked about for the origins of the greeting. "Bloody hell, Eric, you're not much of an investigator."

Some twenty feet away, a figure stepped from a Ford. "You said you wanted a chat, I'm all yours. So what is this chat all about? I take it somebody from upstairs has had a word in your ear."

"Jesus, man, what the hell are you doing here? You were told not to have any contact with anyone without prior agreement, that means coppers or me. I thought that was made clear in the letter I sent to you. You were meant to make an arrangement."

"But you asked for a meeting."

"I didn't mean here, outside my house."

"No, Eric, you meant in an office somewhere so that everything is recorded and then doctored so that I am admitting anything you lot want me to."

"Inspector Sewell, I must ask you to leave immediately. If you do not, I will have to inform Personnel."

"Strong stuff coming from you, Eric. And just what will Personnel do to me once you have told them I have been naughty? Write a letter to my mum? Look, you will talk to me now, where it is nice and quiet. Or we can make it a bit more public, with a lot more noise, say in front of the station with a few cameras; your choice."

Upton wavered, glancing towards his front door. He couldn't see his wife.

"Come on, Eric, get in."

The senior officer stiffly clambered into the front passenger seat, sitting with his briefcase balanced on his knee. "Tony, I don't know what the hell you are playing at. You know I will have to report this."

"Oh, blow it out your arse, Eric. You wanted a meeting, now we are having a meeting. Go on then, off you go. I take it you have been told to warn me off, yes? So how are things back at the factory? All the guys and gals still having a great time are they? And you, still running the place with a rod of iron? Demanding respect, honesty and decency are you, Eric? Still demanding all that old horse feathers. Your strong points, decency and honesty. We've all had the lectures."

"Tony, I do not have any idea what you are going on about. This was meant to take place in my office. Show me your phone, I know what you are like. I'm not taking any risks."

"Right, there's my phone, look switched off. That OK for you?"

Upton grabbed the device putting in his pocket.

"Right, where were we? That's right, you were taking a bung because of my brother."

"Let's not go through that again. I've had enough of this crap, I'm going home."

"Yes, you do that, lovely house. Lucky for your lady wife that she had that rich uncle. Who did she say he was? Yes, that's right, a solicitor with his own practice in Australia, worth a mint. Who was really her uncle? Was he running a legal business in Melbourne? I don't think so, word is he worked in a bar in Wapping. Highly paid work bar work, lots of big tips especially down Wapping. I can see how he made his fortune; lucky wife."

"You can't prove a thing, not a bloody thing." Some of the spittle from his barking reached the windscreen.

"Dear me, did I touch a bit of a nerve, sorry about that. Maybe he worked overtime." Sewell allowed himself a brief respite. "Right, let's pretend you have reasoned with me to see the light and jack all this in. Eric, my old mate, I have seen the light, is that OK? Now that is out of the way, what I want to know is, what is going on?"

"What do you mean, 'what is going on?' I don't know what you are talking about."

Sewell guided his hands around the steering wheel and stared through the windscreen. He addressed Upton in low measured tones.

"Eric, you will not mess me about, do you hear? You will tell me everything that has gone on since I was dumped. If you bugger about, I will finish you, finish you career. You can say goodbye to this house, your pension, the lot. I don't think you wife will be able to find another wealthy uncle who is about to turn his toes up. Do you? You know what I am talking about."

"You've got nothing on me, nothing you can use now."

"Is that what you think? Right, let's go through it. Yes, it was a long time ago, but I can still destroy you. Still remember that night, do you? My mad stupid brother; coming back to you is it? Of course it is. There was a fight, a gang of kids, naturally my brother was there, in the middle of it all, well in it. You got a call from my mum, she needed a favour, a big one. One of the kids got stabbed, dead before he hit the floor by all accounts. We all know Harry did it. Who else but Harry?"

"For Christ sake, Tony, that was years ago."

"As I said, my mum needed a favour. I don't know where I was, out on the beat somewhere. You agreed to nick Harry for some public order offence, drunk and disorderly, something like that. But your notebook showed the time of the arrest as being thirty or forty minutes before the fight started. You got bunged four grand for that, a lot of money in those days."

"Tony, you've got to believe me, I had no idea it was a fatality, I thought it was a wounding. Honestly, I wouldn't have done it if I knew."

"For four grand you would have. A wounding wasn't worth four grand. Old Billy Reynolds was the charge sergeant then. He had more brown envelopes in his time than the whole of the Civil Service. You slipped him a hundred quid to alter the charge sheet to show Harry being booked before the fight started. Billy had to use that correcting fluid. It was a quiet night, a tart and a pickpocket were on the sheet before Harry arrived, he put the details of the two already nicked, after Harry's."

"If you take this anywhere, it means that Harry is in the frame for murder."

"No, that's all been sorted, some other kid got sent down for it. Nothing is going to happen to Harry."

"You've got nothing on me, you're wasting your time; shooting the breeze."

"Do you think so, Eric? Do you think that my old mum is going to part with four grand of her old man's hard nicked money and not have some sort of insurance. I thought you knew her better than that. No, mate, it's all on record, you taking a bung to cover up a murder."
Upton held his briefcase tightly to his chest.

"I don't think you've got anything on record, nothing."

"Is that what you think, then why did you let me jerk your chain for all these years? You know it's recorded, you know my sweet lovely old mum. Do you think she is going to part with all that dosh and not get some form of investment out of it? An insurance policy on the just in case basis, get real."

"I didn't know the kid was dead."

"Yes you did, you didn't get the money until the next day. By then it was in all the papers. You even helped to set up the lad who got sent down for it."

"Tony, you know that lad was there at the fight, he could have done it."

"Could have, Eric, but he didn't. You know that now, you knew it then."

Upton was looking around the car as if seeking an escape.

"If you disclose this, so called evidence, who is going to be in the frame? Old Mary for bunging a police officer and your brother for murder. You are not going to do that, put your family inside."

"Well, I don't think so. You see mum was put upon by you to keep her son out of a fatal stabbing. You said that unless she paid up, you would say that Harry was at the fight and could go down for murder. What choice did she have? It was blackmail, that's how she remembers it."
Sewell let his words find their mark on a collapsing Upton.

"Harry didn't do it because you gave evidence that it was the other kid. The one you sent down when you perjured yourself. The only one in the frame is you, well and truly in it."
Upton's jaw hung slack as he gasped for air.

"It was a long time ago, things were different then. Look, where is all this going? Why are you dragging all this up now, what good will it do you?"
Sewell grabbed Upton's knee and squeezed it. "Eric, old luv, what I want from you, like I said, what I need from you, is information."

"What do you mean, what information?" Upton's words stumbled from his mouth.

"I am being followed. Whoever is doing it is good, very good. Much better than any old bill team. I want to know who they are and how they are doing it."

"I don't know." Upton was heavy with exasperation.

"Eric, I told you, you get one chance at this. Piss me off and I go public on your more entrepreneurial activities. OK? A couple of days ago you had visitors, A Superintendent Mayne and some ACC. There is no such person as Mayne of that rank in the force."

"How do you know this?"

"How do you think, I've still got loyal contacts, I am kept up to date. I am informed that the ACC is called Morris and he is real. So, tell me what went on."

"I can't, I was warned, I could lose my job."

"You will lose a lot more unless you cough the lot."
Upton made a downward chopping motion with both his hands. "Alright, alright, yes somebody, and I don't know who, I really don't, is

conducting surveillance on you. They are using some new techniques, an invisible spray on your outer clothes, they said jacket and coat. Apparently this shows up when special glasses are used. I think it also contains some form of micro pellets, or beads or something like that. They can be picked up by giving off a signal. And as you already know, they can track your mobile. They know that you used a pay as you go phone, they picked up on it, but then you changed it. That is all I was told, that is absolutely everything. I was meant to talk to you to warn you off. I am not sure of the consequences of your actions, but it appears they are prepared to use something fairly drastic. Believe me, I haven't a clue as to who this bloke was, he's definitely not one of ours. Secret services I imagine. I can't even guess at why they are doing all this to you. I don't want to know, I really don't."

Sewell sat with pursed lips and digested the information. "OK, you can go. I'll have my phone back though."

Upton scrambled to leave the vehicle, once outside, holding the door open he looked into the car.   "I have got to ask, have you really got actual information about that bung your mum gave me?"

Sewell leaned back in his seat. "No, Eric, I didn't, but I do now." He flicked a newspaper from his dashboard to reveal a dash cam. "Clever little devices these, film all those dodgy road users. And, do you know what, they record sound as well. So, Eric, I do have you admitting to a serious crime. And you have told me all about your visit from the secret service goons. Thank you so much, it has been a great help."

Upton managed "You bastard" twice. Pointing a shaking finger at the recording device, he stuttered, "That will never stand up in court, that is not evidence."

"Do you know what, Eric, maybe you are right, maybe not. But who knows? It is however, enough to get you thrown out of the job, pension down the tubes, all those years for nothing. Mind you, from what you say, it could be the same if it comes out that you have told me about the secret service surveillance techniques. If I do go public with this, you are dead and gone. Thinking about it, all this would go down well on social media, most interesting. Look, it has been lovely and all that, but I must be off. Bye, Eric, don't be a stranger."

Chapter 20

Atwood knocked and entered the Home Secretary' without ceremony. "Ah, there you are, Norman."

"Christ, Atwood, what do you think this is? A bloody drop in centre for soon to be sacked politicians. I've got a lot on my plate and I don't want you cluttering it up."

"What your office or your plate?"

"Look, get out and make an appointment. Shut the door when you leave."

Atwood made no attempt to leave or to even move. "Norman, we have to talk, it is important for the sake of the party."

"What is it now? You haven't nicked the lead off the roof? Sold Westminster Bridge to some American tourists?"

Atwood lowered himself into a chair. "I don't suppose your little bar is open, I could do with a snifter, a little heart starter."

"No, it's bloody not."

"Ah well, there you go. Norman, the thing is, it's this copper. I think he is really screwing things up. I believe he has the potential to be a danger to our party."

Higgins gasped in exasperation. "He's a danger. It's nothing to do with you then? You are not a danger to our beloved party with all your corruption and screwing the system, eh?"

Atwood shot his cuffs and straightened his tie, "No more than the rest of us, perhaps, but I am in a bigger league than most, more of an entrepreneur I suppose. But look, this copper, you've got to do something about him. I trust you have got the top man, our commissioner, to back off."

"I've had a word."

"Good man, well done, that's a start."

Higgins's head dropped. "Come on then, tell me what's happened."

"It's Darius. At first I thought he had done a bunk, he disappeared one night, no warning, no explanation. I did receive an email, from his lap top, but it wasn't him, he didn't write it, I know his style. Anyway, we agreed that he uses a particular style of address, which is to be used solely for our private business and nothing else. The account is known only to Darius and me, we both have the password, it can't be traced."

Higgins sat upright, his face displaying anger and annoyance. "Jesus Christ man, it's like bloody James Bond."

"You can't be too careful, you don't know what evil bastards are out and about."

"Out and about? They are in here."

"Darius is abroad."

"I hope he bloody well stays abroad."

"Yes, as I said, he contacted me, he told me that our copper friend and a mate, turned up at his flat on the pretence of arresting him and managed to coerce him into disclosing some documents."

"Go on, tell me what these documents were, or are. I imagine they are still in existence. Please don't tell me they show you as having your fingers in the till."

"That's it, that is exactly it. I couldn't have put it better myself."

Higgins voice was weary. "Will you stop pissing about and tell me what they are."

"Bank records."

"Bank records showing your off shore transactions? Bank statements that if anybody could get hold of them would show that you have deposited twenty or thirty times your salary in foreign accounts?"

"Yes, to be honest....."

Higgins interjected. "Now you are telling me that you are honest?"

"Yes, in a manner of speaking, actually, it will be more like eighty to a hundred times my salary. My parliamentary salary, not my other interests."

"Atwood, I really don't want to know. Can we just stick to the matter in hand."

"It's quite acceptable, Norman, my other interests are quite, you know, quite legitimate."

Higgins stood and cradled his head with his fingertips. "Dear God in Heaven, if this gets out, the party will be finished. If we declare it, the party will be finished. Do we cover it up and risk the lid coming off? Or do I ignore it and hope, above hope, that it is not brought to light by the likes of this nosey police officer?"

"Yes it is."

"Yes it is what Norman?"

"The bar, Terry, the bar, it is open. If ever I needed a drink, it's now."

"Good idea Home Sec. I'll join you."

The home secretary tried, not with complete success, to steady his hands as he dispensed large shots. "So, Terry, this copper, the one that you have caused to be sacked, he has them, these bank accounts? I take it that they can be clearly attributed to you?"

Atwood mulled the question over.

"Yes."

"Shit."

"Yes."

Higgins shook his head as a sign of disbelief.

"Right, let's think this through. This copper, as far as we are aware, has kept all this very close to his chest. Not even his immediate boss knows. The other flatfoots he works, or worked, with have been kept out of the picture. So if he could be persuaded to be silent."

Atwood was becoming increasingly hopeful as Higgins's came to grips with the situation.

"And I understand that you have the ability to be very persuasive."

"Terry, do not talk about that or even refer to it. Do you understand? You are treating all this as a bit of a game, a bit of a joke. What would happen if I blew the whistle on you?"

"The party, Norman, the party."

"Bollocks to the party, I could enjoy a very comfortable retirement. I could make a fortune with the media explaining why I thought it was the right thing to disclose a massive fraud even at the expense of the party. After dinner talks all that old malarkey."

The two men sat in silence. Atwood broke the spell.

"So, what's it to be, Norman? Do you send me to the Tower, or do the decent thing? I would like to know as I have arrangements to make. I do have residency agreements with some of my clients. I could take myself off to some foreign part, somewhere warm and sunny."

"Why does that not surprise me? Of course you can, we go to Hell in a handcart and you whoop it up with hula girls on some exotic beach."

Atwood nodded gently to indicate that Higgins's assessment was fairly accurate.

" Right, Mr Atwood, leave it with me. You do not talk about this or discuss it with anybody. Do you understand what I am saying?"

"Do you want me to resign, Home Secretary?"

"No, don't resign. Just get out of my office."

"Home Secretary, just a heads up before you do anything rash. As I said before, I have a few good friends, some of the ones that I know, actually are aware of my interests. In fact they were my mentors in all this. Some of them are still powerful people, very powerful people. I don't know all the names, but there is an agreement that we watch each other's backs. I wouldn't want you to come to any harm, just a thought."

The door hadn't closed as Higgins reached for his phone. "This operation you are running, has it shown anything of note? Anything which might suggest that he is preparing to leave the country? I see. In that case I think you should bring the matter to the agreed conclusion."

Chapter 21

The Sewell brothers, policeman and convicted criminal, were now meeting on a less irregular and an increasingly relaxed basis. As was now usual the gatherings tended to be in the back room of the Three Tuns a pub tucked into the backstreets of the East End of London. Harry, who saw himself as the local crime lord, was accompanied by his two henchmen, Jack and Mickey, who sat beneath his throne. Tony, now a suspended police officer, realised that his recent activities had changed his status to that of a breaker of the law. As the group settled in for that evening's session, the usual small talk was used to lubricate the discussions that were to follow.

"All right, Tony, you OK?"

"Yes fine thanks, Jack, and you?"

"Yeah, I'm good thanks. It's a bloody awful night out there though, it's absolutely lashing down. It looks like it is in for the night."

Harry satisfied that the opening formalities had been dealt with, launched into the topics to be examined. "I got to say, Tony, that was a brilliant result that you and Mickey pulled off, nice one. You did tell me there was an earner in it, and it was a tasty one for me and the boys. Mind you a lot of it was down to Mickey's little box of tricks. You did a good job, Mickey, good result. Look, Tony, are you sure you don't want a cut of it?"

Tony smiled at the halfhearted offer. "No, you're fine, Harry. It was just a bit of luck that the bloke didn't make the meet, cheeky bugger asked if he could have his ten per cent. You're right though, Mickey did a great job, I couldn't have done it without him."

Tony Sewell let the platitudes for Mickey to settle before he spoke. "Thing is, Harry, all I'm interested in is sorting out this politician before they fit me up. I know that this is a major racket with a big time political player. Them up top have a choice of throwing him to the lions or throwing the lions on me. What do you think it will be? Some big nob with connections all the way up, or a washed out copper near the end of his career. What do you reckon?"

Harry's shrug verged on the indifferent. "I know what you are saying, Tony, but what can they do? If you have played it straight, they can't stitch you up."

"Oh yes they can. They will find that I have taken bungs from the likes of you."

This time Harry's shrug showed greater indifference.

"They will drag up a couple of old lags who I've nicked and get them to say I got a payoff for turning a blind eye to other jobs that they have pulled. Or they will say I have not accounted for all the evidence in some drugs case and find some bozo who saw me stick a kilo of coke in my briefcase. There are loads of options, it won't be any problem for them messing up my name so much that it stinks. Anything I say, will be trashed. If they wanted to, they could make Mother Theresa look like a Mafia hitman."

"Or hit woman."

"What?"

Mickey seemed quite pleased with his observation. "If she is a woman, this mother lady whoever she is, then she would be a hit woman. You know, sexual equality and all that."

"Yeah, thanks, Mickey." Tony's sarcasm bounced off Mickey.

"Look, I know what you are saying, Tony, but can they really do that? Can they turn a copper with years of good service into a crook? I don't think so."

Tony gave a snort of irony. "You don't think so, that's what the Met does for Christ sake, stitch people up, that's their job, they are the experts at it."

Mickey's interest in the conversation continued.

"Yeah, that's right, My mum's old uncle Eli always said he was fitted up for a bank job he never did. They took a right liberty."

Wearily Harry raised his head. "Mickey, your mum's old uncle, Fingers Eli Marshall, was found inside a post office after he tried to blow the safe, he had all the gear with him, explosives, cutting tools the lot. Not only had he not even dented the safe, he knocked himself unconscious and could no longer be called "Fingers" as he had blown most of them off. As I recall it, the coppers that night saved his life by getting him to hospital. He tried to say that he had been kidnapped in an ambulance and wasn't anywhere near the post office. That sort of fell to pieces when they found various bits of him, including his fingers, at the scene."

"My mum never told me that bit." Mickey was crestfallen.

Harry turned to Tony. His face made it clear he wanted to discuss the main topic of the night.

"Tony, so what you got? Is it just that stuff that you and Mickey got from his mate's flat? Bank accounts and stuff."

"What I've got is the surveillance material showing Karvonen on several occasions taking money to the launderers. The records show the corresponding amounts, less his own expenses, were paid into overseas accounts. I have the phone records showing Karvonen calling Atwood immediately after the drop every time and then Karvonen going back to Parliament after each handover."

"Isn't that plenty." Harry sat upright at having found the solution to Tony's problems.

"Not really, Atwood is the main man, I need to be able to put him in the frame. How do I do that? He knows we have got a lot on him, but, I have no doubt that he can use his influence to make a very plausible denial. It's pointless going to the banks abroad to make enquiries, taking bent cash is how they make their living. They are not going to screw it up just to please a flatfoot like me. I can't go to the press, the government have got them by the nuts. These days the editors do as they are told."

Harry had not been paying too much attention to his brother's woes. "I hear what you are saying, and yeah, we've got to get it sorted, and we will. But this money laundering racket, it seems a bit tasty to me. These blokes just rock up in the street with a bag full of cash, if we knock them over and have it away, what are they going to do? It's all hooky. If they fancy it, they can come after me, but where they operate, the other side of town, they won't know who I am. They might have a guess. I probably am a name round those parts, they wouldn't dare show their faces round here, that's for sure. So, what do you say, Tony? If your boys give us the nod, we are round there sorting them out. It's a very nice earner, Tony, it's easy, look how much you and Mickey picked up from that bloke you turned over, a nice touch. Just tell your lot to give us a shout and we're going down their place sorting it."

Tony's reply was flat and unhurried. "Sorry, Harry, that's not on, for a start, it puts me right in the frame, then it could bugger up the blokes I have worked with. They've done nothing wrong, they are good lads. I am not messing up their lives. You got a nice bung, that's it I'm afraid, that's it."

"Think about it, could set you up nicely, no risk."

"Not to you perhaps?"

"Tony, it's an earner, have a think about it. Jack, you've been very quiet tonight, what do you reckon?"

"To tell you the truth, Harry, I ain't been feeling too good, my doctor says I got to start taking things a bit easy. To be honest, I'm thinking about packing it in, I've had enough. And the wife isn't so good either."

"What you talking about? There's nothing wrong with you, you're part of the team. You've got years left in you yet. I won't hear of you packing it in. Your missus is always saying she's got something wrong with her, she's just one of those types. No, Jack, you are staying, I won't hear any more about it."

Jack didn't have the heart, or the courage, to pursue the argument. Harry had asserted his position.

"Right, that's it. Tony, have a think about what I said. "

"I don't need to do much thinking. To tell you the truth, I'm getting a bit hacked off with all this, I am considering going in to the Yard and telling them to call the dogs off as I am jacking the whole lot in and I don't give a toss about bent politicians anymore. If you get rid of this one, another ten will take his place. I'm not going to beat them, it's too risky. I could ask for my pension and then sod off to Spain. Nothing to keep me here."

Harry stood, his arms splayed.

"What is everybody up to? Jack wants a note from his mum to excuse him from playing, and now you. A couple of minutes ago you were all for it, now you want to ride off into the sunset, I tell you, Tony, this one's got legs. It could be the easiest job we've ever done. Come on, don't give up on me now."

"I'll think about it, Harry. Anyway I'll be off now. Got to see a man about a dog and all that. Look at it outside, still pissing down. I suppose it could bugger up any team that might be following me. I'm sure I twigged a car behind me; going a bit too slow. I would love to screw them."

About three hundred yards from the pub, where Tony and Harry were concluding their latest meeting, was a parked car. It was empty. However it was rigged with remote controlled cameras in the lights, grill and sun blinds. What it was recording was being transmitted to other vehicles, the closest of which was more than five hundred yards beyond. In one of these vehicles two men sat amongst the debris of sandwich sleeves, chocolate bar wrappers and cardboard coffee cups. The windows were steamed up and the smell of ancient bacon and egg sandwiches continued to brew.

"It's a good night for it, dark and wet, at least we've got all the kit set up."

"At last, took long enough."

"I know, it's always the same, bloody admin don't talk to technical support and they don't talk to us. This was meant to be a priority job."

"It is now. Hang on, we've got something here, the pub door is opening. All mobiles stand by. Delta six can you zoom in as much as you can?" The night scope cut through the rain and the flat dark night.

"That's him, big bugger. I've got a clear view, that's definitely him. Can you get those glasses or scope thing on his coat?"

"Yes, I have the scope on the coat and can confirm the dye markings. The micro bead things are out of range, but it's our target alright. Confirmed to all mobiles, this is our target. Hang on, he's gone back inside the pub. What's he playing at now? I hope he's not going back for more booze, we've been here a couple of hours now. He's back out again and looks like he forgot his hat, now getting into the taxi."

"Description please."

"It's him alright, got a good look when he first went out to a taxi. Usual blue and red checked coat and now wearing a wide brimmed hat. Looks like a cowboy. A wide brimmed dark coloured hat."

"Thanks for that, Delta Six. When he comes past your position, can you confirm he is carrying his usual phone?

"OK. I will confirm he is carrying his phone and that all devices confirm he is our man."

A brief interlude of radio silence followed, then; "To all mobiles, Tango on the move. Wait for confirmation. He's into the taxi. Confirm he is in a taxi, and it is a lift off, lift off, lift off. Travelling towards you Delta One"

The food debris was swept onto the backseat.

"He's gone past our static." After a pause a new slower voice spoke.

"Yes, yes, it's confirmed. He is carrying his usual phone. We will hang back and rely on the trace from the micro beads. Remember, if this pans out, this could be it."

The micro beads on the coat allowed surveillance to be conducted from a distance up to four hundred yards and without the necessity to be in line of sight. The taxi was kept under observation, without incident, for ten minutes "The taxi is going into Canary Wharf. Now stopping near the Jubilee Line station. Get some footmen out to go further up the line, get the bikes to drop them off at stations along the line. A couple of footman to go with him into Canary Wharf. Give us a click on your radio every time you arrive at and leave a station."

The leapfrog continued until a call confirmed he was leaving the tube at Westminster.

"If he stays down, it will be the Circle or District. Do we have sufficient troops to cover it?" This was confirmed.

"Do we have our Goodnight man?"

"Yes, yes."

"OK, if it is suitable, go ahead. Do you understand, go ahead?"

"Yes, yes."

"From the Goodnight man, confirmed the target. I've got good cover. Confirm the devices show it is him. He's on the eastbound platform which is busy , good cover. Do I go ahead? Confirm that I complete the program? Go ahead?"

"Yes, yes, go ahead."

"Confirm description."

"Heavy build, over six foot, wearing a long blue and red check coat and wide brimmed hat. If you have a reader, the coat will show up."

"Yes, yes, I have all that."

The tinted glasses the Goodnight man was wearing confirmed that it was Tony Sewell's coat ten yards in front of him. He moved down the platform towards his target and shuffled forward so as to be immediately behind the glowing garment. A warm stale breeze announced a train was about to arrive. Sewell edged closer to the track. The increasing sound of the rattling carriages and low whine of the engine now confirmed the imminent arrival. The Goodnight man shuffled forward again, closer to the tracks and was immediately behind Sewell. His right hand was inside a plastic shopping bag. As the train drew closer the bag was raised. With the driver's face about ten yards away, a faint 'phut' phut' announced the use of a silenced pistol. Two small holes appeared in the bag. As Sewell pitched forward, two small dark spots in the back of his coat gave off faint whiffs of smoke. The hand with shopping bag reached forward and assisted in the body maintaining its trajectory.

"Oh, God, he jumped, I thought I could pull him back, oh, God."

The silenced pistol was dropped to the bottom of the bag and the assassin calmly walked away. A woman on the platform started screaming. Others registered shock in various degrees.

"He jumped, he just jumped. Some bloke tried to pull him back, but he jumped, poor bastard." A few of the more morbidly curious edged forwards to get a better view of the track.

"Oh, Jesus, what a mess, what a bloody mess."

The gore could be seen oozing beneath the wheels and along the track. Eventually the fire service scraped up as much as they could of the mangled body, then diluted what was left with hoses.

"We'll just get him in a bag then take it to the morgue. No point in any autopsy."

The morning editions of the local papers covered the story of a man who had jumped underneath a train. It was rumoured that he was a police officer. Some editions, quoting reliable informants, confirmed that it was, in fact, a policeman. Sources said that the officer in question had been identified from documents, including his warrant card, found in his coat. Other information suggested that the officer was having severe domestic difficulties which were impacting on his ability to adequately perform his duties. The ubiquitous police snouts came out of the woodwork and, for the standard fee, explained he had been suspended for always being drunk on the job and insubordination. Rumours are he was facing dismissal.

Chapter 22

"Home Secretary."

"Atwood."

"Well done Home Sec, very well done. So that one is sent to bed."

Higgins hung up.

"Yes, Mr Atwood, and he's not the last."

Higgins returned to his default position of standing at his high office window and starring into the yard outside. Behind his back, his left hand loosely grasped the right. From time to time his fingers would stretch and relax. He held this position for five minutes, then he puckered his lips and sat at his desk and grabbed his phone.

"On a secure line. You've seen the papers. Yes, it was the bloke who had been showing undue interest in Atwood. Obviously he is very pleased and very relieved with the outcome. He has already been crowing down the line to me. I have concerns."

"I understand."

Not so very long ago the warm slow voice Higgins was addressing would have been recognised by millions of voters. Higgins continued.

"I feel Atwood is a risk. Now that he thinks he has got away with it, he will feel he is untouchable. He has already made use of the precarious situation of the party to dare me to go public."

"Of course you can't let him do that. It's ironic, a couple of years ago that would have suited my lot down to the ground but..."

Higgins smiled briefly.

"But now, in your retirement and with other interests, things have changed. I was hoping to use some of your contacts. You still do wield considerable influence with some foreign leaders."

"With some, yes. As far as you are concerned, is he a real problem? A problem to such an extent that a solution is needed?" Higgins's response was immediate,

"Yes, absolutely, I feel he is a danger, he thinks that now he wields so much power that nobody can lay a finger on him. He has always been indiscreet. We need a way out of this. Can you help?"

"I am happy to try, Home Sec. What about our officer of the law, our nosey copper? Is his recent 'accident' likely to be an embarrassment?"

"I haven't asked any questions, but I am lead to believe that within twenty four hours or so, it will all die down and go quiet, very quiet. Could I ask you to make a couple of phone calls to sort out this Atwood situation? If that is sorted, we are home and dry. Perhaps we could meet at your club to discuss it."

"Would you set foot in such an establishment setting? Isn't it a bit old school for you, I mean you wouldn't want your public to know that you frequent such lofty premises."

"It's been a long road for me, but I think I have earned it by now. It's time I started to move up into the higher echelons of society. I don't plan to be in this game much longer."

"I have to ask this, did Atwood make any references to me in his discussions with you?"

"No, but he wasn't shy about telling me, without revealing any names, of the powerful people who have been involved in this and who would protect him. He is a real risk, likes to show off, a danger."

"Does he have any idea how much weight his home secretary has in all this?"

"None whatsoever. See you at your club."

Chapter 23

"Ah, Mr Atwood, so good to see you again."

"And you, sir."

"Thank you for coming at such short notice. Please enter, do come in."

The embassy guards stood to attention, not so much for the English politician, but for the Sheikh, who was one of the most influential men from his country. Atwood was guided to a large, lavishly appointed office with pale walls adorned with the flags of the nation and with large framed pictures of those historical figures whose influence shaped the middle eastern country in its formative years. The sheikh, a tall elegant man, though rather overweight, sat behind a large ornate and intricately worked wooden desk, he indicated that Atwood should take advantage of a nearby settee.

"Tea, Mr Atwood? You are aware of our views on alcohol, sadly it is frowned upon. Although I am able to say that I can advise you that we have some very interesting tea. I think you will find it to your liking."

The Sheikh's casual but assured deportment and speech indicated a privileged upbringing and the benefits of being educated at the best British and American universities. A tray bearing two cups and saucers, a milk jug and a tea pot was placed ceremoniously on the desk.

"Shall I pour, Mr Atwood?"

Atwood raised the cup to his lips. "Very nice tea as always, Sir, I would say it was a single malt."

"Indeed. Mr Atwood. If I may come to the point, I realise that your time is precious. A policeman was killed last night, apparently under the wheels of a train, most unfortunate."

"Yes, Sir, so I heard, as you say, most unfortunate."

"Mr Atwood, this policeman, you knew him?"

"What, why on earth should I know this person?"

The sheikh folded his arms and leant across his desk.

"You know people who knew who he was, yes?"

"Sir, I do not understand."

"Mr Atwood, you take advantage of certain business facilities in my country. This can be of a delicate nature. We wish to uphold our reputation as a fair and forward looking people. Some more regrettable practices do continue, but we are systematically closing them down. Because of criticism which may be directed at us, we must take great care so as to be able to defend our honour. As you English say, we keep tabs on everything; everything, Mr Atwood. Your assistant Mr Karvonen left in rather a hurry, we have spoken to him. We have friends in many places. He was most cooperative and was suitably rewarded for his honesty."

"Rewarded, Sir?"

"Yes, we allowed him to transfer all his funds, which are not as nearly as significant as yours I may say, to another establishment in another location."

By now Atwood had half risen from his seated position.

"You allowed him to keep it? I'm sorry, I don't know what you mean."

"Mr Atwood, his account, in our view, was a mere trifle, not much more than pocket money. But, Mr Atwood, yours is not a trifle, it is a lot more than pocket money."

"What is all this leading to? What are you saying? Have I done something to offend you? Is there something wrong?"

The Sheikh, still with his arms casually folded looked from one end of his huge desk to the other. "What you have done, my friend, is to be careless. If we find it so easy to bring to light your interests, albeit in an area of business that we do not condone, then so can others. We do not, Mr Atwood, want any problems which may not reflect positively on our reputation."

"Sir, if it is a problem with my assets, I could withdraw them immediately. I assure you nobody at all will know anything about it. If I may, Sir, I would point out that if your country acts in such a way with my assets that may cause me concern, then others, in a similar situation to me, may have second thoughts about using your facilities. These transactions must be a considerable source of income for your country. Would you really want to close accounts and run these risks?"

"Mr Atwood, we have run such risks in the past and managed the situation without too many problems. In truth, we do not even consider them to be risks."

The merest nod from the Sheikh told Atwood to resume his seat. "Your deposits may be an issue with our people, but no more, at worst, than an embarrassment. Mr Atwood, you are looking troubled. However, there is a way which could protect your assets."

"Yes, yes, anything."

The Sheikh pushed a piece of paper towards Atwood and indicated that he should pick it up. Atwood examined it, initially with an air of mystery, then he registered recognition, horrifying recognition. He slumped back into his seat with his arms hanging limply by his side. The sheikh smiled, a large, uninhibited smile. Atwood struggled to find his words,

"But, Sheik, this is the Zeus stealth drone. It is still in its developmental stage and very much under wraps. It is very much top secret. It's meant to fly further, higher, faster, carry a much bigger payload and has systems that are years in front of anything else. Sir, this is restricted, very highly restricted and very, very sensitive."

"Yes, we are aware of its capabilities; also the desirability. We are not looking for a complete drone, just some small parts for an overseas customer."

"What parts? What do you mean you are looking for parts?"

"The guidance and optical systems."

Atwood was now mopping the sweat from his brow. "But they are the bloody guts of the whole thing. As I say, very, very highly restricted. There is no way could I get my hands on these parts, no way."

Now Atwood was shouting. He thrust the papers back to the Sheikh who's placid demeanour had not shifted.

"Mr Atwood, you are a resourceful and clever man. You have great influence and power, do as I do, use it. It will, of course, be very much to your advantage."

"What do you mean?"

"Mr Karvonen was allowed to keep all his assets."

"Look, if I get caught trying to get my hands on these items, I would go to prison for a very long time. If it means freedom but with a smaller bank account, I will choose freedom. You can keep the bloody money."

The Sheikh allowed himself a soft chuckle. "Mr Atwood, I don't think you understand. We, that is my country, might be of the opinion that the assets in your accounts have come to us by a route that is not entirely legitimate. If, and I say if, we find that is the case, we would have to do the honourable thing."

"Which is what?"

"Why, return them to its rightful owner, your government, to show our bona fides we would, of course, supply all relevant details."

"Oh Jesus H Christ, you cannot do that, you just can't. I am dead, this is blackmail, I'm being screwed."

"Yes, you are. Look, it's not that bad. These drone parts are made by a small hi tech production facility. I have some influence, actually very considerable influence, in this company. Only three of each item are needed, about a million pounds each, so six million. That's not too bad, you see I get a discount. I will arrange payment. To get them out of the manufacturing plant, you tell your people they are needed for test. Imply that the Americans are interested and that there is a huge potential market, something like that. Say it is a joint venture but must be kept very quiet. Once the paperwork for release is authorised, by your good self of course, then there is the matter of exporting them."

"Where are they really going?"

"Initially they will be shown as in transit through my country with an ultimate destination of the United States. That is what the paperwork will show. The actual items will be changed for pieces that look similar and will arrive in America described as something else. Then we can do a deal with those who actually want them."

"But your country doesn't have these things. You will need end user certificates from the Department of Trade just to get them out of the country. They will not be granted." All the sang-froid and hubris Atwood ever possessed had now gone. His stature was slouched, his eyes wide and staring.

In a show of exaggerated patience the sheikh continued. "The documentation leaving here will show American import certification and your country will receive the necessary papers confirming that all requirements have been complied with. These parts will be removed from the development site and will be described as some sort of computer parts. There will be no problems with the Americans who are supposed to be the recipients, that has all been taken care of. However, what I do not have, Mr Atwood, is your signature, your authority to remove these items. I do not have your signature, but you do, which is fortunate and convenient. They may be described as, let me see, yes, water filtration equipment. Our American cousins have been working on these water systems. Why, look, some countries, to whom you supply aid, water is a valuable resource. It is essential that you make the very best use of this valuable commodity. These items will not be sent as part of some horrendous weapon of war, but as control systems for the production of fresh water from sea water and its distribution. That is acceptable, is it not, Mr Atwood? You are helping to improve the quality of many people's lives. The parts will still need an export licence, but I am sure that will not be a problem for you to arrange. So the description on the export documentation will describe the items as parts of water purification processors. To assist you in the matter, we have prepared all the necessary paperwork. It only requires your signature. Please do not worry, as I said, I have considerable influence, very considerable influence at this company. Everything will be controlled. But I do need your signature to obtain release."

For a few minutes there was silence in the room.

"And if I do this, do I keep my money?"

"I do not see any reason why not. Could even be a bonus in it for you, to show our gratitude."

"I see. Where are they really going to?"

"China."

Atwood received this information as though it was a physical blow to his person. The sheikh, in a tone that suggested he was being helpful, continued. "So, to conclude, they will be loaded onto a commercial aircraft as part of its cargo manifest, then they will land in my country. There they will be swapped with items which, more or less, comply with the paperwork. The flight continues to America. So you see, Mr Atwood, it is all very simple and straightforward. All you have do is to bring the items to me with the appropriate documentation and I will take care of the rest. As I say, simple and straightforward."

"Yes, I can see that."

Chapter 24

The door to the house remained firmly shut. The curtains were drawn so as to keep out the eyes of the small handful of reporters and the usual rejoicers of death. A local television crew stood guard around their sound and vision equipment. The neighbours in the street held their ground and remained aloof from the circus that played out in front of them. The sudden death of a policeman, especially a suicide of the most gory and grisly kind, enhanced the clamour to squeeze every last bloodied detail from the nearest and dearest. A reporter grabbed a local as he tried to slip into his front door. "Hang on a minute, mate, is the copper's mother at home? Is she about, or has she buggered off?"

"What old Mrs Sewell? That's where she lives. I don't know if she is in at the moment. I haven't seen she since, well you know since."

"Do you know where she might be if she is not at home?"

"No idea."

"Did you know her son, this copper? Actually, how long have you know him?"

The resident eyed the journalist with undisguised distaste and slammed his front door.

The newsman shrugged his shoulders and as he walked back made a throat slashing movement with his hand to indicate his foray into seeking wisdom and truth had failed. Now the letter box was attacked. "Mrs Sewell, it's the Daily Journal, could we a have just a few words? Just tell us how good a son he was. You must have been very proud of him. What problems was he facing? I am sure as a caring mother, you would have done all you could to help him. Mrs Sewell?"

After a minute of silence there was a sigh of resignation and the sound of the letter box clattering back into its place as the reporter left, only to be passed by a female from a rival paper. Mrs Sewell recognised by those who knew her as one who wouldn't duck the chance of being feted and flattered by anyone. It was assumed she had been moved to a location where, by being supplied with her favourite drink and by not having the means of communication, her silence was ensured.

Outside New Scotland Yard an assistant commissioner armed with a clipboard stood uncomfortably in front of an array of microphones and cameras. He had been instructed by someone who handled public affairs to, "Just knock this one out, it will all be forgotten by tomorrow."

The officer surveyed his audience with the public affairs spokesman riding shotgun. In front police officers were being shepherded to attend so as to make it look like a reasonable turnout by distraught colleagues. The few press representatives, who, with not much else to do, thought that the dramatic passing of a police inspector might make a few lines or a brief mention on local television, had stopped off on their way to a later more newsworthy event.

The public affairs man ushered the assistant commissioner forward. "Your target population."

The officer winced slightly at the use of the esoteric jargon. Speaking as though he was giving evidence in a Crown Court trial, with each word measured and clipped, he launched into his act.   "We are here today to pay tribute to a fallen officer who has given many years of dedicated and expert service. Although of recent, he had faced certain issues brought about, we believe, because of stressful domestic matters. He will always be remembered as a trusted colleague who was a credit to the service. He had previously........"

"Trusted colleague, my arse."

The assembly looked to pinpoint the source of the shocking interruption. A figure was pushing its way through the gathering. The assistant commissioner continued.

"He had previously...,"

"He had previously been known as a complete piss artist."

The assistant commissioner indicated that the officers who stood in front of him in mock grief should deal with the intemperate heckler.

"He had previously...."

"He had previously uncovered a major crime involving senior politicians."

The assistant commissioner hung his clipboard by his side.

"Look, whoever you are, could I ask that you give respect to an officer who was much respected. If you have issues, could I ask that you discuss them afterwards."

"No."

The rebuttal came from a large man now in the middle of the audience who was wearing a flat cap pulled over his eyes. As he spoke he moved up towards the podium, two uniformed officers moved to block his path. The man addressed them, "Hello, George, how is that lad of yours doing at university? Nigel, good to see you. Thanks for coming, very good of you."

The two officers froze with shock. The press, sensing that there may be more of a story than they first thought, took aim with their various cameras and recorders and shuffled forwards. One press woman, asked another. "What do you think? Is it a drunk?"

"Dunno, maybe the dead one was having it off with this bloke's wife. Anyway, we'll hang on for a bit, you never know. Might be worth a few paragraphs."

The man pushed his way onto the podium and removed his cap. He spoke into the microphone. "Hello, for those of you who don't know me, I am Tony Sewell, Inspector Tony Sewell. I am the dead man."

As the information sunk in, the noise of incredulity from the crowd rose. Tony Sewell looked around then again bent to the microphone.

"They killed the wrong man."

The noise billowed again. The press moved in closer, now with increased intent. The man at the microphone stood back to assess the effect of his announcement, then continued.

"I say they killed the wrong man. The person who died was meant to be me, but it was my brother. He did not jump under a train, he was murdered. I demand that a full investigation is undertaken, if there are claims that the cctv cameras were not working, that means a cover up.

I want a full autopsy conducted, an independent autopsy, on what was left of my brother's body. I say again to those of you who have never seen me before, I am Tony Sewell, I am the dead man. Look, ask those two coppers, George Russell and Nigel Beaufort, they know me. We have worked together for years, haven't we lads. So all you press and television lot, get a good shot of me and put it on the news tonight. The story is I had found embarrassing evidence of a fraud based in parliament, with very senior politicians, a major, major fraud, and they wanted me out of the way. I was suspended for doing my job. I am being set up. They tried to kill me."

As he spoke, the microphones were cut dead, a cordon of uniforms screened him from the assembly and a scrum shuffled him through the door into New Scotland Yard. At the same time the two officers he had spoken to, Russel and Beaufort, were sternly warned not to speak and were ordered to go back inside the building. By now the press were clamouring for the full details of the story. The public affairs man, aided by the stunned constables, corralled the press and invited them into London's premier police station with the promise of a full explanation. An invitation to surrender all cameras and recording equipment for "security purposes" not only was robustly rejected, but such a request added further confirmation that there was a burgeoning story. A row of mobile phones went up as news desks were appraised. At the same time, editors were being contacted by the police authorities and the usual promises and threats made in order that some form of construct could be placed on the recent happenings. Within twenty minutes, weightier members of the press started to arrive demanding to speak to their lessor colleagues who were now ensconced deep inside the building.

The Yard's PR section were, by now, demanding of senior officers just what was going on.

"Is this guy really the inspector who was meant to be dead? What was known about a major criminal event taking place around the corner in Parliament? What is our response to be? We can't keep these press folk locked up indefinitely. Their editors have sent the heavy brigade round and they will be banging on the door demanding to speak to their mates, all of whom have probably emailed the events back to their respective offices. Just what the bloody Hell do we do? Give us a clue."

By now Tony Sewell, ringed by uniforms, was on his way to the floor which housed the commissioner and his immediate team. As he was propelled along he saw the irony.

"Hang on lads, take your time. It wasn't that long ago when they couldn't wait to chuck me out, now they are dragging me back in."

He was now holding all the cards. It had cost the life of his brother, an unexpected loss. The plans of those who wanted him out of the way, had now blown up in their faces.

"Oh, if you are thinking about sending a team round to my mother's house, forget it. She's not in at the moment. I thought it would be safer that way; for you lot, not for her."

This time the commissioner met Sewell at his office door. "Inspector, please do come in." His deputy stood by his desk.

"So, I am still an inspector then?"

The commissioner did not reply, but smiled weakly. "Cup of tea perhaps, Inspector?"

"Listen, I'm a dead man." Shortly after he added, "Mate."

There was no reaction. The Deputy Commissioner bustled into the office.

"No, I do not want tea, I want a large whisky, a very large whisky. I think it's about time we got my wake started." Here he glowered at both the senior officers in turn. "Don't you think so? It's the least we can do for a dead man."

A nod from the commissioner saw a full measure handed to Sewell.

"Inspector, I am at a loss. I have no idea what has happened, or what is happening. I did hear about your supposed death, and was most saddened."

"Bullshit, utter bullshit."

Sewell took a generous draught of his drink and studied the glass as the spirit found its mark. "Well, Mr Commissioner, I reckon you are for the chop in all this, don't you?"

"Inspector, you are still a police officer and I am the commissioner. I do think....."

"You know something, I really don't give a toss what you think, call yourself a commissioner, you were actively involved in breaking the law. Sewell's voice was rising as he spoke. "I gave you evidence of a serious, a huge crime. What did you do? Went over and cozied up to your boss and buried it. You made me look like the criminal and then tried to have me wiped out in a suicide nonsense which was a real balls up".

"Inspector, look may I call you Tony?"

"No."

"Right, Inspector, look, I think it would be better if I called you Tony. I am Frank, call me Frank. I feel that the idea of sticking to ranks is a bit passed it now, don't you? Let me say this, and it is up to you if you believe me or not, I will be absolutely truthful with you. I realise that all this is probably not going to help my career. Truly I am at a loss. I assure you I have no knowledge, none whatsoever, of any attempts on your life. Neither do I know of any plot to discredit you, pleased be assured of that."

"Be assured of that?" Sewell spat the words out. "Who had me suspended? You did, and for what? For doing my job. You wanted all the files I had and when I said you would have to put a specific request in writing, I never heard from you again. You knew a lot and you did nothing."

The inspector thrust an accusatory finger towards the commissioner. "You did nothing to stop some secret squad doing surveillance on me. You did nothing to protect one of your officers. Do you know what I would do now if I was you, I would resign. When this blows up and becomes public, as it will, you will be shown up as a useless bloated bureaucrat who is more interested in covering his own arse rather than doing the job you are paid for."

At this point the deputy commissioner interjected. "Sewell, Inspector Sewell, I should not have to remind you who you are speaking to......."

As raised hand from the commissioner indicated that he should be the only one to address the inspector. Sewell turned to the deputy. "You Walden aren't you? We met when I kicked all of this off. I would wind my neck in if I was you, mate. You could be inline for his job when he gets the push."

At this point the door to the office opened. A female uniformed officer half entered looking flustered. "Sir, can I speak?"

"Say what you like, no secrets in here."

"Sir, a rather large number of press people are asking, perhaps I should say, actually demanding, to speak to somebody in authority. What shall I tell them?"

"Walden, go down and put them in a holding pattern, say a statement will be released later, something like that. Tony, I will tell you everything that I know, everything. If you find out that I am lying, I will not try to block you going to the press."

Sewell snorted indignantly. "You have already tried to stitch me up. And how do you think you can stop me going to the press anyway? You are not going to push me under another train are you?"

"Please...." The red phone rang on the desk,

"Commissioner speaking."

Sewell could hear what he took to be an angry voice at the other end.

"Hello, Home Secretary, he's here with me now. What are we discussing? I think it is all about the government trying to kill, sorry, I should have said murder, an officer because he had done his job and was seen as something of a nuisance to your government. I take it that it was your lot that are responsible for all this. And all because he had enough information to blow your party to kingdom come. I think this phone call confirms all that." The angry voice on the line could be heard clearly.

"What does he want, Home Secretary? Hang on, I'll ask him. Inspector, the home secretary wants to know what you want." The voice at the other end of the line rose in tempo and volume.

"Home Secretary, I will call you back. Bit busy at the moment." The commissioner stood in a brief moment of reflective silence. "Sorry about that, Tony, I am only getting to know him and he can be a bit overbearing at times, he will calm down in a while. But you may wish to consider what he said when he asked what do you want. The ball is very much in your court. At the moment it appears you could ask for anything, the sky's the limit. Now, what were we saying?"

Sewell found some comfort with the offhand manner in which the commissioner dealt with the politician. "I think you were about say that you shouldn't shove me under a train, something like that."

"Yes, look, I realise that it must be a bit raw, if indeed it was your brother who died, but could you fill in the gaps? I honestly know nothing of what went on. If it is a government thing, I would be kept completely out of it. Obviously it has to be that money laundering racket that you came to see me about. I fully accept that when you came you had established a case that could rock Parliament."

"So why didn't you do anything?"

"It's complicated. Could you explain the circumstances of your brother's death?" "

Sewell glared his former boss. "I might as well, it will all come out anyway. I knew I was the subject of surveillance, and not by our lot, some bunch of secret squirrels. I was informed that my jacket and coat were marked with a liquid which is visible when viewed with a certain type of eyewear and that they had been sprayed with some sort of micro beads which allowed me to be tracked at a distance."

"I never knew that, I had no idea. How did you know?"

"Chief Superintendent Upton, it seems he had a meeting with MI5 or something like that. They told him it was all top secret, they said if he revealed this to anybody he would, I suppose, fall under a train."

"So how come you found out this information."

Sewell proffered his glass. "I blackmailed him, I suppose you would call it blackmail."

Now passed being shocked the Commissioner limited his reply to, "Really?"

"I was on the beat with Upton many years ago."

Sewell unloaded the ancient story. "He wasn't averse to taking the odd backhander. A bunch of kids became involved in a fight which resulted in a death of one of them. Upton was paid off to keep the one who did the stabbing out of the frame. Quite a large back hander."

The inspector watched for a reaction. There was none.

"And you are going to tell me how you know this. Murder and corruption are serious matters."

"The killer was my brother. The one who is now dead. You can have Upton if you want. I've got evidence. Upton fiddled the paperwork to show that my brother had been nicked for a minor offence before the fight started."

"I see. So what happened to your brother? How come he was the one who ended up dead and not you?"

Sewell seemed stunned as he recalled the last moments of his relationship with his brother.

"It was meant to be a bit of a laugh. I wanted to see someone, a colleague who was keeping me up to date about what was happening in the office. Upton told me about the tracking devices they had put on my clothes. Harry, my brother, thought he would give them a run around, playing the fool as usual. I reckoned they would be waiting for me when the taxi came. It was dark and raining heavily. I went out to the cab and made sure they got a good look at me, then I went back inside. Harry, who looks like me anyway, put my coat and hat on and shot into the taxi. He even had my phone, which I realised was easy to track, and off he went. Then they killed him, they must have pushed him."

The commissioner, after a pause, said he was very sorry. Sewell, now that he had steadied himself, allowed the anger to flow back.

"I want an inquest. I want a proper investigation. My coat needs to be recovered and all this crap they sprayed on identified. I do not want to be told the cameras on the platform were not working that day, I want it proper and thorough."

Frank Withy grabbed his phone. "I want you and as many men as you like to get all the cctv footage from the station, inside and out, where Inspector Sewell's brother died. If anybody has arrived before you and gives you fairy stories about cameras not working, arrest them and tell them they will deal with me personally. Get somebody round to where the body is and guard it, guard it twenty four hours a day. Nobody is to touch it without my say so. Ensure all personal effects are collected and treated as evidence in a crime scene. They are to be kept very secure. If any government or security people try to interfere, arrest them and let me know immediately."

Sewell nodded his appreciation of the immediate action. "And I want an inquest. My brother did not jump. I want a thorough inquest."

"Yes, I will arrange that. So, Tony, what are you going to do now? You are holding all the cards. You could either go for compensation, a bung. I have no doubt that those involved would be very happy to pay you off with a very large amount. Or, as I suspect, you will go for the full glare of publicity, get all this out in the open."

The Commissioner paused to think through his next words. "Look, I have to say this, I am not a fan of this government, or any politicians really, but if you blow the lid off this, from what we both know now, it will have massive consequences, probably cause a general election. The situation is, you a hard working respected police officer, has evidence that a senior member of the government has been stealing very large amounts of money from the public purse which is paid for by the people of this country. The home secretary, when he became aware of this, not only tried to cover it up, but wanted to do so by trashing your integrity and then murdering you by trying to make it look like you committed suicide. To do this a team of, as far as I know, secret government sponsored undercover agents were employed and used advanced surveillance techniques."

"I almost feel flattered."

"Yes, quite. I admit that I was part of this cover up, but only when the home secretary made threats against me."

Sewell seemed mildly surprised.

"I didn't know that, did he actually do that? You're not just shooting the breeze are you?"

"Absolutely not, he threatened to implicate me in some sordid sex scandal and ruin my life if I didn't get rid of you."

"Well done, join the club."

"Yes, thanks. The government must now realise that it could be held to ridicule around the world. For the next few years, the idea of a credible opposition would be a thing of the past as would democracy. As we speak, the home secretary and his team will be working on a strategy to keep all this under wraps, which will be a very difficult task. There is not a lot they can do with you. As you said, they have already killed you once, they can't do that again. It is up to you as to how you want to play it."

"Basically, I want to screw the bastards."

"I can't blame you for that, what they have done to you and your family, is vile. But I would ask you to consider the terrible damage that would be brought down on this country if you showed the government up to be nothing more than a corrupt banana republic. I am not saying they don't deserve it, but do the people of this country?"

"Yeah, OK, Frank, what's your position in all this? Are you on my side?"

"I have no choice but to be on your side whether you go to the press or do some sort of deal. If you go public, I will fully support you. To be honest, I would not want that to happen, but I will give you unconditional support and be very clear on my relationship with the home secretary. He threatened to wipe out my life, my home and my family if I didn't go along with him. I have no sympathy for those involved but I do not want to harm this country."

The commissioner left his words for Sewell to digest.

"So, Mr Commissioner, what happens now?"

"We need to get you out of here to someplace where you will not be bothered by the press or worried politicians, I'll arrange that now."

The police chief barked orders into his phone and told Sewell to find his way to the basement. As Sewell left, the commissioner said,

"I have just decided that, if you don't go public, what my price will be."

The door to the office burst open and two men pushed their way in.

"Commissioner, the home secretary has instructed you to accompany us to his office. That is immediately, like now."

"Gentlemen, whoever you are, there are some things I do not like. Bad mannered people like you two, and the home secretary. Tell him I will see him when I am good and ready. Now get out of my office."

Chapter 25

Mickey Benson didn't have enough time to fully open his own front door before his wife, Lisa, had made her way along the neatly papered hallway to confront him. Without any introduction she launched into the subject that had occupied her mind for the past few hours.

"Mickey, have you seen the news, have you seen it? It's been on the telly and everything. I saw it, I couldn't believe it. It wasn't Harry's brother, the copper, what topped himself, it was Harry. But from what his brother said he didn't top himself, he was pushed. It's Harry, Mickey; he's dead."

He pushed past his wife into the lounge. "I know, Lisa, I know all about it. We just thought that Harry had taken himself off somewhere because his brother was killed. But I thought, that's not like Harry, he wouldn't give a stuff. Yeah, I saw it. Can't say it bothered me that much. Harry was a right evil bastard, he didn't care about anybody and I don't care about him. If he was pushed, I'd like to buy a drink for the bloke that did it. I spoke to Jack, he seems a bit shook up about it. I said, it's a bloody shame that he got topped just now. He owed me, he owed me quite a bit."

Lisa stood, in an agitated stance in front of her husband twisting a scarf around her hands.

"Thing is, Mickey, I went to see him."

"See who?"

"Harry, that time he beat you up. You were in a right mess, I thought he'd killed you. So I went to have it out with him."

"You what? You must be bloody mad, he's a crazy man, he doesn't care who he beats to a pulp.

So where did you see him?"

"Round his flat. It was a very nice place, lovely furniture, all expensive stuff."

"You go round to see a madman and you tell me about his nice flat, you are crazy, totally crazy. So what did he say? More likely he just kicked you out."

"He was quite nice actually."

"Quite nice? He was quite nice? That's just what I thought when he was booting me in the ribs, when I was wondering if I was going to die. As I lay there when I could just about breathe with all the pain, I thought, 'It's alright, Harry is quite nice, he may be beating the crap out of me but he's doing it in a caring way. How can you say that after what he did to me?"

Mickey's volume increased substantially and without warning, he was now screaming into his wife's face. The shock caused Lisa to stumble back. "I know, Mickey, what I meant was that he said it was a bloke thing and it just sort of happened. I know he shouldn't have done it, I know that alright."

She waited until his rage had lost some of its heat. "The thing is, Mickey, he said he owed you money, quite a lot actually. He said it was from some sort of business deal."

"Did he? He shouldn't go shooting his mouth off. And yes, he does, or did, owe me a large wedge. But I don't see how I am going to get that now."

From under a collection of miscellaneous paperwork in the back of a drawer Lisa produced a brown envelope and with a mixture of trepidation and hope proffered it to Mickey who regarded it quizzically. "What's that?" What is it?"

Slowly she surrendered it to him. "It's thirty grand, Mickey, thirty grand. It's your share. He gave it to me when I was round at his place. I've been meaning to give it to you, I didn't want to hide it. I was going to give it to you. I just didn't find the right time."

"You thieving little cow, it must be nearly a week since you saw him and you've had that since then." His voice was flushed with violence. She reeled backwards falling onto an armchair which she felt was more sanctuary than comfort. Straddling his wife, he resurrected his rage. "You don't steal my money, you're a thief, nothing but a common thief."

Terrified she tried to speak but could only produce an incoherent mumbling. Mickey's anger returned to a fast simmer. "Shut it will you, just shut it. I wondered when I was going to get my bung, when I asked him, he just said, 'It's on its way'. I wasn't going to wait much longer mind, I was going to have it out with him, I earned that."

Lisa steadied herself. "There's more, he said there was more."

"What you talking about you stupid cow?"

"Harry, he said there was more money to come. He said there was more."

"I know that, I know it. Don't suppose I will see any of that now. Christ knows where it's gone. Me and Jack were supposed to get our cut, I thought it would come when he sorted it all out. It's all gone now, should have had best part of sixty grand, all for nothing."

"Mickey, somebody must have it, that money must be somewhere. It's got to be somewhere. Who do you think might have it? What about his mum?"

She was now pale and shaking.

"His mum, are you joking? He wouldn't trust her with yesterday's papers."

"Somebody must have it, Mickey, it seemed like a big lot of cash. I was just thinking it could have made a real difference to us, you know a nice holiday, a new extension. We've always talked about that."

"You mean you've always talked about it, new extension, nice little sports car, bloody holidays. I've got to be very careful. If I'm seen throwing money around, the old bill will be down on me like a ton of bricks, you've got to be careful."

Lisa hesitantly started to deliver the words and plans that she had been considering for days.

"I know what you do, Mickey. I'm not daft, not stupid, not as stupid as you think I am. You were a villain when I met you and you've never stopped being a villain. It's not nice for me when you take these big risks. You should get your rewards for the risks and I should have part of that for putting up with it. I reckon it was you with Jack and Harry what done that warehouse where all them booze and fags were nicked;

worth a fortune, over a million according to the press, over a million, Mickey, think about it. Think what we could do if you got your share."

"Ignore the press, they always big it up."

"Yeah, I suppose. But, Mickey, that money is out there and you have earned it. Think, just think where will it be. How do we get it back? Harry gave me thirty grand and with more to come, I think he said a lot more."

"Did he? How much more?" Curiosity and greed were beginning to push his rage to one side.

"I'm not quite sure, but I think it was a lot and you, and Jack, was down for your cut. I'm sure he said something like that."

"Yeah, he must have. That's a point, Jack he might know. I mean he should know, he was like second in command. If anybody has an idea it will be Jack."

Within seconds he was on the phone. "Jack, it's Mickey, we need to talk. Can we meet? I mean like now, as soon as possible. Yeah, it was bad about Harry, no can't believe it. I thought he had taken himself off somewhere because of what happened to his brother, only it wasn't his brother, was it? Yeah, real shame, yeah he was one of a kind. Look can we meet, it's urgent. We can't go back to our usual place seeing as the filth were watching it, maybe they still are, probably listening to us now. Tell you what, do you remember where we used to go on Saturday mornings before the match? Yeah, right, see you there then soon as you like. I'm on my way now. Don't forget to look over your shoulder."

Within half an hour the two men were seated facing each other in a tired looking cafe. Outside the open door, laminated photos, faded and distressed by weather and time, showed the cuisine on offer. Mainly it was a variation of chips with everything. Inside a few diners set about demolishing the large fried meals with enthusiasm. The steamed up expansive windows gave a blurred view to the world outside. Over cups of steaming of tea Mickey opened the meeting. "So, Jack? You weren't followed then, nothing like that."

"If I was I didn't see anyone. It was a bit spooky, you know, all that stuff about them tailing Harry's brother. I don't think they would bother now, not with it all being blown out by the press, no point in it.

Real shame about Harry, his brother is saying the cops murdered him, real shame."

Jack cupped his hands around the mug and sipped his tea. "So, what do you want." Mickey looked around and, being satisfied that no other customers were within earshot, he stretched his torso across the table.

"It's the money, where's the money from the blagging? Did you get some, like a part payment or something?"

"I got something, not all of it though."

Mickey waited for further information, none was forthcoming.

"Like thirty grand, did you get thirty grand?"

"Is that what you got, Mickey, thirty grand?"

"Yeah."

"Me too, yeah thirty."

"But where's the rest, Jack? There is a lot more and wherever it is, we earned that, you and me, we earned that."

"Tell you what though, Mickey, it won't be with his mother, old Mary, she's a thieving cow, he won't have given it to her."

"Too right."

Jack stroked his chin. "So, what do you reckon? What do you think?"

Mickey squirmed further forward. "I'm pretty sure he was dealing with that firm, north London mob, run by Nobby Hayes, you know Nobby, Big Nobby."

"I know him right enough, evil bastard. Don't want anything to do with him. I don't care how much it's worth in bungs. Anyway, it might not be him."

"It is him, Jack, I know for sure."

"How come?"

"I used to download all the stuff on Harry's phone, he would have killed me if he knew. That's what I'm good at, phones and computers, things like that, that's why Harry kept me on. When the job was on, and just after it, Harry had all this stuff on his phone, all rockered up, in code like. I thought it was a load of garbage, but it was all sent to Big Nobby's phone. Now that I think about it, it all makes sense. It said, 'Leave the shopping at my dad's house.' We know that on the night the driver taking the stuff away was from north London and he was going north. When he heard that it was all kicking off and the cops were closing off streets because of all them car fires, he asked for the way to the 406, you get it, the North Circular."

Jack jerked upright. "That was a good stroke, getting that kid to torch all them motors, the cops didn't know which way to look. A typical Harry stroke, you have to give it to him."

"Actually, Jack, I am talking about Harry giving it to us, you and me, our share. We earned it, it's our money, fair and square. Look, when Harry and Big Nobby texted about shopping, Nobby said, 'I'll give you the fifteen quid now and the other fifteen when you drop the shopping off at my dad's house.' He's talking about a hundred and fifty grand up front then another the same again when he's got all the stuff, that's about right for that load. The press said it was well over a million, maybe a million and a half, but they just want a story."

"You didn't clock my phone did you, Mickey? I'd be a bit pissed if you did."

"I never, Jack, never, anyway you never had much on yours, you hardly used it."

The two men gathered their thoughts, then Jack posed the obvious question.

"So, Mickey, what are you going to do? I got to say I don't want anything to do with Big Nobby, nothing. He's got no soul. I looked into his eyes once, there was no bottom to them. I don't care what you got planned, you are on your own."

"What I was thinking, no just hear me out, Jack, was that we go over and see this bloke and tell him that Harry discussed it with us and that we were all going over to collect the dosh. We can say we had to hang back a bit because of Harry's decision to head butt a train, now we are doing what he asked us to do."

"Like I said, you are on your own. Listen to me, if you've got that thirty grand, hang on to it. We both got a very nicer earner from when you and Harry turned over that bloke's flat; most useful that. Listen, Mickey, get yourself out of this business, You've got quite a bag of dosh in your pocket now, get a job, run a stall on the market, anything. Lisa is a lovely girl, she's worth more to you than all the bent money you can get. You will end up inside at some time. I've already told my missus that I'm packing it in. She hasn't been too well lately. I said that

I would look after her until," here he faltered, "until she got better. But I won't be going back, I'm getting a bit past it. Look, I suppose we got away with that last one, that's because the way Harry set it all up. I'm not being funny, Mickey, but you're not Harry. I'm packing it all in for good, I've had enough. I just want to go home to my wife."
Mickey missed the slight catch in Jack's voice.

"I've done the crime and done the time. No more, I'm packing it in. If I were you, son, I'd do the same. Go home to your wife, spend your money. Live in peace."

"Blimey, Jack, that was a bit heavy, all I'm saying is that we go over and talk to Big Nobby, give him the spiel, if he says no, we turn around and walk out, that's it."

"Mickey, Nobby will eat you up and spit you out in little pieces. That's if he is in a good mood. Take it from one who knows, keep away. Go home and get a life."

"I'm going to see him, just to have a word like, that's all. What can go wrong? Thing is, Jack, now that Harry has gone, you were always the second in command, so now you are the head of the firm. You're in charge, you give the orders. That's the way it happens."
Jack sat back and gazed into the distance. "I never thought of it like that, as far as I was concerned, Harry was the boss and that was it."

"But you are the boss now, Jack, you are in charge, you've got to sort things out. If you don't we will have some gang of deadbeats trying to take over. We can't have that, it's up to you to show them who runs our patch."
Jack slowly blinked at the idea of being the head of a crime syndicate. "I never thought of it like that. I suppose it would make sense, but it's always been three of us. If we carry on I would need to recruit another one to keep the numbers up." Jack was now juggling ideas, his head rocking gently on his shoulders. "We could just carry on as two and see what happens. As it happens, there have been one or two jobs I've been thinking about, nothing big, but safe, we haven't done a bookies for a while. They used to be dead easy, we would box it off with the manager, he would get his cut for letting us know when they were going to bank the takings, then we would be in, bosh, sweet as a nut."

"That's it, Jack, now you are talking. We could do with another body to make the numbers up, you could sort all that out, you know all the names round here. We might find somebody as things happen. You are the boss now."

"Blimey, who would have thought that, Old Jack in charge of his own patch, running his own show. That would get a few heads turning. You're a handy lad, Mickey, you could do all the enforcing, that is if we had to."

"No problem, I can handle myself and they know it."

Then Jack's head lowered and he was silent. Mickey sat still not wishing to risk breaking the spell.

"No, it's no good, I'm not going to do it, I've told the wife, I've got to look after her. I am out of it."

"When will your missus get better then, will it be soon? If it is only a week or so, we could pick it up from where we left off. You look after her, then when she's all fixed we can talk it through."

"That's an idea, Mickey, when she is on the mend, I'll get in touch. I'll give you a nod. " He abandoned his attempt to accompany his message with a smile.

"That's alright, I can hang on for a bit. But I'm going to have it out with Big Nobby, just chat it through that's all."

"I suppose you are the boss now, you're in charge. If I'm honest, Mickey, I don't think I'll be coming back, I've had enough, a few close shaves, quite a few. I don't need any more of that. If you must see Big Nobby, just talk to him, be polite and don't push it. If he says, 'No' say 'Thank you' and leave. When are you going to see him?"

"I'll give him a bell tomorrow, go up and see him."

"Be very, very careful. He is a real animal. Tell you what, Mickey, give me a call before you go and when you get back. I don't trust him and watch that temper of yours. Remember, show him respect

The next day, Jack received his phone call. Mickey explained that he had sorted a meeting with Big Nobby Hayes. "Listen, Mickey, be very careful. He's evil. Don't let him wind you up, he'll try all that."

"I ain't going to do anything, just talk, I'm going to ask if I can have a fair share, I've even thought about saying I could work for him to earn a bit, you know as a bit of muscle."

"The last thing that gorilla needs is muscle, don't push your luck. Go over on the basis that it is very unlikely that Big Nobby will part with anything. But, I suppose it's a good idea to say you can do some work for him, goodwill like. Just keep cool and, like I said, watch your temper. Where are you seeing him?"

"At his club, you know he owns this strip joint; tomorrow about twelve midday."

"Has he still got that place? It's a right dump, it must cost him a fortune just to pay the old bill off. OK, mate, be lucky."

Mickey stood outside the door of the club. The exterior tawdriness was carried through to the interior. In the lobby an old lady with heavy arms and swollen legs was armed with a mop and bucket slopping with grey water. She did not give him a second glance. His heart was thumping in his chest, a mixture of fear topped up with a considerable amount of growing anger buzzed through him. During his journey that day, his conviction that he was entitled to the lion's share of the robbery proceeds, ballooned ever larger in his mind. He steeled himself and entered the club with a show of bravado and a considerable swagger. A man sitting at the bar asked, "Are you Harry's kid then?"

He spoke with his back to Mickey. The first thing that struck Mickey was that Big Nobby wasn't that big. Stocky and powerfully built yes, but not big. Shaven headed, conspicuously adorned with gold. Gold necklaces, bracelets, rings and a watch not much smaller than a town hall clock. His round bald head showed several jagged scars. He was in the company of two men, both of whom fitted the stereotype of a vicious thug.

"Actually, I am, or was, one of Harry's associates. You Big Nobby then?"

The floor was sticky, the room smelled of stale beer. Cold harsh strip lights peeled away any veneer of welcoming comfort.

"So you are an associate. If I thought we were having important people round, I would have got all dressed up. Sorry, Associate, I am just in my working clothes, I am so very sorry, it's not what an associate should have to put up with. You are probably used to much better than this."

Hayes looked around for approval of his barbed humour from the two men who were with him at the bar, both of whom acknowledged his implied command. The sarcastic darts pumped Mickey's anger to new levels.

"And yes, I am Nobby Hayes. So what do you want, sonny."

"Actually, Nobby, now that Harry's snuffed it, I run the patch, it's my business now. If you ever want to meet with me, you know, maybe to talk over a job or something, give me a bell."

Only now did Hayes turn to face his visitor, he didn't hide his contempt. Mickey proffered a slip of paper. "Here you are, Nobby, these are my numbers."

Hayes took the paper and, without looking at it, screwed it into a ball and threw it to one of his companions.

"Here, Jake, put that where it belongs, flush it down the toilet, that's right, sonny, the toilet. That's where you belong, right down round the bend. And another thing, you don't call me 'Nobby', it's Mr Hayes."

His two men showed their appreciation of the boss's leadership by breaking into laughter. He swivelled on his stool and presented his back, once again to Mickey.

"Come on, sonny, let's hear it, Mr Hayes, come on, My Hayes. I can't hear you, you'll have to speak up."

The laughter in the club increased in volume.

"Like I said, Nobby,". The announcement of the name was slow and emphasised. "I am the boss of Harry's old patch, I think that means some respect, don't you?"

A blanket of silence and stillness fell over the room. Then the three men collapsed into uncontrollable laughter. Mickey braced himself as though he was about to enter a physical confrontation. "I want my money, Nobby, I earned it, it's mine, I think you should hand it over. You don't want any trouble do you?"

The mirth quickly drained away. Hayes's two attendants stood and faced Mickey, but waited for a signal from their leader. He held a hand up to indicate that they should hold their ground. Hayes also stood up. Now pointing a finger at the young upstart, he spoke in a slow and low voice.

"Sonny, I think you better get out while you can still use your legs."

Mickey's renewed anger flashed through him like an electric shock. "You think I'm scared of you and your old age pensioners. I could do the three of you now, come on if you want it."

Hayes casually nodded to his staff, who then, with well-practiced movements, produced a baseball bat each from behind the bar.

Mickey's eyes were blazing. He screamed out, "You are pathetic, absolutely pathetic. Come on then."

His attempt to further the conversation was halted when the door was pushed open.

"Hello, Nobby. You alright then? It's been a while hasn't it?"

"Blimey, Jack, Jack Hamilton, what you doing here? Come to hold the boy's hand then?"

Mickey's interruption was curt and abrupt. "Listen, I don't need anyone to hold my hand. I am well able to handle myself."

Jack tasted the atmosphere. "What's going on, what's up?"

Hayes made an attempt to smile but was overtaken by a wheezing cough.

"Have you come over to hold his hand or what? I think you'd better take your boy home, slap his legs and send him to bed with no supper."

Jack walked towards Hayes with his arms raised in surrender. "Nobby, he came over today to have a chat, just a chat. Isn't that right, Mickey? He's a good lad, blows up a bit at times, but don't we all. He was meant to ask you for a bit of a bung, for the warehouse job that we did with Harry. I told him that if you said 'no' to turn around and walk out. He even said that if ever you needed an extra body at any time, he could help you out. Didn't we say that, Mickey, when we spoke about it? Anyway, I think we are sorted. It's good to see you, Nobby, it's been a while."

As he spoke, Jack's attention was focussed on Mickey and slight flicks of his head suggested that the young man should not hang about in making his exit.

"Yeah, yeah, good to see you, Jack and all that old bollocks, now take the kid and get out before we do the both of you."

Mickey's frame stiffened and he stood square to Hayes. Jack rushed over and grabbed Mickey's arm. Mickey screamed into Jack's face,

"Why did you come here? I don't need you. I can do it myself, these are just nobodies, I'm in charge now, not you, it's my patch."

Hayes moved towards the two men. Jack was by now trying to drag the younger man away. As he did so he shouted over his shoulder,

"Good to see you Nobby. It's been a long time."

"I think we've done that bit."

Mickey was, by now, almost sobbing with rage. "What you doing here, Jack? I can handle myself."

"Thought you could do with a bit of company, and, of course to have a catch up with Nobby."

"I don't need babysitting, you best be off, go on, sod off. I have come for my money, it's mine, I earned it."

Jack grabbed both of Mickey's arms and faced him head on. Looking over his shoulder.

"Thing is, Nobby, he has got to learn the rules. We'll be off now."

"Remember, no supper tonight and no sweets tomorrow."

Mickey tried to shake himself free from Jack.

"Mickey, come on, we are out of here. Don't want any trouble, Nobby, we're off, we're out of here, no trouble. "He pushed Mickey to the door. "No trouble, son, we don't need any trouble."

Suddenly Mickey broke free from Jack's grasp and strode purposefully back to Hayes.

"It's my money and I want it."

Hayes waved the belligerent young man away, "On yer bike, sonny."

The two men with baseball bats moved in on him. From within his jacket Mickey produced a pistol and pointed it at Hayes. "I said it is mine."

Jack shouted, "Mickey for Christ's sake no, put it away."

As he reached Mickey's outstretched arm holding the gun, he grabbed at it. There was a loud report and a smell of gunpowder. Hayes, seemed to have been punched backwards and landed in a shapeless lump on the floor. Mickey waved the firearm at the two men who remained standing but who were now backing away. "I told you it was my money, I bloody told you."

Jack, the blood draining from his face, was immobile with shock. He fought to find his voice.

"What have you done you stupid bastard? You stupid, stupid bastard, we are done for. That's it, it's all over. My wife, I won't see her again. She's dying. It should be you dying. I won't see her, ever. You said you were only going to talk to him, nothing else. We are both going to be banged up for what you done. This time it will be a long stretch. Why did you have to bring a bloody shooter for? You said you were only going to talk. I came here as a friend. Oh, Christ, we've had it now, we're finished. My wife, my wife, that's it, I won't see her again. What have you done?"

From the floor by the bar, Hayes could be heard groaning, he struggled to right himself, but the effort proved too much.

Chapter 26

About two hours or so of leaving Big Nobby's tattered, seedy club, Jack was at his house sitting by his wife's bed. She was asleep. He gently took her hand and held it softly in his. "Jack, that you, Jack, love? I was dreaming, nice dreams. It was a beautiful sunny day and we were walking along a beach, perhaps we could do that tomorrow, have a little holiday. We had some nice holidays. Do you remember that time we went to France? That was the best holiday ever, I loved that time there. Right down south, it was a beautiful place, lovely and warm and sunny. We used to walk from the hotel to where all the restaurants were. We never knew what we were ordering. You got something that smelled horrible, but you ate it because you didn't want to offend the waiter. Then we would stroll back and stop off at a couple of places for a glass of wine, then back to the hotel."

"Ah yes that hotel, I will always remember that hotel." Jacquie giggled slightly, "I wonder why? "Anyway, you're home early? I don't normally see you at this time. Got a day off?"

"That's right, Jacquie, a day off. I thought I would come home and tell you how much I love you and what you mean to me. And that is everything."

"That's lovely, Jack, why thank you. Are you alright, Jack, you look a bit upset? What's bothering you?"

"What you talking about? Nothing bothering me, nothing I tell you."

After a moments silence Jacquie raised the subject that had concerned her greatly in recent days.

"Jack, you know what we talked about, you know, a while ago about you and what you do. Have you done anything about it?"

"Oh yes, I have. I have packed all that in, I've told Mickey that I am now retired. So you are married to a retired man, from now on you have got me to yourself."

"You don't know what that means to me, it means everything, I am so happy, I'm thrilled." Now her mood softened. "When, you know, when I am not here, will you go back to it"?

"No, Jacquie, no, that's all gone, all gone, it's behind me now, finished."

"Jack, I am so pleased, I was worrying about who would look after you if you got into trouble and all that. Have you really packed it all in?"

"Really."

"So we can spend what time I've got left together. All the time and not worry about what could happen?"

"That's right, we'll be together and we won't have any worries."

"Jack, love, that's all I want. I am so happy now, I couldn't be happier."

"Jacquie, can we sit here and not talk, not say anything, just sit here. How you feeling today?"

"I thought you weren't going to talk. Yeah, I'm alright, actually more than alright now. If I'm honest I get a bit scared, but now I know you will be with me, it will be alright. We can enjoy our time together."

"That's right, Jacquie, we're together now, we will always be, the two of us, like the old times."

"I'm getting a bit tired now, sorry if I drop off, it's all these tablets and stuff, they knock me out."

"Before you drop off, you know I love you."

"Course I know that, and I love you too, my funny, now retired, Jack."

He watched as she drifted into a deep sleep. Tears filled his eyes and rolled down his cheeks. He sat unable to take his gaze away from his sleeping wife. In the distance the sound of sirens and flickering blue lights were moving closer and closer. Soon they were in his street. He bent over and kissed his wife. From his pocket he withdrew the pistol he had earlier wrested from Mickey's trembling hands. The sound of the sirens and the blue flashing lights now filled the room. He put the gun to her temple and squeezed the trigger. Then he lay down beside her and put his arms around her in a comforting embrace.

"That's right, Jacquie, we will always be together." A second bullet left the chamber. The police cars screeched to a halt immediately outside the house. Officers with guns drawn took cover behind the vehicles.

"This is the police. We are armed. We are armed. Hamilton, come out with your hands raised. Come out with your hands raised." The blue lights flickered through the bedroom curtains.

Chapter 27

Atwood's attire had become somewhat dishevelled, his normally bright features now careworn and jaded. He had been staring at his phone, but now decided it was time for action.

"Hello, Jaimmarsh Research, how may I help you?" The female voice was young and perky.

"Oh, hello, could you put me through to the MD, Mr Lyons please?"

"Who shall I say is calling?"

"I am Terry Atwood, the MP with responsibility for overseas development. Mr Lyons will have heard of me. Hello, is that Mr Lyons, Simon Lyons? It's Terry Atwood, I think we have met when I was on a parliamentary committee for supporting the defence industry."

"Yes, I remember, Mr Atwood, you were most helpful."

"Please, call me Terry, Simon, I'm a bit pushed for time, Division Bells and all that. This is about Zeus, but I am on a secure line. We have had an enquiry from a friendly source, a very acceptable source. I am not at liberty to disclose who it is, I will just say they are officials of an extremely wealthy country. Somehow they have heard rumours about the Zeus project. Apparently they are working on similar equipment, but are having problems with their stabilising and guidance systems. Long story short, they are willing to pay top dollar to be allowed to produce it under licence if our systems are suitable. What they are looking for is to manufacture using their space industry. It could be a very big earner, very big indeed. Probably some of your best men may have to work alongside theirs to show them the ropes."

"That sounds very interesting and profitable."

"As you are well aware this is a very sensitive project, Simon, and we have to exercise the greatest security. All this has been cleared with the appropriate committee which I head up. What the prospective purchasers have asked for, is the guidance and optical units. They would like three of each. For security reasons they are to be described on all export documentation as parts for a water filtration system. It has all been cleared with the various authorities. It has been agreed that these parts will be hand carried by our security staff. It is vital that word does not get out to other sources that we have the capability to produce this equipment."

"I see, is this all legal? I don't want the DTI round my neck."

"Don't worry about the DTI, this has all been cleared at the highest, and I mean highest, level. Actually this sort of thing is not so unusual, it happens quite a lot. These don't always come off, there will be a lot of hoops for both sides to go through. But, if it goes ahead it will really help with the export figures. So, if you could produce documentation describing them as discussed, I will arrange the export papers and the End User Certificates. Payment will be made via a third party and will marry in with some of the other, less sensitive items that you make."

"If you are sure that it is all above board. Actually we do make parts for water filtration, mainly for Africa."

"There you go then. If necessary I will send one of my assistants down to collect the bits and pieces with the documentation. Because of the sensitivity I may well collect them myself, could always do with a trip abroad. If my blokes do come, they will show you their official ID, but to be on the safe side, call me before you release anything, get your switchboard to contact me directly. I will be able to verify the identity of my people. How soon can you sort all this out?"

"A couple of days I suppose. We may have to use parts that we have trialled. Is that OK?"

"Sure, not a problem, obviously, the utmost secrecy and security is essential."

"Do you know, I always thought that when you politicians got involved it would take yards of red tape and hours of discussions."

"Not with matters like this, Simon, we have to move quickly. There is too much at stake if we lose this deal."

"Are you sure this is acceptable?"

"If it helps, I have to be in your neck of the woods soon. I could drop in and you can get it from the horse's mouth."

Five days after the conversation and two days after Atwood had made his fleeting PR visit to Jaimmarsh where he was handed a small package containing circuit boards.

Atwood's taxi was cutting its way through the London traffic enroute to the embassy and, he hoped, his final meeting with the sheikh. On instructions he was carrying, in his briefcase, the packages. Despite the risks involved with making phone calls, Atwood had contacted the embassy directly.

He received the assurances that he most anxiously sought; his money was safe. It had crossed his mind to withhold these small, but very valuable, computer circuits, until cast iron guarantees were given. He recalled the sheikh's assurances.

"Of course, Mr Atwood, and be assured, your money is safe. Maybe there will also be something for the arrangements."

Atwood looked, but really didn't see those familiar sights of the City as the cab rattled along.

The sheikh's promises offered some degree of optimism, but the issues and the risks were rebounding in his mind.

"Once I drop this stuff off, I am out of it. No more sheikhs, no more deals. I've done enough, earned my little stash. The old sheikh was really pushing it, very risky; old bastard. If the wheels came off now, Jesus where would I end up? I could always twist the home secretary's arm, he couldn't risk a stink. If it comes to shove, I will say that Higgins was aware of these deals, but did nothing about it. What if I said that he wanted his cut? That would blow a bit of a draft up the government's frock. I think I will retire, health grounds probably, get a bit of sympathy, I deserve that."

As the taxi rolled to a halt at a red light, a large dark saloon cut in front and stopped abruptly. A passenger from the car indicated to the cab driver to remain where he was and not to move. "What's going on? Do you know these blokes, Governor? They are not crooks are they? You haven't been up to anything lately. Who are they anyway?"

A second man from the saloon got out and showed an identification card to the driver. By now the traffic was building up behind the two vehicles and horns were being leaned on. This appeared not to cause the slightest concern to the men from the saloon. Atwood's guts twisted into knots.

"Oh, shit."

There were now two grey suited men standing by the cab. The door was pulled open.

"Mr Atwood, Mr Terence Atwood?"

"What? Yes, what is this?"

"I think you had better come with us, Sir."

One grey suit grabbed Atwood's briefcase.

"I'll take that."

"What? Look, I am a member of parliament. I hold a very senior position. Unless you bugger off now, I will......"

"We know who you are, now unless you want us to handcuff you in the street, I suggest you get into that car. By the way, you are under arrest."

As the saloon pulled away, a voice could be heard shouting, "What about my fare? It's nearly seventeen quid, who's paying that then?"

Initially during the half hour journey, Atwood was vociferous in letting his captors know that he was a member of parliament and exercised considerable influence. Threats were made about the men's futures. However, his continuing protests were not met with any rebuttals at all, rather a stony silence. The volume and frequency of his remarks diminished. He had, from the outset, realised probably why he had his collar felt, it was one of two matters. Either it was his banking of public funds, or much more seriously, taking steps to illegally export highly sensitive military equipment. He prayed to himself. "Please let it be the rip off of the foreign aid budget." He could handle that. The potential smuggling charges were a different matter. He was fighting to refute the obvious, that he had been set up by the sheikh. If that was the case, his future was going to be very bleak. But, then again, why would the sheikh go to all these efforts merely to deprive him of his financial acquisitions. For the sheikh they would be pretty much small beer. Perhaps it is the money after all. He thought of one last shot.

"I think I should tell you that I am a close colleague of the home secretary. He has direct control over the police."

The man in the front passenger seat turned to face him, and for once he spoke.

"Yes, so he tells us." The man continued to stare directly at Atwood and then announced,

"We are not police officers."

The shock of this aside tightened the already twisted knots in his stomach.

The vehicle pulled into the rear of a dowdy grey office building where he was bundled into a windowless room.

"Sit." The two men who had been his travelling companions took seats opposite him.

"Right, Atwood, don't ask for our names or which department we work for, we don't disclose any of that. We could go through a question and answer session but that would be a pointless waste of time. We know the truth and you will only lie about it, and no, you cannot have a lawyer. At the moment that's the last thing you need. I will tell you what you, and we, already know. You have taken steps in a criminal attempt to illegally export highly sensitive and restricted military equipment. If this stuff fell into the wrong hands, it could affect the military balance and the security of this country."

Atwood inwardly reeled at this disclosure. This could, and probably would, mean considering his age, the permanent end of his freedom. Though close to fainting and with the bile rising in his throat, he groped for some form of retaliation.

"I am not saying a word until I see my lawyer."

"Quite frankly, Atwood, I don't give a toss whether you speak or not. Now the facts are that you approached a senior official at Jaimmarsh and lied to him in order to smuggle out of the UK parts of a military drone. We've got all the paperwork, statements, the End User Certificates that you arranged, the lot Also Jaimmarsh have been very helpful. You are, in the parlance of the trade, banged to rights. Up the creek without means of propulsion."

"I demand to see the home secretary."

"He doesn't want anything to do with you. What is going to happen, is that you are now going to resign from parliament and resign your position as an MP."

"Why should I resign? Nothing has been proved in law."

"Why should you resign? Good question, I haven't quite decided on a reason yet. Let me see, how about sexual misconduct against junior female staff? No, you would only be told to sit on the naughty step for a day and then be welcomed back into the fold."

Atwood found the strength to raise an ironic smile. "Sexual misconduct against female staff? You haven't done your homework."

"No, it would have to be something a bit darker than that. Unfortunately, we can't use the real reason, the drone. That is covered by the Official Secrets Act, there is no way we can risk making any details, or even its existence known to anybody. I've got it, how about a bit of shoplifting? Yes, that would work. Let me see, you go into stores and pinch ladies' underwear. When the police searched your apartment, there was loads of it. Hundreds and hundreds of pounds worth, all sorts of stuff, bras, frilly knickers, the lot. That would do it, a pervy thief."

Atwood was going further down into the pit of despair.

"That is ridiculous, I have nothing like that in my apartment, nothing at all."

His interrogator leaned forward and smiled. "Do you know what, Atwood, you are absolutely right. There is nothing like that in your place, nothing at all."

He turned and nodded to his colleague, then turned back to Atwood.

"But there will be soon. Do you have any preferences, lace, black, white, pink? I tell you what, we will do a nice selection. Don't worry, it will all be good quality material, the best brands, I wouldn't want to make you out as a cheapskate."

"This is outrageous."

"Not as outrageous as selling secrets to the enemy, so that's it, Atwood, the police will search your place, but not just at the moment, we will have to wait for the evidence to arrive. They will gather all the stuff you have stolen, once it arrives that is, then you will plead guilty at a magistrates' court. Get a fine and a suspended prison sentence, then off you go."

"And what if I don't?"

"That might be a bit of a problem. Any trial, that is if there was to be one, would have to be held in a closed court in respect of the drone parts. You will be found guilty and the sentence would have to be a very long one, something like twenty years at least I imagine. That is if the government actually want the bother of a trial. It will be a bit awkward explaining to the press why a prominent politician has been given a very long stretch and is in solitary confinement. However, by explaining it, the chances of it becoming public would be too risky. We will not be able to state the exact circumstances. As you know these parts, and the drone itself, are highly restricted, very sensitive indeed. You are a nuisance, Atwood, we just want to get rid of you with as little fuss as possible."

"How did you find out?"

"The manufacturing site is very sensitive. It is essential that it is very closely monitored. But they don't know that. Most of the staff there don't actually know what is being developed on site. Although one or two very senior members of staff cooperate with us if they feel the need."

"If they are so secret, how come my dear friend the sheikh knew all about them?"

"Sheikh, we haven't heard of any sheikh. No sheikh involved. Don't know what you are talking about."

"Oh, so that's how it is?"

"That's how it is."

"Can I keep my money?"

"What money?"

Atwood had to think quickly. "Investments, savings, that sort of thing."

"What investments are these?"

The interrogator did not appear to be overly interested in extraneous financial issues.

"Oh, nothing really, bits and pieces, inheritance mainly."

"That's nothing to do with us."

"Will I be able to keep my passport."

"I do not see any reason why not. Planning a holiday are you, Atwood?"

"Maybe."

"Right, that's it, Atwood, magistrates' court in a week or so. You enter a guilty plea, job done. I must warn you that if you try something like going public, your feet will not touch. The press will be instructed, in the clearest terms, not to disclose any of this, D Notices and all that. Any efforts by you to try and screw this up, will have very serious consequences, very serious indeed. Before you go, you will have to sign this interview of you under caution where you admit the offences of shoplifting."

Atwood's look of incredulity was fleeting. "My interview, my confession?" Then the reality of the surreal proceedings registered. "Of course, and I thought I was the crook here." An idea grew in his mind. Maybe if he could again draw the sheikh into it, influence from a powerful man could be inserted into the mix. "What about accomplices? Are you saying I did this all by myself? How could I have done? Are you arresting anyone else?"

No reaction was shown.

"We have what we need, once your statement is typed up, you can pop off. A word of advice, keep well away from ladies' underwear shops. You don't want a second offence against you."

Terrence Atwood, pleaded guilty and had, as promised, received a suspended prison sentence and a fine for shoplifting. His defence counsel stated that, "My client has worked loyally for his party and for the public good for many years, but recently had encountered increasing stress because of the mounting pressure brought about by running his office. These actions were entirely out of character and my client expresses extreme remorse. He fully accepts that his political career is now finished and now wishes to lead a quiet life away from the glare of the public."

The papers were full of the story, which burst into life, then, just as quickly died down to become an occasional item only to be replaced by another scandal selected to feed the nation's desire for prurience.

Chapter 28

In his office, the home secretary's phone buzzed. "Hello, Home Secretary, that all went rather well. At least he is out of the way now."

"Yes, thank God for that, he was becoming too arrogant, too indiscreet which is always dangerous. More importantly, which is what I suspect, is the point of your call, is that it has freed up considerable assets that now are available."

"Good news indeed, Home Sec. Has it been sorted as we discussed?"

"It has indeed. I think we handled it in the most appropriate way. He was too much of a risk all round. The sheikh, as always, was willing to co-operate, he did an excellent job. Don't think our Terrance knew what hit him. Anyway, the sheikh, being an upright sort of bloke, has now realised that the funds were not legally obtained and they have been repatriated. I'm having lunch with him, tomorrow. Why don't you come along? He is always pleased to see you."

"I might. So the funds, have they been moved yet?"

"As we speak, into two accounts. I made a gesture to the Sheikh, he was most appreciative. I felt sure that you would approve."

"Yes, of course."

"Right, Home Sec, I shall make a call to make sure the assets have all arrived safely. What is Atwood doing at the moment?"

"Just about hanging on I would imagine. By now he must realise that the cupboard is bare."

"I have no compassion, Home Sec, greedy little man."

"Quite."

After his trial, Atwood's calls to the sheikh were all turned away. When he summoned up the courage to check his overseas accounts, he was not surprised to find that they had never existed. His rage at this loss eventually, with the growing acceptance of his fate, dissipated. He put his large manor house in Sussex on the market, ring fenced his legitimate, and other assets, and took a flight to Majorca. In the quiet, comfortable northern town of Pollensa, he reacquainted himself with his airy town house a few minutes walk from the main square. As he unpacked, he thought,

"Well, Terrance old luv, this is it. Might as well get used to it."

That evening he made his way to the Plaza Major and found an alfresco seat at his usual restaurant, the Ocho Mesas. The owner, having recognised him, with a portly deftness pirouetted and danced through the tables and past the other diners and made towards him. "Terrance, it is good to see you again."

His greeting was understated, but warm and genuine.

"You too, Miguel."

The two clasped hands. Eventually Atwood spoke.

"Miguel, has there been much talk, from your customers about the publicity I attracted in England?"

"Terrance, here nobody cares, they come they go, they are on holiday, nobody cares. Let me bring you a glass of champagne, on the house of course. Will you stay in Pollensa for a while."

"Miguel, I think I will stay here for a long time, a very long time."

"That is good, Terrance, in that case I will bring you a second glass of champagne also on the house."

As Miguel clapped his hands to instruct one of his waiters to bring the drink, Atwood reflected.

"Perhaps I could get used to this."

Miguel reappeared at the table, with restrained nonchalance said,

"Terrance, if you are staying for a long time, I think you should have a bottle of champagne, on the house of course."

"Why thank you, Miguel, that is most generous of you."

"Not at all, if you are going to stay in Pollensa for a long time, I will soon get my money back."

"In that case, make it a bottle of the good stuff."

Chapter 29

The message from government sources, claimed it had been a simple and unfortunate case of mistaken identity. Part of the official release read, "For whatever reason, Harry Sewell had borrowed, or had taken his brother's coat, which contained, among other things, Inspector Tony Sewell's warrant card. Unfortunately, because of the incident at the tube station, and the extent of the resulting injuries, accurate identification was difficult. The two men, being brothers, looked very much alike. As such, confusion respect of their identities was regrettable, but understandable. We are unable to comment as to the circumstances which resulted in this distressing tragedy. But we have reason to believe that persons from Mr Harry Sewell's immediate circle of acquaintances may be involved. Official sources have kept in close contact with Inspector Sewell with excellent mutual cooperation. It is now known that, at the time of his brother's death, Inspector Sewell had been suffering from acute stress and his outbursts were irrational and completely inaccurate. The Metropolitan Police have greatly assisted in procuring appropriate assistance and treatment for him."

The media scrum to whom, on the day, he revealed himself as not being dead and the subsequent press attention meant that Tony Sewell could not go back to his home address and was now, in effect, part of a prisoner protection scheme. Sewell was left very much alone as he didn't need protection from criminal gangs, just senior politicians. He bought two more 'pay as you go' mobile phones for cash and was using them to continue to keep in touch with Mark Stephens, his former constable. Initially Stephens registered concern at the contact, however this drifted away when Sewell explained that the commissioner was now an ally and was planning to right the wrongs visited on him by the residents of parliament

Withy now arranged his meetings with the home secretary at his own convenience. Although the politician knew the police chief held all the cards and now had considerable sway, he found it hard to moderate his stance and to acknowledge his shaky ground.

"Now then, Frank, how are we going to sort out this bloody awful mess? What are your proposals?"

"Norman, it is not my mess to sort out. It is yours, and it is a huge mess. Personally, I can't see how you will get out of it. You may not have shoved the wrong man under that train yourself, but you, either expressly, or by implication, authorised it. All to save your political skin. The press statement that you released on behalf of the Met, rings about as true as a politician's promise."

"Maybe, but it will have to do, it will all blow over anyway. Have a drink, Frank."

"No."

"Look, Frank, there are things we have to do, you know, for the good of the country, and this was one of them. If we didn't act, that copper could have done enormous damage and finished this government off and let the other lot in and given them free rein. That is not an option, I could not allow that to happen."

"So, one of your senior cabinet members works a racket by stealing huge amounts of tax payers' money. To cover it up and to keep him in the clear, you kill, sorry, murder the officer, except you murdered the wrong man. So, how are you going to keep the lid on Sewell, he can't stay gagged forever?"

"We are working on that. Anyway we don't actually know he was murdered, he may have jumped."

"Look, Norman, if you are going to treat me like an idiot, I will leave now and go straight to the press. I could tell them that you threatened to falsely implicate me in a sex scandal if I didn't back you up and discredit Tony Sewell. I think that's when you pointed out to me it would mean the end of my career, my pension, my house and, likely as not, my marriage."

"Frank, that was just talk, that's all."

"Not from where I was sitting it wasn't, you meant every single sordid word. And you, standing up on your hind legs and spouting that crap. What was it, that's it? You pledged, 'To pursue all crime, no matter who is involved without fear or favour, nobody will be immune from the legal process.' That's how it went wasn't it?   And then he was murdered."

The home secretary's unease was palpable. Before he spoke he steadied himself by leaning heavily on his desk. "We don't know that, probably never will. You cannot keep on saying that."

"Well, Home Secretary, I do know for certain. We have secured the dead man's effects. His clothing, the coat he wore which was in fact his brother's."

"And?"

"He wasn't pushed off the platform, as you have instructed the press to imply, the coat has two bullet holes in the back, both fired from a very close distance. Your boys assumed that because it was a suicide and because the body was mangled to a pulp, that nobody would take any interest and just cremate the bits that were left. I think, I hope, the autopsy will recover the actual bullets. Now that will be interesting, that will back up nicely what Tony Sewell said. His brother was murdered and he was murdered by the government. Do you feel another press release coming on?"

"Autopsy, bloody autopsy, no you can't."

"I can and I will. Under the circumstances I do not think that any medical examiner, in the light of all the recent publicity, will try for yet another cover up. The bullets, Norman, we are looking for the bullets. As we speak, the remains are on their way to be x-rayed, talk your way out of that. Will I still be framed for some weird assault? What do you say, Norman?"

"Yes, yes, I admit it, I said all that. But that was only to get you to sort this bloody copper out. Nothing would have happened to you. It's politics, just politics. Sometimes we have to use the sledgehammer to crack a nut. You would have been left alone."

"For God's sake, man, you have committed murder. Why should I believe that after the shooting, even though it was the wrong man, that you would have any compunction in trashing my life."

"Listen, Frank, we as a party, have come through a lot worse than this. We will come through this."

"How? By reducing Sewell to a gibbering wreck and telling the world he is insane and not to be believed."

Higgins was rock like, his unblinking eyes fixed on Withy. "If necessary, yes. We have a team on it already. The likely story will be that the inspector's brother was a well-known violent career criminal. Our sources will say that we have established this was a gangland killing, thieves falling out. Happens all the time, we can always tidy up any loosed ends."

"Loose ends like tearing up Atwood's bank statements, Sewell has all those. You may be forgetting, this all started with Sewell proving that Atwood was a major fraudster."

"It can be fixed, it is being fixed. Atwood has been fixed, he is out of the picture. The press will not take this any further, we've made sure of that. It had to be done, Atwood is finished, we will never hear from him again."

"So I hear, a very subtle touch. You seem to be rather good at this sort of thing, rather polished."

"Yes, Frank, we are, and you would do well to take note of that."

"Oh really, I can still blow you out of the water, I know where Sewell is, where he is staying. I am working on him to trust me, he is on his way to thinking I am his best friend in all this."

The Home Secretary's eyes were still boring into the Commissioner's. "Frank, you could do yourself a lot of good in all this. Nothing has been released yet, but it will be announced that, on a democratic vote of course, I will be the new leader of the party. In eight or nine months, I could be the next prime minister, think of that, Frank, unlimited power. I would have to look after my friends."

"Or shoot those who are not."

Chapter 30

"Hi, Tony, it's the Commissioner here, sorry, I should now say Frank. I have just had a meeting with the home secretary. Can we meet somewhere to talk?"

An hour later the commissioner acquainted himself with a small pub in a side street off The Strand. It had been many years since he had been in such premises, but had made considerable use of these establishments as a young constable on the beat. Sewell was quietly amused to see his ultimate boss, not in a neatly pressed uniform, but in slacks and a jacket, making himself at home in premises that he would not have seen the inside of for many years.

"Right, Frank, what's the word?"

"The home secretary is shitting himself, not to put a too fine point on it."

"What about my brother? What is happening?"

"A post mortem is being arranged."

"Forget it, Frank, I know the medics, in the past I've used a good one, straight as a die, I've asked him and he has agreed to do it. I don't think anyone is going to object, do you?"

"Under the circumstances no. A piece of information for you, they in parliament tried to cover all this up. You have seen the press releases?"

"I have, now I am a ranting madman."

"Your brother's coat, or rather your coat, now has two holes in the back. You are right, he didn't jump. On that basis I was going to arrange matters, I asked for X-rays to locate the bullets. As you know, the body was, well, it isn't a pretty sight."

Sewell spat his words out. "Bastards, absolute bastards. They did murder him, I knew it, I absolutely knew it. I see they sorted Atwood out, but for Christ's sake I hear he has been done for shoplifting ladies frillies, is that the best they can do? He should have been done for fraud, stealing the public's money, abuse of his office, should have got seventeen to twenty."

"I'm with you on that, Tony, but it's the way these politicians work. Get rid of him for good but limit the damage."

"He's free man and my brother is dead. If it wasn't for Higgins Harry would still be around. What about the money, all the dosh, has he got all that? It was millions."

"Apparently, a couple of days ago the home secretary got in touch with the embassy of the country where the account was held and explained origin of the money. It seems the embassy was only too ready to assist and, in the interest of entente cordial sort of thing, all the funds have been released and returned to the UK."

"Where to?"

"I don't really know, some government coffer somewhere. Higgins has had to play it down a bit. They cannot really say it is the money that Atwood squirrelled away. They said it would be funnelled back into the appropriate accounts."

"That's OK then. What about Harry, how do they propose lying their way out of that?"

"Sorry, Tony, they clammed up on that. Of course they will have something up their sleeve. Political assassination, the Russians got the wrong man again, gang land revenge, that sort of thing. Let me say this, I fully accept that you brother was murdered and that you have been, with my assistance I admit, treated disgracefully, but we are up against the government. They deal with all sorts of wrongdoings and are expert at covering up. Russian spies, industrial espionage, crooks like Atwood, keeping the lid on it is their day job. I know you are mightily pissed off with all this and no doubt that you could probably do a lot of damage to our lords and masters. But they could leave you screaming in an asylum if they choose, or something worse, be very careful. Look, it was indicated to me that you could be made an extremely generous offer to buy your silence. You would be able to retire in complete luxury and live a very comfortable lifestyle. They indicated it could be a lot of money, we are talking a million plus."

"Yes, they bung me to keep quiet, then in a year or two, I have a heart attack or suffer some other fatal collapse or something of their choosing. They will always know I could drop them in it."

"Tony, there are ways, you know, to keep your information safe. You could give it to a trusted source, who would release it if anything happened to you."

"What type of source?"

"Something like a newspaper, not here in England, but abroad, some place that is not too enamoured with England. If you do a deal, you let it be known that you've got insurance against anything untoward happening to you. I have done business with the editor of a fairly major French paper. He can be trusted and he would jump at the chance of a story that would let him piss down the leg of the UK government. I can arrange it for you, it will not be a problem. Then you know that if you happen to fall underneath a bus…"

"Or a train."

"Yes, quite, then the story will receive full coverage."

Sewell juggled the idea in his mind. "Thanks, I'll have a think about that. By the way, the bullet holes in the coat, I had heard the rumours. Anyway thanks, it shows we might be on the same side after all."

Withy nodded his head and splayed his hands to accept the measure of trust. Sewell looked down then slowly raised his head. "So, Mr Commissioner, if you were me what would you do? What do you think my options are?"

"Two obvious ones, take the settlement they are hanging in front of you. Or go public, go to the press, tell them everything that has gone on, the money laundering MP. You could release the evidence you have. The surveillance logs and the bank records are pretty compelling. I take it you have access to all those?"

"Yes, they're safe, and you."

Withy was taken aback by the question. "Sorry?"

"I said 'and you'. You are part of the evidence chain. My meeting with you, my reports, your meeting with the home secretary. That's all evidence, very good evidence unless you'd rather not disclose it."

The police officer showed signs of discomfort. "We'll see. Don't forget that I have been threatened as well. Right now, I am pretty much out of a job too, or could be soon. Made to take early retirement because of my inability to perform my duties. Be shunned by former and present colleagues. If you do go down the road of public disclosure, the government will be pretty hacked off, even if this lot lose the next election, they will still carry a lot of weight. They can do deals with their opposition, you know, call in favours."

Sewell spoke. "So, what if I do demand an enquiry into Harry's death?"

"Harry's death? Maybe it was a gangland killing. Your accusations about a government conspiracy could quite easily be kicked into the long grass. They will stick to their press coverage story. Repeat it often enough, people will start to believe it, then, very quickly, everybody gets bored with it. The cctv footage at the tube station will identify the man with the gun as a foreigner, Bulgarian or Russian hitman, paid for by a London mob. The hitman goes home, the London mob guys are as safe as houses, something like that. Gone, never to be seen again.

"Do you think it was security services?"

"Almost certainly, your outburst at that press meeting will be put down to a disaffected copper who was on the verge of being kicked out of the job for heavy drinking and incompetence."

"You think so, come on Frank, you are the top copper. How many of our blokes that you know of have been sacked for drinking and not being very good at what they do? Not many, if any. If that was the criteria for sacking, half the bloody force would be gone. Come on get real."

"I take your point, but this will be aimed at the public, they don't know what goes on."

Sewell slowly rolled his glass between his fingers and seemed to study it carefully. "Go on then, what's next?"

"When I spoke to the Home Secretary, I could see that he was really concerned about all this. He will have a team working on the basis that you may do a kiss and tell, blow the whole thing wide open. No surprise there, they are not too keen on that. The consequences are enormous, here and abroad. A government covering up a corrupt cabinet member who is screwing millions of public funds, you may even convince the press that your brother's untimely demise was sanctioned at a high level, who knows? If that was made public, and it stuck, which is the unknown, God knows where it would stop. There is the connivance of other countries, perhaps heads of state. It would, in all probability drag in the other governments who are involved in overseas aid. Pound to a penny, journalists in America, Germany, France and so on, would start digging to see if their politicians are as bent as ours. This government would be trashed, we could be, in effect, a one party country. If it was discovered that members from the other party were filling their boots. We could have the loony mob front running the show."

"Aren't they doing that now?"

"Do you see what I mean, Tony, what I am getting at? What the home secretary told me is that for your silence, you can name your price, he is talking millions. You would be given cast iron assurances as to your future safety, like I said, I can arrange that. Clearly he wants a sort of non-disclosure clause. If you blabbed, all bets are off. A file somewhere will show you as a mentally challenged out of control corrupt officer and that you come from a family of well-known career criminals. Your word would be meaningless. The money would be grabbed back."

"What about my brother, Harry, what about him?"

"If you mean an autopsy, no reason now to lie. Harry was shot in the back, the bullets recovered. As I said, a gangland killing, he fits the bill."

"Yeah, thanks, no need to rub it in. And you, Frank, still head of the Met, what's your angle in all this? What are they going to do to pay you off? I mean you've got them by the nuts. Nobody can say that you are a mad incompetent copper from a long line of East End villains. Your word carries a lot of weight. They can't say you are making it all up, especially if we did it together."

"Me, I am a servant of the people, that may sound weird, but that's how it is. It was made clear that if I didn't play ball, I would be finished. If I did, I would be left alone. Not much more than a year to retirement, I don't want to rock the boat; but enough of me. I have been asked to sound you out about you taking an offer of to buy your silence. I think you could push it into the millions. As I said, you will have safeguards. You can take your time. Let me know when you decide."

"So, Frank, in all of this, you get nothing and expect nothing. Is that what you are telling me?"

"That's it, what I get is peace of mind and to be left alone to prune my roses, that is more than enough for me."

Sewell appeared mildly surprised. "I suppose, Frank, that is not a bad place to be. And you say that all of Atwood's overseas bankings have been paid back?"

"That is what I was told, by the home secretary himself no less, back into the government's kitty. As soon as this was made known the overseas bank paid the assets back straightaway, that is after some urging from those in charge of the country."

"And you trust him, the home secretary, the same bloke who tried to screw you and me?"

"Yes, Tony, on this matter I do. And I hope that, perhaps, you can trust me too."

Outside the pub, as the two men walked off in opposite directions, Withy reached into his jacket and withdrew a small device which he clicked to 'off.' He then slipped it back, patted his pocket down. "I'll get all that typed up."

Chapter 31

"Michael Benson, you have been arrested on suspicion of attempted murder contrary to common law." The sergeant did not look up from his desk and continued to enter details onto a screen. He paused and looked towards the arresting officer who took his cue to address the charge sergeant.

"On the tenth of July of this year it is alleged that you discharged a firearm at the Double Cup Club, Enfield, in an attempt to murder Robert Hayes or other persons present. Robert Hayes received a bullet wound and is currently in hospital. Michael Benson was arrested by and cautioned by me at the Ferryman public house, Wapping. He made no reply to the caution."

Mickey turned to the uniformed officers flanking him. "I never done it, I tell you I never done it."

Being escorted to a cell, he shouted out over his shoulder, "I ain't going to say a word until my brief gets here. Call him now, go on call him, Cliff Howarth at Howarth and Boyd. Call him now, the number's in my phone."

The cell door slammed behind him, Mickey slumped onto the thinly padded mattress. Although it was an occasion that was not unknown to him, this time the stakes were much higher than the usual run of offences that had seen him removed from the streets in the past. Having his collar felt for theft, assault, breaking and entering and the like, were part of the trade he was in. But now, attempted murder, this was several steps up from his past misdemeanours. So, at least, Big Nobby was still in the land of the living. Though still not an ardent fan, Mickey sincerely hoped that Big Nobby would remain a fellow citizen allowing, perhaps, the opportunity to face a lesser charge. As it was. The fear of the occasion made his heart thump in his chest like a large steam hammer. He held his head in his hands. "What have I done? Jesus? Have I cocked it up or what? This is the big one, I'll go down for seventeen at least. How do I get out of this?"

About an hour after his initial incarceration, he heard keys in the locks of his cell. "Hello, Mickey. And how are you today?"

"Hello, Cliff, I think I might be in the shit this time. It's attempted murder."

"So I hear." The solicitor sat beside his client putting his unopened briefcase on the floor. "So, in a minute I want you to tell me the SP on this one." His voice suggested that his origins were the East End of London. He made no attempt to hide the accent he was brought up with. "Right, first things first, have you said anything to the police, anything at all?"

"Honest, Cliff, I haven't said a word, I got nicked in my local, I thought the lads might give me an alibi."

"An alibi, blimey, you are an optimist, you might as well have performed in front of a cast of thousands. No, mate you are placed at the scene, no point trying to fight that one."

"It was an accident, honest, Cliff."

"Listen, Mickey, it is important, very important, that you do not make any admissions to me. All you do is to answer my questions. Listen to them carefully. Do not say anything that can be construed as you saying you are guilty."

"All right, but I am shitting myself. They are saying it's attempted murder, if he dies, it's murder, bloody murder, Cliff. I could go down for....."

"Mickey, shut up, shut it. First thing, it will not be murder. Big Nobby is only wounded. Apparently the bullet cracked some ribs and caused internal injuries. But he will make a full recovery."

"So I heard, I seriously thought he had copped it, I reckoned he was dead."

"No, Mickey, in some ways it's a bloody shame that Big Nobby is not making his way to that big strip joint in the sky, but you can't have it all I suppose."

"So, does that help, that he is only wounded?"

"Not much, if you carry a gun then point and discharge it at somebody, not that I am saying you did, but if a bloke did that, it is a serious offence. A legal representative who found himself in that situation, would have to work hard to get charges reduced, not that we are in that situation, are we?"

"If you say so, Cliff."

"Yeah, shame about poor old Jack."

"I know, he was trying to help me out. Has he been nicked yet?"

"Nicked, Jack nicked? Haven't you heard? He's dead."

"What do mean Jack's dead? He can't be, what happened? Heart attack, stroke?"

"You haven't heard have you, Mickey? He blew his brains out."

"You are joking, you're having a laugh."

"No the best choice of words, Mickey, and his missus."

"And his missus? What happened to her?"

"He blew her brains out as well."

"He never, what did he do that for?"

"Mickey, that is a good point, a very good point. Now I am going to make some notes. Remember answer my questions, do not tell me anything that is not an answer to a question. Do that and I think you might walk away from this, but be very careful. First I have to make a call."

An hour later the accused and his legal representative took their places in an interview room opposite two plain clothes officers. As they settled themselves, the lawyer gave his client a covert knowing wink.

"For the benefit of the tape I am Sergeant Webster with me today is Constable Squires. Michael Benson I remind you that you are still under caution. Right, Mickey, why did you shoot Big Nobby?"

Howarth's interjection was snapped out. "Officer, please. I thought this was a process to establish the facts, not to make wild assumptions about my client."

Webster rather dramatically and forcibly exhaled to show his level of frustration. "Right, Mickey why did you go to Big Nobby's club the Double Cup?"

"It was a business meeting."

"What sort of business?"

"A friend of ours was recently killed, murdered by the government, probably done by coppers, you lot."

Howarth quickly interjected, "Not now, Mickey."

Mickey continued. "Alright, alright, our friend, Harry Sewell was killed. We thought that Big Nobby might have owed him some money from a previous business deal."

"What deal was this?"

"I have no idea. Before he died, Harry said that he must go over to see Big Nobby to sort the money out. He said that Big Nobby owed him. I thought it would be nice to be able to give Harry's old mum a few quid, a little treat like."

Webster referred to his crib sheet. "What time did you and Jack get there?"

"I got there about half twelve, something like that."

"Who was at the club when you arrived?"

"Obviously Big Nobby and two other blokes, I don't know who they were, I think they worked for him."

"Did you previously arrange with Big Nobby to meet him?"

"Oh, yeah, it was all set up, proper meeting."

"What happened when you first arrived?"

"I just went in, Big Nobby was waiting and we started talking; about the business; the money."

Constable Squires, somewhat to Webster's annoyance cut across. "How did Big Nobby seem, I mean was he happy that you were asking him for money?"

"Come off it, Constable, you know Big Nobby, how do you think he would take it. Meanest bloke I'd ever seen. He was a bit pissed off and told me to get on my bike. Then Jack came in."

Webster took the reins back from Squires. "Is that Jack Hamilton?"

"Yes."

"So you and Jack went over together, on this, what you describe, as a business meeting?"

Howarth was now becoming concerned that the officers were leading Mickey into a 'yes no' situation where Mickey was at risk of answering questions without first giving due thought.

"Gentlemen, you must be aware that my client and Mr Hamilton travelled separately to the premises, then returning in their own cars. You did know that didn't you?"

The police officers looked at each other with a degree of surprise. Howarth took advantage of the officers' stumble. "Tell me you knew they were in separate cars. I mean you are investigating this, a very serious allegation, professionally. You are aware that separate vehicles were used? I must say, it is very concerning that you drag my client in here, accuse him of attempted murder and you do not even have the basic facts, very concerning. Are you fitting events to suit your own purposes?"

"Come on, Cliff."

"I am Mr Howarth to you."

Squires tried to assert himself after Howarth's reprimand. "Alright, Cliff, we will get the cars sorted out. It doesn't really matter anyway, we know Mickey did it, he pulled the trigger, we've got witnesses; he did it."

Webster tried, but could not hide his deep concern at his junior officer's lack of professionalism. He knew what was coming next. Howarth remained outwardly unperturbed. Inside his pulse quickened. "So, Constable Squires, you know that my client pulled the trigger. You know this to be at an evidential level. How do you know that?"

Webster moved to speak but Howarth's continuance stopped him. "Constable Squires, you said that you know he did it. If you know this, and you seem loathed to tell me just how you know what my client did and didn't do, shouldn't you now stop this interview and charge Mr Benson with the offence for which he was arrested?"

Squires was shocked and puzzled at the same time. His sergeant now had an opportunity to contribute. "Mr Howarth, our apologies, I think it was a slip of the tongue by Constable Squires. He has only recently joined our team from being in uniform."

"Sergeant, your constable here has just shown prejudice and has done so without any evidential basis. He clearly said, during the interview that he knew my client 'did it'. By that I take it that he meant that he knows that my client is guilty and has evidence to support that opinion. Under the rules, the interview must cease. You either charge my client and we proceed only with what has been said today. I think that amounts to Mr Benson saying he met the victim, nothing more, that's it, no evidence of any offence. Or you release him."

Webster by now had cleared his head and sought rationality. "Cliff, it was a cock up. I'll give you that, although the constable is inexperienced, it should not have happened, alright. If Mickey walks out of this station now, he will be re-arrested and interviewed again. What is said in the interview will go before a judge and he will decide as to whether to admit it in evidence or chuck it out and whether or not it was prejudicial, but he will still face being interviewed."

By now Mickey was on his feet with his mind set on freedom, his lawyer motioned for him to retake his seat. Howarth was now in speech making mode. "Gentlemen, this interview, although only started has lurched from incompetence to prejudice in record breaking time. In the interest of justice, I will allow it to continue, but I must caution you to tread very carefully." The officers did not take heed of the lawyer's growing confidence. Mickey was still most displeased at his freedom being thwarted. Howarth spoke. "Right, shall we continue?" The sergeant did not address the constable, but the look clearly meant, "You do not speak." The sergeant tidied the papers in front of him, then recommenced. "Right, Mr Benson, we have established that you were joined at the club by Jack Hamilton and that you both travelled in separate cars. Is that correct."

Mickey looked to his lawyer who gave an affirmative nod, "Yes."

"What happened then?"

There was another nod. "What? Oh, right, you see Jack had been going on about Big Nobby owing him big time. I don't know why he was owed, or why he thought he was owed this wedge but he did go on about it, quite a lot actually."

"OK, so what happened in the club?"

"Jack arrived about a few minutes after me. I was chatting with Big Nobby. Jack comes in and straight off him and Big Nobby are at it, slagging each other off, Jack was really getting the hump. Then, bugger me, he pulls out this gun and points it at Big Nobby. At first I thought Jack was just trying to put the frighteners on, then he went all serious. I thought, 'bloody hell' he's going to do it."

Webster's look of confusion changed to anger. "You're having a laugh, you had that gun."

Howarth allowed himself a smile. "Sergeant, I think we have been here before, not so very long ago."

"No, he had the gun, the staff at the club told us that not more than a few hours ago."

Howarth smiled again. Mickey was sticking to his script. "No, Jack had it. I see that he was getting serious and then he pulled the hammer back. He was shouting, "You're a dead man, Nobby'. Then I dived at him to stop him doing something stupid. But it was too late, I actually had hold of his hand when the gun went off."

Howarth's plan was working. "Sergeant, I am sure that if you did forensic tests, you will find powder burns on my client's person and clothing, this confirms his account. In fact, in all probability, Mr Benson may well have saved Big Nobby's life. I mean, from what I hear from where Jack was standing, he couldn't have missed. It is likely that Mr Benson prevented more than just the one shot being fired, I think he is a bit of a hero."

Webster was on his feet. "No, no, no, Mickey, you had that gun, you pulled the trigger, Nobby's two minders told us, like I said only a couple of hours ago."

Howarth, judging the timing to be right, moved in. "Sergeant, you have already demonstrated the rather tawdry style of investigation you conduct, I feel it is getting worse. If you care to speak to those staff members now, you will find that their account of events tallies exactly with my client's. They told me, less that an hour ago, that when they spoke to the police, they were in shock and were confused. It all happened so very quickly. They say that the investigating officer pushed them into saying it was my client who had the gun."

"You what, Howarth? You bloody what? You lying bastard, just like your old man. He was a lying bastard as well. He had his collar felt a few times. You're all the same."

Howarth had made the perfect catch.

"So, Sergeant, is it my father who is now suspected of wrongdoing, or is it me? Or is it both of us? This really is not going terribly well for you is it? May I point out that you have called an officer of the court a liar, I take it you have evidence of this?"

Webster leant back in his chair and wiped his mouth with the inside of his hand. There was a long pause in the room. He leant forward with fists clenched as a rage swept over him.

"I'm going to charge him, 'your client' is going to be banged up. He's not getting away with this."

In contrast to Webster's heated state, Howarth was calm and controlled.

"Sergeant, I do not wish to tell you how to carry out your duties, if you do, by any chance, happen to make enquiries you will find that the two witnesses, who were present at the time, will support my client's innocence, as will the victim, Big Nobby himself. Further to that, it is now known that Jack Hamilton left the scene still in possession of the gun. Sadly he, allegedly, later used that same gun to kill his wife and himself. If you do insist on having Mr Benson charged, you first have to convince the charge sergeant that there is sufficient prima facie evidence to support the charge. If it does go to court, it won't get past first base. Now does my client leave here now without any further action? Or do you want to demonstrate more harassment and prejudice?"

Howarth and Mickey walked from the police station to a bar across the road. In a quiet area Mickey, at last, found the breath to speak.

"I got to say, Cliff, you played a blinder, you run rings around them flatfoots. I really thought I was stuffed. It was a shame we had to use Jack like that, still I don't think he would have minded."

"Probably not, knowing Jack, why do you think he topped himself and his wife?"

"Cliff, this is the gospel, as he run out of that club, he says to me, 'she's dying'. I heard that she wasn't too well, but I didn't think it was that bad."

"Oh, I see. Maybe he realised that he stood to go down for a long stretch on this one and that she would be on her own. Nice bloke Jack, I liked him, a gent."

Mickey took a large swallow of his beer. As he placed his glass back onto the table, he asked the question that had filled his mind. "Cliff, Big Nobby and them two goons in the club, how come they said it was Jack?"

"It was Jack wan't it?"

"Yeah, I know all that, now officially it's Jack. I don't see why they dropped Jack in it instead of me. But why? I would have thought that Big Nobby would be well pissed off with me, so how come the alibi?"

"Mickey, you've had some good news today, now the bad news. If you got locked up, Big Nobby could not, personally, get his hands on you. I had a word and pointed out to him the advantages of you being on the outside. That is he will be able to rip you to pieces. He saw the merit in that when I put it to him. He told his blokes what to say. Now that you are a free man, he can come looking for you, and he will. If I were you, Mickey, I would run. I would run as fast and as far I could."

Within minutes of being given this advice, Mickey was on the phone to his wife.

"Lisa, pack a bag as quick as you like. Put all your valuables and stuff like that in."

"Valuables? are you joking, I'm married to Mickey Benson, where would these valuables come from then? Right, I'll pack up all my valuables. That's all done then, what next?"

"Lisa, just chuck everything in the car and start driving. Grab that money you got from Harry. Look, under the stairs, fish out my old football kit in that sports bag. Chuck the kit out but bring the bag. Make sure you bring the bag."

"Mickey, what is all this? Why do we have to go right now? What's up? Anyway, what's in this bag of yours?"

"We have to go, I'll explain later. Don't forget that bag."

"I heard about Jack and his missus, why did he do that?"

"Lisa will you get off the phone and start packing. Be out of the house in ten minutes, no more than that."

Lisa cut into Mickey's orders. "You know with Jack, and his missus of course, wasn't he owed money like you were? I mean he must have a fair bit, he never spent much. I was thinking, as you are his friend, his last surviving friend, shouldn't that money be yours? Jack would probably want you to have it. It's not like he has got anybody else to leave it to and he was very close to you. You don't know where he kept it do you? I know he would want you to have it, especially as it won't be any use to his poor wife now. Do you think it might be worth having a look round his house? You never know, he might have something."

"Lisa, get off the phone, get packing and get out and drive north. I will call you and get you to pick me up. Listen very, very carefully. If you do not get out the house within ten minutes you will be visited by some men who will do a lot of damage to you, a lot of damage, to get at me. Look if you want to stay and fanny around looking for Jack's pound notes, carry on. If you do stay, you will not be able to spend it, or anything else for a long time; if you are lucky that is. If you stay, you are on your own. I'm off. Maybe I will see you later. If you don't go, leave the sports bag under the stairs."

Chapter 32

Sewell punched a number into the cheap burner phone he had been using for discreet communications. "Hello, Raj, long time no see. How are you, keeping busy then?"

"Bloody hell, Tony, good to hear from you, you're famous now, the dead man who isn't dead."

"Yeah, thanks, Raj, I see that you hung on to the mobile I gave you. Actually, now it doesn't matter a toss about safe lines any more. There's nothing they can do to me and a lot I can do to them."

"We guessed all that. We, me and Mark, we both saw you on the telly when they were crying about you going under that train, then you took the stage, front and centre. Listen, I'm sorry about your brother; condolences and all that."

"Raj, to be honest, we weren't all that close, although it got a bit better at the end. You and Mark are still on the money laundering?"

"I see that you have still got your ear to the ground then, Tony. You're right, we're getting some good stuff. Obviously your bloke is out of it now, but the others are turning up as regular as clockwork. I thought it would have all been kicked into touch with all the publicity."

"Not really, no reason why the villains would know that any of this was down to their racket. They wouldn't have heard anything about it. Look, I need to know something. Are the launderers using the same bank?"

"Yes, the same old one is favourite. Still haven't got a clue as to where it all ends up, but we have got enough this end for convictions. "

"That's good to hear. Listen have we still got that manager looking after us? He hasn't got himself nicked for fraud or dealing coke yet?"

"No problem, he's still there. Still terrified he might get found out and shipped back home. If we need anything, you know the latest figures, he just looks them up and gives them to us. He's used to us now."

"Raj, I would like you to do something for me. It's all part of this job, but I need to see some files, some different files, it's all related. If it's what I think it is, it might show that some more big names are involved."

"Don't see that as a problem, Tony, just give me the details and I will sort it."

"Thanks, Raj, what I want is the details from a couple of accounts. Atwood's has been emptied. I need to know where his money went. Where it all ended up. I just want to see where all his dosh went, just the files, nothing else."

Two days later, in the quiet of his current abode, Sewell scrutinised his recently acquired documents, then he scrutinised them again. He reached for his phone.

"Commissioner's office please, Mr Commissioner, your favourite inspector here."

"I thought you had been quiet for a day or so. What can I do for you?"

"I have details of some accounts that I have recently acquired."

"I won't ask how."

"No, it's alright, almost legitimate."

"I am almost disappointed."

"I need to trace some off shore accounts. Are you any good at that sort of thing?"

"It should not be a problem, we have fiscal liaison officers in most locations of interest. They team up with customs who do the drugs and their financial stuff. Between them they seem to able to get most of what is required. Do you have the details of what you want?"

"It's very sensitive. If it is what I think it is, there might be a few sweaty bum pieces in high places. I think it is better if we meet rather than talk over the airwaves. After all, you might be thought of as being on my side and somebody just might be earwigging."

Within the hour, Sewell stood to greet Frank Withy as he approached the bench in Victoria Embankment Gardens, a few minutes walk away from his office. "So, Tony, why have you dragged me out here?"

"We can talk and nobody can listen. They might be able to see us, but they can't hear us."

"God, it is years and years since I did any of this covert meeting stuff. I used to enjoy it, real police work. Right, what is this all about?"
Sewell handed over a small file of papers. "They are copies of accounts. I've got the originals somewhere safe."

"I see you are still reluctant to part with the real stuff."

"Oh, that? Well, you were the enemy then, maybe you still are, who knows. Are you on my side, Frank, or are you just shooting the breeze? I don't really know. Are you working for the other side, your bosses, the politicians?"

"Tony, time will tell, only time, my friend."
Withy flicked through the papers. "Go on then, what's this all about. What have you got?"

"I'm not a hundred per cent sure, say ninety five per cent. I know for certain, courtesy of Atwood's assistant, into which Middle Eastern bank Atwood's cash finally ends up, or used to end up, now a former account. From there I have traced two accounts where the assets have been moved into. The amounts involved match, almost to the penny, the total of his account. One is in British Virgin Islands, the other in Bahamas. Like I said, I've got these from Atwood's account, which shows it being emptied then closed, then it never has existed. Within hours of Atwood's being closed, all of this happens. The funds are then transferred into these overseas, non-official accounts. They are shown as being companies, but, in reality, they don't exist, maybe nameplates on a door somewhere. I cannot find any trace of them, which is normal when you are on the fiddle. Can I ask you to get behind these companies and find out who the principals are? They may have used other accounts to hide their identities. I won't tell you what I suspect right now."

"The home secretary told me this money had been returned to the government, let's hope it has."

"Look Frank, if I am right and something really bent is going on, this might blow up in your face, or it might give you the upper hand. Are you still facing being pensioned off?"

"I don't really know, the powers that be, whose laps this is all in, are worried that any move might rebound on them. Getting rid of me might be considered losing control of you. As it is, it leaves me with a certain amount of freedom. I'm not all that worried, I will keep my pension and, with your help, I have got a few aces up my sleeve. I'm pretty sure I will get an honourable discharge. I'm looking forward to my roses and sailing. Leave it with me and I'll get back to you as soon as I hear anything."

When Sewell heard from the commissioner, it was suggested that they occupy the same seat in the same gardens as they had done previously. As before, Withy had covered up his uniform with a coat. Without speaking he took his seat. "You know, Sewell, as we sit here, they are probably watching us from my office."

"Does that bother you?"

"No, I suppose not. Probably scares the shit out of them."

"Tell me, Frank, do you ever think about having a go, I mean really blowing the wax out of their ears or are you just going to let it all drift?"

"I don't know, I haven't got your balls, or your anger I suppose. I am not looking for revenge, I just want to survive. If I can walk away from this with my pension intact, that would do for me. I have worked bloody years for it, I deserve it. But I hate it when they try to make me look like a total prat."

Sewell leaned forward resting his arms on his thighs. "I see. So what have you got for me?"

"It is interesting, very interesting, but I guess you were expecting that."

Sewell did not respond. "Tony, this is explosive stuff. I had it done on the QT, old friends, a few favours owed to me. Can I ask you to try to keep it under wraps?"

"If you want, I'll try, no promises, it will probably come out some time. So what do we have?"

"As you already know, the account details you gave me is, or was, Atwood's, the one he was using to stuff all his bent loot into; it was close to ten million. About a ten days ago, it was emptied and then closed, but I was told that. However, it wasn't just closed, now on paper it never even existed. Now why is that? Was there something that made you suspicious?"

Sewell sat upright and leaned into the back of the bench. He gave a nod of confirmation. "Sort of. Did it all transfer into these two accounts?"

"That's right, then the money was moved through a series of accounts and funds. The usual when somebody wants to cover their tracks. But, it's what our officers do, and they have done a cracking job."

"Frank, can we skip the plaudits and get on with it?"

"OK, apparently it was all well-hidden, but then both holders bought large amounts of shares to be placed into trusts. We traced the individuals through share registers."

"Frank, for Christ's sake get on with it, I take it one beneficiary was our home secretary, Higgins."

"Yes, that's right. How did you know that?"

"Never mind, I'll tell you in a minute. Who was the other one?"

"It is Lambie, Spencer Lambie."

"What, the former prime minister? Must be about twenty years ago now. But he was on the other side to Higgins. So he was at it as well. I wouldn't have put them down as soul mates."

"When my officers looked through the records, Lord Lambie, as he is now, was a senior minister involved with the overseas aid committee. There is no suggestion that Higgins was. We assume he had some sort of influence and was suitably rewarded. Higgins and Lambie have been seen socialising recently, so they know each other."

"So, Atwood's ill-gotten gains are now the ill-gotten gains of our lords and masters. Do you know what, when I was a copper on the beat, round these parts years ago, I used to worry if I took a bottle of whisky from a landlord as a Christmas bung. My god, these guys make me look like a Sunday school teacher. So, Frank, what do you think we should do with all this? Any ideas?"

"You are the ideas man. But listen, I haven't finished yet. All the money that went into the two accounts, and then funded the value of the shares, very suddenly, like as of yesterday, both funds were transferred into some obscure government coffer. As was to be expected, they got wind of our enquiries and went for damage limitation. Our two politicians, if pushed, will come up with some story of confusion or a plot against them. Some old horsefeathers like that. I'm not surprised that word got to them that their nest of worms was being prised open."

"And?"

"We have the records of the share purchases? How can they explain that? " Withy pulled his coat tighter around his frame against a stiff breeze. "So, Tony, what made you think to kick open this particular parcel?"

"It was when you told me Higgins had said that all the money had been repaid into official funds. I mean, how could he have done that so quickly? Why would Atwood release the information that would give access to his loot and allow all it to be ripped off? Why would he disclose what bank he was using? I mean, he wasn't that worried about Higgins knowing about the scam, but Higgins didn't have any of the details of where the cash finally ended up. We got all that from Atwood's assistant, Karvonen. Apparently Atwood stuck two fingers up to Higgins and dared him to go public. He knew Higgins couldn't do it as it would wreck the party and his own chances of staying in a job. Now we know that Higgins had a greater interest in keeping a lid on it." Sewell paused and gathered his thoughts . "As we now know Atwood was publicly humiliated, which in itself was obviously a government stitch up. I thought that was the deal. But there is no way Atwood would part with his money, or would even have to part with it. It all happened too quickly. One minute Atwood has his trousers round his ankles getting a spanking for pervy shoplifting, the next Higgins is saying the money is actually back here. In the first place, Higgins would have to know where Atwood had his ultimate account. He had no idea where it was held, apart from somewhere in the Middle east. Then he makes all the arrangements for its return to the UK. There is no way Atwood had to, or would, tell anybody about the details of his account. He's already been got rid of, he's had his punishment, so why not hold onto the assets. I know the details of where and when and nobody else does apart from his former assistant who has now done a bunk, and as far as I know, doesn't want anything more to do with it."

"Inspector, I have to say that was a very clever piece of deduction."

"Quite, thanks for the compliment. Anyway, Higgins would have to have all that information, then liaise with the bank and the officialdom. He would have had to go through diplomatic channels and all that guff, that doesn't happen in a couple of days, it takes weeks. So when Higgins said that within a day or two, it was actually back in the UK, my copper's nose started twitching. No, something was done to Atwood to make him let go, some sort of blackmail, but how? Obviously the shoplifting charge was done to shove him out of his political circles. They must have had his arm up his back about something, but not the money. OK, he is officially a member of the flashing mac club, but why part with the money when there was no need? If you think about it, Higgins didn't want Atwood to disclose the banking details, because if he did and it became public knowledge, he wouldn't be able to get his hands on it once they had dispatched Atwood. Higgins knew all along where the funds ended up. He's been working with this embassy chief."

"Do you need to know all this, Tony? Haven't you done enough?"

"I want the whole story, you never know what else may fall out if you shake the tree hard enough. I would have thought that you, as commissioner, would have chased this to get all the details."

Withy shrugged and pulled his coat tighter. "It's because you don't want to piss off your bosses, isn't it?"

"Maybe."

"I will tell you, Frank, what I am pretty sure of is that the Middle East embassy chief here in London, has to know all that is happening in his country's banks. He is a very big hitter. According to Atwood's assistant, it was the embassy chief that originally made the arrangements, he has his cut as well. He is the one who could pull all the strings and set things up. Atwood's assistant more or less pointed us in that direction. I think it is time I had a look at this bloke."

"Be very careful. Diplomatic immunity and all that, these Arab states can be very, very sensitive. We do massive arms deals with them, worth billions. If you start trampling over their vegetable patch, your feet won't touch, you will be a properly dead man."

"I see, make it official."

"Tony, I have taken your side on the matter of your brother and Atwood's fiddle. I cannot, and will not, become involved with anything to do with the embassy, absolutely not."

"Fair enough, Frank, I don't blame you. Actually, I think I might leave this one well alone. So, what do we do with the home secretary and our former prime minister? Do we blow their schemes to the press?"

"If you think about it, you would be doing the same as exposing Atwood's entrepreneurial activities. Higgins could, in all probability, cover it up, though his credibility is wearing a bit thin. As much as I hold these people in utter contempt, I personally do not wish to harm the place where I live. I do not want to go down that line."

"I hear what you are saying, but they still murdered my brother. Can I let that go?"

A couple, arm in arm, approached the two men. They both sat upright until the young man and woman had passed and were a distance away.

"From what I hear you and your brother were not very close; far from it, different characters altogether. You, a senior police officer, he a career criminal. He hasn't done you many favours. You were, in your day, a much respected officer. You should have been promoted but..."

"But, my brother was bent, so maybe I was. I take it that was the thinking."

Withy nodded his head slightly. "Something like that. I've had a look at your records and it seems that Eric Upton, now to be former, chief superintendent, always held you back, damned by faint praise."

"There's a surprise. Can't you promote me now, you being the top man? Can't you dub me with your sword or something and say, 'Arise, Chief Inspector' and go and sort those toe rag villains out?' Won't you do that for me, Frank?"

"I'll put it in my diary and let you know." Withy leaned back and scanned the surrounding area, then he directed his gaze back to Sewell. "All this stuff that you are chasing, it's not for justice or anything like that, what you are talking about, really talking about, is not your brother. You are not looking for justice, you don't give a toss about that if you are being honest. It is revenge isn't it? Revenge for what the system has done to you. You are a little man who always wanted to be much further up the tree. You know that revenge for his killing is not really worth screwing this country. Be under no illusion, if you do blow this wide open, I wouldn't like to think about your future, that's if you have a future. One way or another you will be destroyed."

"Oh, I know that, I have no doubt about it."

"So what will you get out of it, even if you shaft some politicians. Your options, as I see it, is go public blow the government to buggery and then yourself. Of course you will receive platitudes and bunches of flowers, probably at your funeral. Or, get them to pay for your silence. As I told you, you could get millions. Think about it, go and live wherever you want; luxurious life style. What difference does it make to your brother?"

"You know something, Commissioner, it sounds like you are selling me the government's line. Why should I worry if all the politicians of this country all get caught flogging the family silver? Maybe it will change things for the better, maybe that's what is needed. If I take this bung that you are dangling in front of me, won't I be part of the whole squalid system? Whose side are you on anyway?"

"I'm not on anybody's side, I'm looking after me. If you don't trust me, that's up to you. So far, I think it is fair to say I have played it straight."

"Well, maybe you have. But, if I followed your orders then, we wouldn't be sitting here now. I would be in some dole queue looking for a job as a night watchman. Do you think that's a fair summary, do you, Frank?"

"Yes, fair enough, I did do those things to you. But I was being shafted as well. Go on then, tell me what you would have done if you were told you were going to be fitted up for some sordid crime? Come on, Inspector, state your action."

The two men let their respective angers boil then simmer, but not completely cool.

"Tell you what, Tony, if you don't like it, I will keep out of your way. You do your own thing. All I am doing is acting as a go between. Suit yourself, I thought that the two of us together carry more weight than being two individuals. Look, I'm off back to the office, you know where you can find me."

Withy rose and straightened his coat. As he was about to move off, Sewell spoke. "I'm sorry, Tony, I didn't catch that."

"Tell them, tell Higgins and Lord bloody Lambie, that we have the evidence of them emptying Atwood's pockets, make sure they know. Tell them, if they want to sort it, that I want one of them to speak to me directly and admit it."

"Tony, can I say this, not necessarily as a friend. You need to sit down and think things out. You are all over the place. You don't know what you want. Anger is the poison of reason."

"Very poetic, Now I have thought about it, I am going to get to the bottom of this. I will find out where this money came from and where it went to. See, I'm still a copper,"

Both men strode off in opposite directions. As he walked away, Withy could not resist patting his coat pocket.

Chapter 33

It was one in the morning, the latest music of the day was pumping out at a violent volume, reducing conversation to having to shout directly into your audience's ear. The strobe lighting that defined the area reserved for dancing flickered hypnotically but did not reach into the further recess of the night club. In the private rooms, the noise was muted. Sewell, accompanied by Mark Stephens and Raj Patel caused a minor flurry when they gained entry to the premises by flashing their warrant cards. The indifferent and quietly groaning mountain of meat who acted as doorman, when pressed by Sewell, thought it better to let some off duty coppers in rather that have the usual commotion about being arrested. Also, there was always the possibility that if these officers of the law overindulged and demonstrated the art of indiscretion, they could well be turned into valuable and useful assets. Once inside the officer's chain store attire marked them out from the rest of the clientele in that their dowdy outfits fell far short of that of the strutting peacocks, who with fixed knowing smiles, prowled the area showing off their attributes and demonstrating what was on offer.

As they crossed the bar area, pushing past dancing gowns and suits, Sewell bumped into an immaculately attired man who was groomed to perfection. The dancer's insouciance slipped as he snapped, "Oi, watch it." The mannequin surveyed Sewell with growing contempt. Sewell stood back, hands raised as a silent apology. This act of contrition did not appear to placate the dancer's ego.

"Are they letting any old tat in here these days? Have you come to do the washing up?"

The man's words were swallowed by the all around noise, but his fellow good time folk understood the gist of it and allowed themselves supercilious, sniggering grins. Angrily Sewell grabbed the lapels and addressed the tailor's dummy. The man responded in like manner taking control of Sewell's ear. "He's in the room marked 'Rose Petal' up the stairs. His muscle on the outside is carrying." Sewell, in perpetuating the pretence, pushed the man away and made for the stairs with his two comrades in his wake. On the lower steps a bored looking minder who was leaning on the bannister and guarding the rope that acted as a boundary to restrict entry to the chosen few. He shook his head and languidly put his arm out so as to impede progress. Raj, accepting the proffered limb, flicked one end of a set of handcuffs around the wrist and the other onto the bannister. The man's shock was quickly overtaken by embarrassment. The few revellers who noticed his predicament were mildly amused, some wondering if this was yet another service being offered. At the top of the stairs Sewell found the door marked 'Rose Petal' where, on the outside stood a large, very heavily built minder. As he, together with Mark, approached the door, the minder pushed out an open hand with a view to deterring visitors. This did not slow the approach. In an act of almost nonchalance, the man took hold of the officer's jacket and drew him in. Mark accepting this gift, grabbed the man's little finger then, quickly and forcibly, snapped it upwards and back. As he did so he heard the faint crack as the digit broke. Suddenly the minder thought that standing en pointe would ease his excruciating pain, it didn't. Maintaining his grip on the damaged extremity, Mark twisted the arm behind the suddenly inconvenienced door attendant and with his free hand, patted the man's jacket and soon found the object of his search, "Very nice." He put the pistol into his own pocket. "Well, my friend, you are carrying a firearm in public. Got a licence?"

The man, between winces gasped, "Embassy, diplomat, diplomatic immunity."

Sewell nodded to Mark to handcuff his victim. "Listen, mate, you are not a diplomat, you are a lackey, no immunity, nothing. This door, is it locked?"

The driver's attempt to refuse to answer was defeated when Mark applied further pressure to his little finger. Now still standing on his toes he hissed out, "Yes, yes, here in my pocket."

Sewell threw the door open and strode in. The smell of cannabis filled the air. A befuddled sheikh was recumbent on a bed and showing a fetching line in socks and boxer shorts and nothing else. Lying beside him, looking diminutive in contrast to his considerable bulk, was a young girl attired in fewer garments that her male companion. Their bewilderment, Sewell guessed, caused by the ingestion of various substances, showed no sign of diminishing. Raj, whose latest introduction was still attached to the woodwork, joined Sewell and, with his mobile, started to record the scene. Sewell addressed the girl. "Hello, love, what you doing here? Is he helping you with your homework?"

An immaculately suited and evenly tanned male, barged into the room, "What the hell is going on here. What do you think you are doing?" He turned to an assistant who had just caught up. "Julian, call the police, call superintendent Matthews, tell him it's urgent. We have thugs on the premise."

Sewell decided to assist. "Look, Julian mate, that will be Sandy Matthews, he's about as much use as a concrete parachute, I always reckoned he was on the take. Go ahead, Julian, you can tell him that the police are already here, tell him I am Tony Sewell. I tell you what, when he hears that, there is no way he will get off his backside and put in an appearance. Look, while you are talking to him, tell him so far the count is an assault on a police officer, a bloke carrying an unlicensed and loaded firearm, the supply of class A and B drugs, Oh yeah, and trafficking of under-aged children for the purposes of prostitution. Go on, don't just stand there, call him."

Julian wavered, looking to his boss for a lead. None was forthcoming.

With the two managers seemingly unable to counter Sewell's assertiveness, he was now exerting his authority. "And you are?"

"I am Giles Fraser, I am the manager here."

The diplomat, in a haze, who could do no more than mindlessly rumple the duvet on the bed, knew that something was happening, but was unable to sufficiently declutter his mind enough to comprehend what it was. He blinked at the flashes from Raj's phone as it recorded the scene. "Is it a problem? Do you want me to pay? Where is my driver? Shall I pay now?"

Julian was now demonstrating the finer points of hand wringing. Giles Fraser attempted to rescue the situation by attempting to shore up his managerial status. "Tell me again, who exactly are you?"

Sewell assisted. "The old bill, the filth, the police. I am Inspector Sewell. I am not on your payroll or anybody's payroll. I wouldn't even think about bringing in your protection racket boys, you will both lose badly. So what have you got to say about this little lot? He has paid you for these 'facilities' hasn't he? Like I say we've got assault, guns, class A and B drugs trafficking of minors; nice place you run here. Giles, mate, haven't you called Sandy Matthews yet. Come on, get your finger out. That goes for you as well, Sheikh."

Fraser surveyed the area again. "Inspector, what do you want? You haven't just turned up here to catch a fat, coked up Arab who has a predilection for, what some might call, innocent fun. What is it really all about? Whatever it is, I am sure we can facilitate you. And that is not a bribe of any sort."

"What I want, Giles, is a word with our fat friend here, that is when he rejoins our planet, a word on our own."

"What's the deal? If I arrange it for you, what happens to me, the club?"

"Giles, I don't give a toss about your club or the chinless wonders downstairs who think they are the beautiful people. I need this room until the Lord of the Tents here is able to bite his fingers again."

"You've got it. I will have my staff bring sandwiches and drinks."

Sewell threw the young girl's scattered garments towards her. "Get dressed, love. Get her to Social Services."

Dawn had filtered its light through the trees and buildings by the time the sheikh was resurfacing and collecting his scattered wits. In the corner he saw his distressed driver handcuffed to a large chair and three men eating sandwiches. He propped himself up and, in the most casual of tones spoke. "Hello, gentlemen, and how are you today? I take all that food is on my bill? May I ask who you are and why my driver, miserable wretch that he is, is handcuffed? Was that part of the night's entertainment?"

Sewell took his time in finishing a smoked salmon offering. "We are police officers, your man, in the corner has been arrested for carrying a loaded gun. Before you say anything, he does not have diplomatic immunity."

The sheikh made an apologetic shrug in the direction of the miscreant who, in turn, could do no more than make a mournful gesture and display his newly acquired bracelets. Sewell continued through a mouthful. "And you, you were found to be under the influence of prohibited drugs and in bed with a minor, very naughty."

"Yes, I may have been very naughty as you put it, but I, unlike him over there, do have diplomatic immunity, so, gentlemen, I think I will get dressed and leave now."

Now partaking of coffee, Sewell addressed his two constables. "He says he's got diplomatic immunity. What do you reckon, Raj? Do you think he has?"

"Probably has, boss. I wouldn't be surprised if he has. Looks the type."

"Alright, you have got immunity, we can't arrest you. You are free to leave."

"Thank you. What about my man? I cannot see that it is going to benefit anybody by pursuing this business about a gun. We do not want bad feelings between our countries, do we?"

"Do you know what, I guess you are right, so, no action about the gun. He can go as well."

"Thank you officer, I do not see what you hoped to gain with all this fuss. I do know some of your senior people rather well you know."

"Yes, I do know. You are friendly with our home secretary, Norman Higgins. And you know, or at least used to know, Terry Atwood a member of the cabinet."

"Yes." The word was stretched out. "Officer, may I ask your name?"

"My name? You have probably heard of me. I am the one who is supposed to be dead. I am the one who can prove that Atwood had his fingers in the cookie jar. I am the one who can prove that he used one of your country's banks to launder the money he stole. I can prove all that. My name? I am Inspector Sewell. But you can call me Tony." The sheikh was climbing unsteadily into his clothes. The name made him stumble slightly.

"You are quite correct, we cannot arrest you, you have that spot on. What we can do is to place on public media, all the photos and film we took of you last night. Clearly out of your head on a variety of substances with all the paraphernalia lying around and, evidently enjoying a good old romp with some kid. She must have been all of fourteen. There is also the matter of your armed stooge, he's not very photogenic but it's a nice gun, people will like that, it's interesting."

Raj, taking his cue, panned round to the minder and to Stephens who held the firearm in a helpful display. "There you go, nice bit of footage, that will attract some attention. Do you think you can stop it, Sheikh? You can try, but before you do, I imagine it will cause a lot of interest back in your own country."

The sheikh stopped wrestling with his trousers and sat on the edge of the bed. "Inspector Sewell, what did you have in mind?"

"I propose a deal. You give me the information I want, and I will not publish the film or the photos. But hear me, if I think, for one minute, you are holding back on the truth, or try to mess me about, you will suddenly become very famous. Right, what happened to Atwood?"

"Inspector, do I have your word that none of this...this information about me will be made public? Your word as an officer and a gentleman."

"I give you my word. What's in it for me to splash your life around? I want to know about Atwood."

"You know, Inspector, that my country does billions of pounds of business with yours, billions, Inspector. If we encounter any, what may be regarded as problems, your country would lose all that trade, major ramifications between our governments could follow"

"Look, I am not the least bit interested in any of that, I really, really do not give a stuff. I want to know what happened; it's make your mind up time. Either you start talking now, or I am out of here and you get a new fan club; it's your call."

"Very colourful, Inspector, I have your word?"

"We have been through all that. Am I leaving now or do you start talking?"

"What do you want to know? Get rid of my driver."

The door slammed behind the driver with Stephens guiding him.

"Right, what happened to Atwood? How come one minute he was up to his armpits in twenty pound notes, the next he is going guilty on some ridiculous charge. Then all his money is withdrawn, but not by him. Somebody had something on him, something big enough for him to get a criminal record and then very suddenly become a lot poorer. So let's have it."

The sheikh studied the floor for some time before an intake of breath. "Alright, first no telephones, nothing is to be recorded." The officers placed their devices on a coffee table. The sheikh, once he had satisfied himself his words would not reach posterity, spoke.

"Mr Atwood became embroiled in supplying, or attempting to supply, a foreign power, I believe it was meant to be China, with top secret details of some missile, a drone I think they call it. Very top secret as I understand. This drone is still being developed, apparently it is very sophisticated. Mr Atwood was caught in the act. I understand, from certain sources, that a full blown trial would have seen him being handed a very, very long sentence, but such a trial would incur considerable risks. It wouldn't do for any details, or even the existence, of this thing, to become known. I am informed he was offered the option of admitting to a crime that would effectively remove him from public office for good. Or he could face, a problematic and uncertain future." The sheikh smiled at Sewell, who did not return the gesture.

"How did you know about this top secret gizmo if it was so highly restricted. What is the project?"

" Zeus, it is known was Zeus. I have certain interests with the company, I know people."

"What you are saying is, you pulled the strings and then shafted Atwood."

The sheikh splayed his hands, "Perhaps."

"Obviously you were working with our home secretary in all this."

"Inspector, I would not like to answer that."

"You just did. So you stitched up Atwood and emptied his account, he had no place to go. He is forced to admit to this ridiculous frilly

underwear theft, then all his illegal loot is sent to accounts held by Higgins and Spencer Lambie, the former prime minister."
The sheikh had now succeeded with his sartorial struggles. "Really?" I had no idea who the other one was."

"I see, they had Atwood by the dangly bits and he chose the soft option. So you can confirm it was Higgins who organised, through your good offices, to sort the money that left your country in one hell of a hurry?"

"We like to be efficient. I was asked if I could use my influence to repatriate it to where it belonged. I saw it as part of engendering good relations."

"You sent it to two bent politicians, a current home secretary and a former prime minister. You did it by way of offshore accounts."

"My dear Inspector, I, or rather my people were, facilitating a request from a very senior and highly regarded politician. I did not see it as my position to ask the reasons. Now, I think that is all I have to say, I really do not know anything more."

The police officers reached the street and savoured the fresh air. Raj raised the obvious question.

"Tony, what, I mean how? How did you know that bloke would be in that club tonight? And how did you know where he would be?"

"Raj, I've still got some mates in Vice, we look after each other. You do realise that a large amount of bent cash comes from places like this. It is kept quiet because some big names are involved. Can't say any more than that."

"Oh, right, I see. So, Tony, so what do we do now?"

"What we do, or rather what I do, is to load up all that footage and send it worldwide."

"But you gave him your word."

"Raj, do you think a scumbag like that deserves any consideration? If he could have been arrested, he would have got years for using that young girl as a piece of trash then throwing her away. So he's going to be famous."

"Tony, remind me never to play poker with you."

Chapter 34

"Withy, get your arse over here now, don't bother with any of that crap about being sacked and spending the rest of your life in tatters. My office, now." Higgins slammed his phone down before Withy was able to formulate a reply.

On this occasion, Withy approached the home secretary and seated himself whilst displaying a look of utter contempt. Higgins was beyond expecting, or caring about the niceties he would usually consider proper.

"Your bloody copper has got to be stopped. He's on the verge of wrecking this country. He's a madman, a bloody madman. Do you know what his latest little venture was? Only trying to blackmail the head of the one of most important embassies in the country, he could cost this country billions in lost sales. I tell you the man is out of control, he thinks he is untouchable."

"Home Secretary, if he thinks that, who do you consider is to be blamed?"

"Don't get all smart arsey with me."

Withy did not demonstrate any undue interest. "And what exactly did this 'blackmail' consist of?"

"Haven't you heard? Have you not seen it? Good God, man, what do you do all day in that bloody ivory tower? Which I may add costs millions to run."

"Sticking to the point would be useful, if unusual."

Higgins spun his computer round to face Withy. "Have a look at this. This is your copper trying to destroy every last one of us."

The commissioner took in the contents of Sewell's handy work without showing any reaction.

"Norman," for a split second the use, by the commissioner, of his first name jarred with Higgins, but matters of a much greater note had to be addressed. "What I see and hear is that Atwood has been framed for some secret arms production racket, something he was pushed into doing. I realise the man is a crook, but it still is an injustice. Then he was made to confess to stealing ladies underwear, most ingenious. Is that the type of thing you had planned for me? That is what you promised me not so very long ago."

"For God's sake, man, let it go, nothing is going to happen to you. That is if you play your cards right."

"Norman, I feel that if there is a stick to grasp you will, without hesitation, grab the wrong end. You are not in a position to dictate to me, it is rather the other way round. I notice in the clip you have shown me, there is nothing to suggest that you were involved with sharing Atwood's booty. I watched the recording this morning. Why did you not show me the part where the sheikh says he transferred the money to you and to Lambert?"

Higgins threw his pen across his desk. "Look, that can be easily explained. It was for accounting purposes. It is not what it looks like."

"So the Accounts Committee have nothing to worry about?"

"We will talk about that later. At the moment we have a country to save."

"Not a reputation or two then, Norman?"

"Frank, we have to get this sorted. If you help, you will see a benefit."

"And if I don't, it's off to the Tower?"

"Look, let's cut the crap, yes, you have me over a barrel. At the moment that is. Get this sorted, we will all be back to square one."

"What do you want, Norman? Push Sewell under another train? You are right, he is dangerous, very dangerous and very, very pissed off. Can you blame him? It was you that started all this, blaming a police officer for doing his job and letting one of your mates, who has stolen millions, off the hook. It's your nest and, at the moment, you are up to your armpits in shit, and it's getting deeper. Why should I help you?"

"Frank, the other side are having problems, major problems. This election is getting closer and there is a better than even chance we will get back in. Think about it, Frank."

"I am thinking about it. I am wondering what it will be like to be governed by a bunch of ruthless crooks."

"We are no worse than the other lot. You saw that their former prime minister got, well almost got, his bung, that's the way it works. Frank, work your magic, go and be a copper and sort something. There must be an angle somewhere, I'm sure you are the one who could flush it out." Higgins paused and lowered his voice. "You will be rewarded, Frank, very generously, I promise you that."

Chapter 35

After the shooting of Big Nobby Hayes, a routine search of his premises was conducted by local uniformed police officers and a couple of CID men from the same station. Some of whom were personally acquainted with Big Nobby and had enjoyed being very generously entertained in his seedy premises. Until it was found, from an evidential point of view, that he was an innocent victim, an assumption had to be made, not without good reason, that he may have been involved in some untoward activities at the time of his shooting. In one secure lock up, a considerable quantity of spirits and tobacco products were found. When questioned at his hospital bed, he assured the investigating officers that the booze and baccy where legitimate and were for his club.

"Yes, there are a lot of them, but I buy in bulk then sell to other outlets at a small profit. Officer, on my life, they are dead straight, when I get out of here I will show you the invoices, it's all legit. Look, to show my appreciation of the way you boys got this all sorted, if you want a bottle or two or a carton of smokes, help yourself. It's a little thank you. Please, guys, help yourselves."

As was expected, drinks and cigarettes were accepted as a gift from a thankful citizen. Now the issue of the law sticking their noses into his affairs was less of a problem. Having accepted Nobby's generous and understandable offer, and having lightened his load somewhat, an officer of the law was not likely to point the finger if he himself had benefitted from the crime. It was not much more than a week after the shooting of Big Nobby, when, during an office celebration in an East End London police station to mark the end of a successful investigation, that a bottle of whisky was pulled from a desk drawer. "Come on, who's for a top up?" Cheers and laughter greeted this most generous offer. An inspector from the Crime Squad, gratefully accepted. As his glass was being replenished, he grabbed the bottle and examined the label. A cross check against his notes confirmed his suspicions. "Rob, where did you get this from? It's from that warehouse job, you know the one where we reckoned it was Tony Sewell's brother."

Big Nobby was visited again. This time he remembers buying them from Harry Sewell, "The one who got done in by some bunch of villains." Big Nobby assured those present that everything he bought from Harry, was genuine. "It's a shame you can't have a word with Harry, not with him being dead." Not wishing to doubt Nobby's word, but staying on the safe side, further and more extensive searches were conducted. These uncovered greater quantities of alcohol and cigarettes which were then detained and secured in police premises.

The buzz went around the office. The sergeant who had investigated the warehouse theft and who had tried to doorstep Harry, was spoken to. He explained there was no chance of getting past one who knew so much about the law, albeit, learned from the wrong type of experience. In passing, he recalled threatening to make a visit to Harry's mother, but the warnings were sufficient to deter him. "Well, he's not around anymore, let's give that miserable old cow Mary Sewell a tug. Nothing to lose. She's got previous, and knowing Mary, she will have a bit of a stash somewhere. We did get some whispers that she had some of the stuff. Don't know how much though."

"What about Tony Sewell, what's he going to think? He won't be happy at us turning his mother over."

"If he's an honest copper, he's got nothing to worry him. Anyway, I hear he has a lot on his plate, with him meaning to be dead and all that."

Mary Sewell's top lip, in a snarl, creased upwards until it almost made contact with her nose. "What do you bastards want? My son, my lovely Harry, is not long in his grave, murdered by you lot. Now you're round here giving me grief."

"Yes, we saw how very distressed you were when you sold your story to the press. Wasn't that two days after Harry snuffed it?"

"Bastards."

"Yes, I can see your point, but these bastards have got a search warrant."

"Nothing here for the filth, I don't know what you want."

"The warrant was granted on the basis we have reasonable grounds to suspect that stolen property is on the premises. That will not be a first, will it, Mary?"

"You watch your mouth. You are wasting your time so you all might as well be off. Go and annoy another old pensioner."

After thirty minutes, the team of four police officers formed a huddle in the lounge. "So what have we got."

"Two unopened bottles and one about half full in the lounge, an empty one in the bin along with some of the fag packets. They all match the stuff from the warehouse."

"Dave, you've got something."

"Yeah, upstairs in a bedside drawer, three packets of smokes, all from the warehouse."

"It's not a lot. Let's have a word with her, she won't cough to anything, she never does."

Mary, hovering by the door, listening, took this remark to be her cue for an entrance.

"You cheeky buggers, them fags and that booze, I got off a man in the pub. Before you ask, I have never seen him before. Don't think he is from round these parts."

Outside, the team of officers gathered in the street. "What do you think?"

"Sarge, it's sod all. It's not worth wasting our time. She's going to stick with 'the man in the pub' excuse."

"OK, Dave, I will call it in. Who is running this now?"

"Funnily enough, it seems to have gone right up the ladder. It's Chief Superintendent Walker. I think it's because of her son."

The sergeant was about to dial a number when, a beckoning arm from a premises across the street caught his eye. He looked over and mouthed the words, "What me?"

The arm movements became more demanding and were now accompanied by a rapid nodding of the head. "Hang on lads." On reaching the house, the front door was opened, but nobody could be seen. He peered into the dark hallway and saw the owner of the inviting arm. "Come in, son. Come on quick, I don't want her to see me. Vicious old cow, nasty piece of work."

"Look, Mr....?"

"Roberts, Ted Roberts, don't think I know you. I have met your lot in the old days. All that's gone now that I behave myself."

"Right, Mr Roberts, I am Sergeant Deacon. Something I can do for you?"

"You've been turning her place over haven't you? I know what it's all about. It's them fags and booze, isn't it?"

"Might be."

"Harry done that job, I am positive. See, after he turned the place over, they had to stash all the gear somewhere. I mean, they couldn't go selling it straight off."

"Mr Roberts, this is very interesting, but is there a point to it?"

"In a minute, son, see, she put the arm on Mickey Benson, little toe rag, she made him bring a load of the fags and booze round here, to her place, tons of it. Mary was flogging it off, selling it to anybody in the street, not me though. I wouldn't go near the old witch. See, Harry was a good bloke, I liked Harry, liked him a lot. He looked after me. I would never grass Harry up, or anybody else, But her, nasty old cow."

"Are you saying that Mary sold a load of this stuff around here?"

"Yes, loads of it."

"I see, Mr Roberts, and when did all this stop, there doesn't seem to be anything for her to sell now."

"The old bitch was doing it up to about five days ago, I could see the punters going into her house."

The sergeant was quiet, deep in thought. "Mr Roberts, when is the next rubbish bin collection?"

"I can guess what you are doing, it's tomorrow morning. All the bins are put out tonight."

"Mr Roberts, that has been most helpful, thanks a lot."

"Hello, Commissioner, how are you?"

"Fine, Chief Superintendent. And what can I do for you today."

"It is about Sewell, that is Harry Sewell, the chap who was killed, brother of Tony Sewell."

"Ah, yes, I have recently become acquainted with Tony. Is there a problem?"

"I've got a team looking into the warehouse job that everybody assumes, quite correctly in my book, that Harry pulled. Some of the team fell over some of the stuff that was stolen. I don't think you will want to be appraised of the details as to how they got hold of it."

"Right, OK."

"Because of the circumstances a search warrant was obtained for Harry Sewell's mother's house."

"That was brave. Go on."

"A small amount of the stolen stuff was found in her house, but not enough to get excited about. But a local volunteered some information, apparently he has an intense dislike of the woman. He claimed that Mary got hold of a load of the booze and fags and was flogging them to the neighbours. As a result of that, our boys did a bin run late last night in her street and in the surrounding area. Some of the bins had either empty bottles or cigarette packets. All of them had Mary's finger prints on them."

"Interesting, I know what you are going to say next."

"Yes, Sir, do we take it any further? With Harry now having left us and all the racket with Tony, I was wondering if it would be prudent to leave it?"

"Good point."

"Sir, there is also the business of Harry's sidekick topping himself and the other one seemingly doing a runner."

"What happened?"

"It seems like Harry's two mates, a Jack Hamilton and Mickey Benson, small time crooks, went to have it out with a Robert Hayes, Big Nobby to his friends. From what we can find out they went to see Hayes, who was supposed to have bought a large amount of the stock but had not coughed up for it, with a view to getting some of the proceeds. By this time Harry was dead and his two boys wanted his share. It all kicked off, Hayes got shot but was only wounded. Hamilton and Benson did a runner. But when Hamilton got home, he shot his wife then himself."

"Why was that?"

"We are not sure, but the wife was seriously ill. Maybe that had something to do with it."

"Did this Hayes actually have this alcohol and tobacco."

"Yes, our local uniform went over to see Hayes; he's still in hospital. He claims it is all legit. I've got to say that I don't think our boys asked too many questions about what they found. But they had the foresight to take some samples and when these were checked they were confirmed to have come from the warehouse."

"Took samples, Chief Superintendent? Is that what they call it these days?"

"Yes, Sir, like I say, it's probably better that we don't delve too deeply into that. The thing is, Sir, with all that has been going on, I don't know if this should be progressed. I mean, if it is likely to be political, we could leave it alone."

Withy rose from his desk. "Chief Superintendent, you are correct, this is political and very sensitive. I cannot stress that enough. For reasons that I will not go into, it is important that we find out as much as we can about this case. Can I ask you to do something for me? Whatever your methods, no questions will be asked."

Twenty four hours later, Chief Superintendent Nick Walker was in the commissioner's office.

"How did it go, Nick? Any problems?"

"No, Sir. I put the arm on Hayes, told him that we have sufficient evidence to send him down. With his previous, that could be for a long time. I told him that if he cooperated, there would be no charges, no further investigation and that he would walk away. He saw sense. In all we recovered quite a haul. It's all in a lock up now."

"Well done."

Chapter 36

Two days later, Tony Sewell entered the commissioner's office without formality. "Hi Frank, how's it going?"

"Inspector Sewell, I am the commissioner, you will address me accordingly."

"Piss off."

"No, Inspector I will not 'piss off' you will listen. We have recovered a substantial amount of the product stolen from the warehouse theft carried out by your brother."

"Your point is? And piss off."

Sewell, somewhat taken aback, did not notice Withy's demeanour. His delivery was robotic, his face a blank mask. Rather than address Sewell directly, he gave the impression of talking to somebody behind and to the right of the inspector.

"An examination has shown that several of the bottles have finger prints on them. Your finger prints."

This verbal grenade stunned Sewell into momentary silence. "What? You what?" He gasped for words. "Oh, I see this is the stitch up. Try it if you want, I think you will find that I am holding all the cards."

"Do you think so, Inspector? Perhaps I should mention that we are preparing to arrest your mother. It is clear that she harboured and dealt with a considerable quantity of the stuff. From what we can ascertain, she was a prime mover in this very serious crime."

Another silencing blow to Sewell. Withy's attitude did not change. "My mother, what the hell has she got to do with it?"

"As I say, we can prove beyond doubt she was involved. It was a major crime, we will be looking for a custodial."

"Do what you like with the old bitch, no jury round here is going to bang up a seventy five year old pensioner."

"Actually, she is seventy six."

"OK, if that's how you want it, I will go back to the murder of my brother, the bank records and the sheikh's filmed recordings."

"I don't think so, Inspector. Let's look at the facts. You come from a family of known hardened criminals. Your father had several custodial sentences against him. Your brother, now sadly deceased, was a violent and persistent criminal. Your dear old mum has had one or two spells inside as well. You are from criminals, you are a criminal, it runs in the family. As we now know, your brother was killed as part of a gangland vendetta."

"This is all crap."

"The, so called bank records that you possess are forgeries. We have experts who can confirm that."

"How can you confirm anything when you haven't even seen them, nobody has."

"They will be confirmed as forgeries."

"Like my prints will be found on the booze?"

"Exactly, your footage of the sheikh, which has now been removed from the various sights, was taken in a darkened room, the images are of a poor quality. The man in the footage is an impersonator. The real sheikh is very, very unhappy and is threatening to sue you. Obviously he will be able to afford the very best legal team. It appears that, all along, you have very irrationally, tried to put together an elaborate hoax, against the British government in order to blackmail it."

Sewell sought a response. "What about you? You told me yourself that you were threatened by the home secretary. He was going to kick you out of the job."

"You see, Inspector, more lies. That never happened. Another figment of your twisted imagination. So, there you have it. You and your old mum are banged to rights. A family of established crooks, being established crooks. We also have your phone records which show calls from a well-known active criminal."

"What? I have never spoken to anybody like that on my private phone. Do you think I would use it to contact villains? No, you've got that wrong."

"It was about three or four weeks ago, in the evening, that was the first one, later a couple more."

"That is absolutely wrong, no way did I speak to anyone like that, I never have done, never." Sewell paused and reflected. "Three weeks ago, in the evening? Wait a minute, I did have calls from a bloke who said he was an ex copper. He wanted to give me information about a file that had my name on it. That wasn't a villain, it was a bloke who had been on one of my training courses. He knew all the details. He claimed his partner was a serving officer."

Withy tilted hid head and now allowed himself the semblance of a smile. "Is that so? Our surveillance show, beyond doubt, that at that time phone was registered to one Sam Wentworth, a known villain, a very well-known villain."

"What," the word was drawn out. "So I have been stitched up from the start, how very professional."

"We also have footage of you in your local, picking up a folded newspaper that was left for you by somebody we have identified as being from a criminal gang. When he was recently arrested, he confirmed that, inside the newspaper there was an envelope that contained a considerable amount of cash. It was a bribe."

"You have really stitched me up, call yourself a leader of officers. You are nothing more than a crook, corrupt and a crook. When you go home tonight, tell your wife, tell your children what you did today. 'Well, family, today I broke the law and screwed a totally innocent man so much that I ruined his life. But don't worry, it was the most convenient thing to do'. I really should publish all this."

"Go public if you like, but who are they going to believe?"

Sewell blanched and his skin was tight around his face. He had just had his absolute power dashed from his grasp and now faced and extensive term in prison. "You can't do this, you can't."

"My dear Inspector, it has been done. Think what your future has in store for you, and your mum of course."

Sewell, watching his life swirl away like a receding tornado took a last chance on grasping for a defence, rebutted with the one irrefutable fact that he held. "I still have the recording of the phone call from you where you demanded all the information I had on Atwood. You lied then, why should anybody not think that you continued to lie, like you are doing now. That recording will not go away. Are proposing to tell the court that too was fake. That conversation is secure."

"If you mean you lodged it with my French newspaper editor acquaintance, I think you will find there is no such recording."

"Ah, yes, your French mate. Thing is, Frank," the name was spat out, "I never really trusted you, it looks like that was a good move. Your phone conversation is secure, very secure, with one of my contacts. Nobody that you know and, even if you did, nobody that you could put the squeeze on. You were not the only one recording what was said at our meetings. The bulge in your pocket was just about the size of an official device. So, do you still want to take me to trial. You have no idea of what I have collected. You always were too much of a wobbly copper to come down on one side."

Although the thought crashed into Sewell that all his previous statements about accepting the likely consequences of tilting at a very large windmill, were, at that time, acceptable. The reality was different. This was his last desperate shot at securing freedom.

Withy's face tightened. He looked around his office though searching for a prompt. He continued to parrot his lines. "However we do realise that a trial would be unpleasant and that it is possible, just possible, that something nasty might fall out and bite us on the bum. With that in mind, I am authorised to make you an offer."

Sewell tried to remain expressionless as he realised he was gaining the upper hand. "Go on, make me an offer."

"First you retire, full pension and lump sum. If you are prepared to drop these ludicrous stories you have been peddling, the government has, as a matter of expediency, suggested an amount of seven hundred and fifty thousand pounds for you to go away and not come back."

Now Sewell knew that his risky attack had found it's mark. "Frank, you are a book man, not a street fighter, you know that if I had a half decent lawyer, you, or your politician friends, wouldn't stand a chance. Make it a million." There was not the slightest hesitation.

"Alright, a million. It is suggested that you leave England and settle abroad somewhere."

Eight months later the headlines blazoned, "Another term. They are back again. The new prime minister, Norman Higgins said. 'This a great day for democracy, but much work remains to be done.' It is thought that Mr Higgins will name his new cabinet within the next few days."

Later the New Year's Honours list showed that the outgoing commissioner of police, Sir Francis Withy, had been appointed to the House of Lords. This being a reward for his leadership qualities and for the reforms he brought in to strengthen and improve criminal investigations.

A year after his last meeting with Frank Withy, Tony Sewell left his sea front apartment near Malaga. The bare minimum of dowdy furnishings spoke of his indifference to comfort and the need for colour in his life. All contact with former colleagues and his daughter had long since ceased. The only thing he had on his hands was time, his days and nights were long and empty. His habit of saying goodbye and hello to the framed picture of his former wife had withered and then expired. It was late afternoon when he closed the door behind him and, as was now usual, made for the string of gaudy tourists bars. It was his only way of dealing with the crushing boredom and loneliness.

Four hours later he was swilling down yet another brandy in an "Authentic English Pub" along the tourist strip. The drinks were neither savoured or assessed, rather they were consumed with a degree of urgency and anxiety. Now his face was puffed and blotchy, his head was unsteady and his deep set eyes, bloodshot. In the bar, he tried to attract the attention other customers and, with a lopsided leering smile, attempted to lure them into conversation. His rambling, dribbling delivery caused those within his spitting distance to leave. The bar owner, a large Mancunian sporting the compulsory gold accoutrements, threw down the tea towel he had been twisting for the last five minutes. "OK, that's it, Tony, on your bike, you are out of here.

You are like this every night now. You, my son, are barred. My customers are leaving in droves, go on off you get."

When the message eventually filtered through, Sewell registered surprise. "Right, if that's what you want, I'll be off. Spend my money somewhere else. I used to be a police officer you know, an inspector. Did I tell you I could have brought down the government? I had them, I had the buggers."

"Yes, so you've told me, and every punter who comes in here. Very good, why don't you go back and lock them all up."

Sewell lumbered out into the night and, with his ravaged face and rictus grin, he turned to a couple about to enter the bar he had just vacated. "I'd be a bit careful if I was you mate, the boss is in a bit of a mood tonight. He gets like that sometimes." He tried to hold himself erect and concentrated on walking as straight a line as possible. "Yes, you know what, he's right, I think I'll do that, arrest the lot of them." Then, as best he could, he set a course to his empty apartment.

In London the new Commissioner of Police in his first day, was settling into his new office. In his safe he found a sealed envelope addressed to The Commissioner of Police, New Scotland Yard. The contents were typed and weren't signed and had no marks to identify the author. It was stamped and had a central London postmark. He did wonder how such an item could have been placed in his safe without it being opened by one of the administrative staff.

The note said, "There is very persuasive evidence that suggests Higgins, the current prime minister and former home secretary together with Spencer Lambie, former prime minister, are involved in large scale money laundering involving public funds. Enclosed are copies of statements and material which support this view. If you do start an investigation, take extreme care. There are very powerful figures, mainly high ranking politicians, who will also be involved and have much to protect. An enquiry based outside the UK would be advisable."

Printed in Great Britain
by Amazon

18642005R00154